DEMON IN THE ATTIC

T.C. LUPPI

To Debora (in memoriam) and my husband Pedro, the guardian angels I was given on Earth.

My most sincere gratitude to all my loyal readers who make sure to read everything and let me know they loved it, no matter how crazy things get; you know who you are.

Special thanks to my author friends, who are almost as nice as they are talented, particularly Travis Baker, a brilliant and kind soul, and Nick Moorefox, the author I aspire to be.

And all my love to my *other* friends, the ones who don't even like horror that much but are reading this anyway.

VELOX BOOKS
Published by arrangement with the author.

Demon in the Attic copyright © 2021
by T.C. Luppi.

All Rights Reserved.

This book is a work of fiction. People, places, events, and situations are the product of the author's imagination. Any resemblance to actual persons, living or dead, or historical events, is purely coincidental.

No part of this book may be reproduced, stored in a retrieval system, or transmitted by any means without the written permission of the author and publisher.

CONTENTS

Pauline's Dress	1
Shadowfuckers	6
The Sygil	12
Twelve Years as a Boogeyman	16
Telomerase	26
Eighteen	34
I Was Sold by My Parents	40
I Was Hired to Murder Myself	47
Forgotten Pickup	52
The Doors of the Universe Are Closed	55
My Twin Lives Under the Bed	67
The Family Experiment	72
Are You Fine?	91
The Lost Planet	96
The Domino That Doesn't Fall	101
Babysitters	108
Invisible Hairs	114
One Girl at Night	122

Pumpkin Spice	128
Someone I Know Might Not Be Alive	133
Orphanage Rules	138
Remember Me	144
Ava Disappeared	151
Spiders	154
The Euthanasia Service	158
Demon in the Attic	166

PAULINE'S DRESS

Pauline was a sweet woman who lived across the street. We weren't close as kids or teenagers because she was around five years older than me, but our parents were friends. I think she babysat me when I was younger, too.

When my mother learned that Pauline was engaged, she sent me to help with the bridal shower. Poor mom, she thought I was *like that* because I was too often around boys and needed to learn to be more feminine, but she's got that backward.

We soon became good friends, and that's when I first learned that Pauline and her soon-to-be husband had made a blood oath.

"The first one to die comes and takes the other as soon as they can," she explained to me, swirling the ruby ring gently around her fingers.

"Isn't that too dramatic? What if you end up divorcing and marrying other people?"

"We won't. We are soulmates!" she assured me. Her naïveté made her incredibly beautiful, but it felt really wrong being 21 and thinking that I was so much more mature than a 26 years-old.

I didn't pursue the matter, but she kept talking about him in a dreamy tone. *Aiden would like this*, *I wish Aiden was here*, and so on. Her dreamy tone almost made me believe that soulmates existed and that you could make the person you love the most follow you in death by just willing it.

I met Pauline's friends, and we all ended up having some quality girl time. Pauline explained to us all how she believed that you can wake up in the afterlife and start controlling things with your mind.

"Of course your memories will be hazy," she clarified. "But that's why we made the blood oath. So we can remember."

"And how will one get the other back?" I asked, entertaining her.

"I like to believe that we'll both grow wings!"

It was all terribly silly when I think back, but Pauline had something about her that made everyone pay attention and marvel at her words. She could convince you of almost anything.

Despite the age gap, I ended up becoming her closest friend. Maybe we were finally at an age where it didn't matter anymore, or maybe she just liked my honesty about everything, when her other friends only cooed in excitement and complimented all her choices.

Since I was in college but lived with my parents and didn't need to work, I had a lot of spare time to accompany her to wedding dress fittings, cake tasting, and all the little things that were the world for brides.

But Pauline was a pleasant bride-to-be and never freaked out; she was just thrilled about marrying the man of her dreams, and wanted to make it pretty if possible.

Little by little, I grew to understand her devotion to Aiden. And he was just as crazy about her, if not more. When they were together, the world felt like a brighter and warmer place. Like marshmallows slowly melting over my heart.

Before Pauline and Aiden, I never knew such a pure feeling could exist; they were the first people to ever make me believe in true love and that some matches are made in heaven.

The day of the wedding came, around half a year after her bridal shower.

It was neither a big nor a small wedding—it felt like both Pauline and Aiden were able to invite exactly everyone they wanted around on their happiest day. Not one more, not one less. I felt somewhat honored to be there.

Still, the happiest day never came.

When Pauline arrived, belated as any bride should, there was whispering and disquiet; Aiden wasn't there yet.

Her smile didn't falter, because she was completely sure that he would never bail on her, and all of us agreed. But I could tell she was worried. The bridesmaids—her two closest friends from high school—started making calls to try to find out if the groom had a sudden illness, the only possible explanation for his absence.

Soon the bridesmaids realized that Aiden's parents were there, but not his brother. They informed that their other son was supposed to drive the groom as part of his best man's duties.

The nervousness in the atmosphere grew as the groom's family and the two women made call after call, trying to find Aiden. We all desperately wanted to find out it was just a trivial incident and laugh it off.

But, as you might imagine, it never happened.

When the devastating news came, everyone wanted to comfort Pauline, everyone wanted desperately to protect her precious heart, but it was too torn apart to notice anyone else.

It was all too fast and scary... A sports car ran a red light straight into the Mirage... The man in the passenger seat was dead on arrival... The driver was taken to the hospital but his state was critical.

It was all so hard on everyone. Aiden's brother ended up surviving, but he'll be tetraplegic for life due to severe injury to his spinal cord. As far as I know, he's also miserable because he wishes he could be the one who died; I feel almost as terrible for him as for my friend, widowed before becoming a bride.

Right after the wedding that never happened, Pauline and Aiden's parents dealt with selling the house they had just bought, and Pauline continued living with her parents. They both still worked office jobs they couldn't quit, so her other friends and I started taking turns keeping her company while they weren't home.

I did my best to be there for my neighbor and friend, but *she* wasn't there. She was living in delusion, and the only thing you could see leaking into reality was her desolation.

I never saw such a deep and heart-wrenching sadness. Pauline refused to take off her dress. She would spend the whole day by the window waiting for Aiden and the whole night crying because she missed him desperately. Every single day.

She was hopeful it was a matter of time until he woke up on the other side and remembered to bring her along. That's why she wouldn't take off the dress—he had died in his wedding suit, so it was only natural that she was up to par.

Pauline held on to the wedding dress not only as the best way to have Aiden find her again, but as a last memory of the time she was happy, a memento of all the has-beens and never-weres in her interrupted future.

Her parents and every single one of her friends tried to coax her into changing her clothes. We promised she could always keep the dress close for when Aiden came, but she knew that we didn't really believe he would. It was like promising your kid that you'd buy them a Happy Meal some other day.

I felt devastated and guilty for not believing her comforting tale, but not even I could be completely honest and shatter her heart even more.

No one dared to penetrate her grief and force her out of the dress. Pauline spent the day in it, slept in it, even bathed in it; since we live in warm and arid weather, having it dry wasn't an issue, only everything else.

The once beautiful organza and silk were now ragged, grimy, and smelling. But she still refused to take it off. She started to believe that Aiden wouldn't be able to spot her in the crowd if she wasn't wearing it.

It was impossible to change her mind, and even though she was seeing a therapist three times a week, she wasn't improving. Her mourning and trauma were turning into a darker, more permanent mental illness.

She started talking to Aiden, then explained to us that he was nearby already, so we should start saying our goodbyes.

"I can feel him coming, his warmth is so close now. It's just taking a while because flying is really hard when your wings are newly acquired, and time doesn't work like we know it on the other side."

When she said things like that, it was the only time that her eyes sparkled with life. I wanted to believe it so badly. I think everyone else did, too—the reality was too cruel, too unnecessary.

Then one morning, Pauline disappeared for good. No one saw her leaving, and no one saw her at all after that.

The only thing that we were able to find, in the small grove behind the house, was her filthy wedding dress. It had two large holes poked on the back like it had grown wings.

***

After finding the dress, everyone who loved Pauline was relieved; her mother readily admitted that she actually believed that Aiden somehow had come back to take her. Others weren't so fond of the supernatural explanation, but thinking that there was a chance that it happened brought us a sense of closure.

It's not that we were happy about her death, but we conformed to the possibility of her finally finding her peace and her much yearned happy ending.

She was an angel, after all. Why wouldn't she grow wings and escape her flesh prison?

The family held a beautiful memorial service in her honor, and slowly we all started moving on with our lives.

Now, you might ask what I believe in. I would laugh bitterly because I don't have this choice to begin with.

Being the person who spent the most time watching Pauline those days, it was only natural that I was the one to find her dead in the bathtub. Hiding and subsequently getting rid of her body was the hardest thing I have ever done; tampering with the dress, though, was eerily healing.

Still, I think she would be pleased to know that I faked her rapture.

A romantic and mystifying death fitted her way more than suicide.

SHADOWFUCKERS

I have been a nude model for 2 years. It started off with sexy cosplay, then I photographed Suicide Girls style, and finally, when I had people up to pay enough, solo porn.

I used to live in a crappy kitchenette, but once I was successful enough, I was able to afford a nicer place. Things got better when I moved in with my new roommate, but also weirder.

I'm not using our real names or our artistic names here because I'm scared as fuck.

My new roommie, Savannah, was a cheerful and sweet girl. Her perky personality had flocked plenty of followers and fans, way more than I had myself, and she was making some good money; for instance, she was a homeowner at 22.

Her place was huge, and she decided to rent her extra room for an attractive price, as long as the other resident was fine with her vast collection of sex toys being displayed in the living room.

I thought that was hilarious, and we immediately hit it off, so the other resident became me. The fact that we were both nude models helped our friendship, but to be fair I had met some other girls in my field before, and most of them were a stick in the mud.

Savannah was nice, tidy, and amazingly respectful of my personal space. She didn't act like she owned the place, even though she literally did. We both had a good few months before things started to go south.

"So, Ayla," Savannah approached me over breakfast. "Would you be willing to collab with me? I have a request for a private two-girl job and I thought it made sense to invite you first, since it will be so much easier to arrange our schedules."

I wasn't doing much, just my nightly streaming, my regular sets and my sets for patreons. I asked more about the job.

"Well," she laughed. "I have to tell you it's one of a kind. It's nothing dehumanizing or anything, but it's weird as fuck. This guy... he jerks off to shadows. He wants us to pretend we're fucking them."

"Fucking the shadows?!" I asked, and laughed loudly. She confirmed, laughing too. It was insane but relatively harmless, like when some guy paid me 5 grand to legally bind me to not show my feet to any other man but him for a whole year. That's the reason I never take my socks off unless it's before a shower, and haven't been to the beach for months.

When Savannah told me how much the client was willing to pay for such a thing, I was immediately in.

"It will be so embarrassing, but kinda fun, right?" I said.

"Yeah, and with that I can finally stop taking private requests and focus on other things," Savannah replied, happily. She's sort of a do-it-all artist—model, photographer, painter and so on, and nude modeling was simply the more profitable way to fund the rest of her passions.

A few more e-mail exchanges with shadowfucker@[redacted].com and he had approved of me and discussed the details with Savannah. He wanted two videos a week—on Mondays and Thursdays, and each should be at least 30 minutes long.

A very reasonable request, considering that, with my share of what he was paying, I could drop everything else and still live comfortably.

He would send us the equipment before the first week, then outfits every two weeks.

I was the one to receive the large box from UPS, as Savannah wasn't home. I knew she had a P. O. box to avoid disclosing her real address, but this one came straight to our place.

Weird, but considering how big this client was, I could understand her making an exception for him, and said nothing about it.

Later that day, we opened the box. It contained some light strobes, a few large but hollow wooden and metal objects, eight sets of costumes—wigs included—a photograph and a small package marked *otherworldly condoms*.

"Wow, imagine being this lunatic!" Savannah grabbed the little package laughing, then opened one of them.

They looked nothing like regular condoms; they were more like those plastic bags you use to freeze stuff, but the material was so much thinner and slightly iridescent.

"That's probably something he made up to make it more realistic, right?" I asked, then read the instructions aloud. "When having sex with the shadows, make sure to protect your whole groin with otherworldly condoms. They can unfold to thrice its size."

The outfits were actually cute, and we spent some time deciding when we were going to use each of them; the client had perfectly guessed our sizes.

Then the photograph finally caught my attention.

It showed the right way to arrange the equipment in the room, but funnily enough, the room depicted was incredibly alike to Savannah's studio—our third bedroom. Unlike me, she didn't often shoot in her own bedroom, preferring to use a mostly neutral room where she could set up scenarios or just take cleaner pics and videos.

I couldn't help but feel that the picture had been taken exactly in her studio—*at the very place we lived.*

***

The day of our first video came—a Monday. It didn't take us more than 15 minutes to set up the whole equipment in the studio exactly like the picture showed. The objects projected large shadows on the room, and the lights were set to slowly move on their own, so our interaction with the shadows was like the strangest sexy dance—but at least it made everything feel more realistic, instead of having us stand still for half an hour pretending to fondle the same empty spot.

Despite thinking that it was wacky, Savannah was a professional, and she diligently used the otherworldly condoms as requested. I used them as well, and for 35 minutes, we pretended to fuck shadows.

I felt utterly ridiculous, but being used to doing solo videos, I knew very well how to do it. The color of the lights and the outfits really helped set a soothing mood that made it all less shameful.

Savannah then turned off the cameras and looked at me.

"It wasn't awful, was it?"

"It was okay," I agreed. I could make a fool of myself for some good money.

"Do you want to shoot a second one and end this week early?"

Before I could reply, her phone buzzed loudly.

From: <Unknown Number>: Remember, shoot twice a week. Separately.

We stared at each other in confusion.

"Maybe there's a mic hidden in the equipment?" I suggested. "Or somehow it streams to him real time?"

We searched the whole room but found nothing.

I didn't think much about it. Rich people are controlling. They know things, always. The client knew when we were going to film the first video, and of course he figured we would consider doing everything on the same day instead of having to disassemble the set and reassembling it again.

I went about my day, and nothing strange happened. Savannah seemed much more alive because now she had time for her hobbies, and I was doing well enough to start sending my family some money, something I had wanted to do for a long time.

We were to send him the first video on the day we recorded the second and so on. On Thursday, Savannah told me the client loved our first video, and looked forward to the next. To get us a little more comfortable with our weird thing, we had some wine and put on jazz music.

"Setting a mood for the ghosts!" she said, and we laughed.

This time things went smoothly, but I kept hearing some humming while we pretended to fuck the shadows. I was sure it wasn't coming from the music.

I asked Savannah, and she didn't hear anything. "Maybe you're a bit drunk? Slow down on the wine next time, home girl!"

For video number 3, I was completely sober and asked Savannah to do it without music. She agreed, and in the total silence, I still heard the humming.

It was a humming that wasn't there before, and it didn't come from the light strobes either. I was so focused on it and intrigued that my face looked really unsexy in the video—so much that, a few hours later, Savannah's editor called to ask if there was an issue.

"She just keeps listening to some humming. Yeah, I'll tell her to see a doctor. Think you can mostly show her from behind? Cool, you're an angel!"

Savannah looked more worried about me than anything else, so I promised to see a doctor. Maybe something was wrong with my ear—even though I only had this bizarre sort of tinnitus while we were filming those specific videos; at least now I could afford some quality healthcare.

Between the filming of videos 3 and 4, I got my ears checked, but they were perfectly normal. Savannah reiterated that it was totally cool if I wanted to give up on this freaky fetish-video thing and she would get another girl for that, no hard feelings.

But I didn't feel like the videos were the problem. There was just this weird *thing* I couldn't quite understand.

On video 4, Savannah was tipsy and seemed to be really enjoying herself. I felt a little guilty that she was clearly overcompensating for the fact that I was worried and gloomy on the previous video.

The humming evolved to whispers. And for the first time, I heard—no, it was more like understanding from the context, with the intuitive side of my brain—a few words.

"I actually like this."

At last that's what I foretold that the whispers said. It probably sounded more like *sfslsosls dlsowllss swowllls*.

***

Once again, I didn't tell anyone. I was almost convinced that I was actually being crazy. It was just an eerie feeling because I was stripping to and groping empty spaces twice a week. I'm sure things like that end up messing you up in the head.

On the Friday after recording video 4, we got a new box with outfits. There was another photograph, instructing us to rearrange the lights and boxes too, I imagine, create different shapes with the shadows.

I couldn't restrain myself this time.

"Savannah, don't you think this pic looks exactly like your studio?"

"Yeah, that helps a lot, right?" she smiled, and then slowly realized what I meant, her smile withering. She grabbed the photo from my hand. "Oh, now that you said it, it's quite alike. But of course no one broke into the house, right? I think that's a standard room."

But she sounded shaken.

I think that's the reason she completely forgot the otherworldly condom.

***

We made the preparations as usual; changed the setting as the photo instructed, dressed up, put on our wigs and make-up.

The whispering immediately started, and for a moment I got lost in it, trying to understand. A buzzing sound, then another.

"There's food today."

"It tastes good."

Then Savannah screamed.

I didn't realize she wasn't wearing the otherworldly condom either—not until I saw her groin covered by the blackest of blacks, then her legs disappearing into the darkness of the shadows.

Like she was involved by long and thick pieces of deep-black fabric, her torso and head disappeared too. She didn't seem to be in pain, but in shock—everything was so quick and uncanny.

I reached out for her, but there was nothing there; my hands grasped nothing but thin air.

I immediately turned off the strobe lights, turned on the normal lights, and moved all the boxes around. They were still hollow as ever, and Savannah was nowhere to be found.

I then searched the entire house fruitlessly.

It's ludicrous to say that, but shadow-people took my friend.

I sat on the floor and cried, worried about Savannah and about what I would tell the police about her disappearance.

I was a mess, and decided to cancel my live-streaming that night for personal reasons.

As soon as I opened the browser, an e-mail notification popped on my screen.

From: <shadowfucker@[redacted].com>

It's not your fault that your friend neglected my one rule.

I like you, Ayla. The editor tried to cut off your face from the last couple of videos, but I realize you are accomplishing something I was never able to: learning the shadow-people language.

Keep working for me and all your financial concerns will be taken care of, especially regarding your teenage sister and her two children. I'll deal with everything related to Savannah's disappearance as well.

Find me a new second girl for the videos, the cash and outfits will keep coming. It's up to you to instruct her to always use the otherworldly condoms, and make sure you are both protected—it surely was a pretty traumatic experience for you but, as for me, I don't mind feeding them.

THE SYGIL

I've been researching Mesopotamia my whole life. I remember being fascinated by that civilization ever since I was a pre-teen. Unlike my friends and schoolmates, I spent my time daydreaming of Sumerian kings and the Euphrates River—a weird child.

I then grew up, went to college and became a Sumer researcher. I'm not a particularly prominent historian, but I'm one of the very best in the world when it comes to translating Sumero-Akkadian Cuneiform writing, especially from around 2,800-2,500 BC.

Former teachers often recommended me for these very specific jobs, so I was the obvious choice when this specific 4,600-year-old document was found.

I wasn't expecting a lot when I was invited to translate these newfound tablets; I mean, I was personally excited, but also sure that the contents would be mundane enough. So far, I hadn't been lucky enough to find anything more interesting than recordings of the harvest of a few years.

My employer was a little private museum in Istanbul that specialized in artifacts from the Gilgamesh dynasty and prided itself on having acquired these new items before the British Museum could put their hands on them.

I was welcomed at the airport by the owner's second assistant, a flamboyant and clever Arabic man who spoke English with almost no accent. "I've been assigned to accompany you during your stay, Madame. Please inform me of your every need."

Eymen was a pleasant man around my age, the Turkish version of an English butler. He gave me space to work but politely reminded me of making at least two meals a day when I was too deep in my work. His presence helped so much with my productivity, since I didn't have to waste time preparing or fetching my own food.

Still, no matter how great an experience it was, I'm terrified of my findings.

The following is my translation of one of the tablets.

***

We humans are being killed daily. The Sygil are an inferior species in every way, some humanoids barely more men than monkeys, but they have something we lack—something that should be a curse and yet, somehow, is their biggest strength: they don't know when to give up.

They surprised us with their resistance. And they are so numerous; the Sygil took a habit of procreating like the rats or ants, and now they are as numerous as the stars in the sky. They always had plenty of children, like savages do, but most of their offspring would die of disease or being attacked by the predators on their precarious houses.

That way, their numbers were always around the same, unless they were in war between themselves—which happened constantly, for simple resources like water. But now some of the Sygils, merely through observation and the trial-and-error method, learned of our medicine and architecture and they started to flourish and prosper—too much.

After invading and overpowering their fellow Sygil from other tribes, a group reached our empires and slaughtered us. We hit them back, with our better horses, better weapons, better built men. And we slayed them, but despite that, they never, never stopped. They are indefatigable.

While still there are two or three of them, they still have the will to fight. We don't know who they are fighting for, since not a single one of them will be able to seize the spoils of their unlikely victory.

I wish I could understand why they never give up. We're taller, stronger and dotted with brains they probably think only a god could possess, and still, they fight.

Just because they learned how to walk in two legs a while ago they think they can rule the world; despite the fact that their reasoning is puny and their sciences are non-existent. They don't even know how vast the world is. That's laughable and sad.

Like their ancestors—even inferior hominids—their life is only worth after procreation, so their children dead before mating age are useless and forgettable. This primitiveness is what enrages me about them the most.

The Sygil wants to learn our other secrets and to be ruled by our King—they want to be us.

Tired of seeing my sisters and daughters die, I'm utterly ashamed to admit that I was scared and reached out to the King. I advised him to strike a deal with the Sygil.

At first, he refused; but after a lot of our blood was shed, and only around a few hundreds of us remained, our king Gilgamesh finally surrendered to the inferior species so the rest of us could be safe. We would retreat to our underground city, and live safely for generations to come.

The King would stay with them on the surface to rule them and develop their society, and remain there with them for precisely 4,560 years before we fiercely take our world back.

Of course, they agreed. They don't even understand how much time that is; but it's not a lot for us. We never die, we are simply reborn on a new body of a new generation, every time wiser, sturdier, purer. The more they kill us, the stronger we arise.

We are moving to our fortress deep inside the Earth by the ending of the forthcoming Araḫ Addaru Arku month. We will make no mistakes this time; we'll keep the Sygil under constant surveillance and learn all their secrets.

Next time, we won't have any weaknesses; just like they almost did to us, we will destroy them all mercilessly.

***

I was shocked to realize that *we* are the Sygil. King Gilgamesh was said to have extraordinary powers and wisdom, and he's one of them—one of the *real* humans. Which means there's a way more advanced civilization living underground on this planet as you read this.

By chemical testing, the museum expert was able to determine the age of this tablet with incredible precision. The Sumerian Calendar is very similar to the Gregorian Calendar we use nowadays; it has 12 months, alternating between 29 and 30 days, following the moon cycles, which have 29.5 days.

There's a 13th month with 33 days called Araḫ Addaru Arku that only happens every 3 years; it was added to compensate for the discrepancy.

It wasn't hard for me to convert 4,560 years for them to our Gregorian calendar, using the tablet's age as the year zero.

And I found out that the real humans, with their superior brains and hatred for us across millennia, are coming back to reclaim their land soon. How soon? According to my calculations, the 4,560th Sumerian year is next year.

TWELVE YEARS AS A BOOGEYMAN

Boogeymen are born from normal people; people who have let the evil enter and break their minds.

It starts with seemingly innocent bad thoughts. Someone has let their dog poop in your front yard and you half-jokingly wish they were hit by a bus.

You newborn son can't get a full night of sleep. You love him, but you wish just a little bit that he didn't exist.

You look at your boss, yelling at you for being late and sleep-deprived, and imagine yourself twisting his neck, very, very slowly, until he cannot breathe.

You sometimes feel a lack of memory, like some minutes went by and you didn't even notice, or someone had an entire conversation with you that you can't remember, but you blame it on your stress and on sleeping poorly. Your boss is putting you through a lot this week.

Your neighbors don't say good morning to you anymore. Even the over-friendly neighbor is different. He timidly waves at you, but in a colder way.

You say something that sounds normal to you when you're mad, but the whole room is looking at you like you're crazy.

The water and the food start to taste weird. And the smell. The sulfuric smell will never leave your nostrils anymore, although no one else feels it. Like your very soul is rotten. You go to the doctor and with a shaky voice he asks that you never come back again.

He won't tell you what you have, he didn't even charge you. You suspect the smell comes from inside, so there's no amount of baths and lotions that can solve it.

You go to churches and temples and synagogues and mosques, but no one can help you. No one can find what's wrong. There's no devil, no vengeful spirit. The poison is in your very being.

You realize nothing of it can ever go away again. You only had to feed **It** once or twice before **It** learned to feed **It**self on you.

You find yourself in the middle of the night in the living room. You don't remember getting there. You're fully dressed, covered in sweat, and holding a butcher knife in your hand. There's no blood, but it *could* have been bloodied moments ago.

The next day, you watch and read the local news, praying that none of the vicious actions they describe are yours.

You start a diary, because that's what people descending into madness do. They write to document their decay.

But when you try to write, you notice you have no control over your hand anymore. You write what **It** wants, not what you intended to. You know **It** craves violence, unspeakable acts that make your stomach churn, so you lock yourself away from everyone you could hurt—which is everyone in the world.

You know you're dangerous and others will be safer without you around. But **It** controls your every move, so **It** unlocks all the big padlocks every night.

That's the reason you can't even die—**It** won't let you. You're not in control of your body anymore. You're locked outside of yourself. **It** has taken over.

You're not you anymore. Your friends abandon you, your family despises you. Your eyes hurt and you hate the light. Your fingers are numb, everything is numb, because your body isn't yours anymore.

Maybe Humanity's greatest fears of all are Being Forgotten, Being Misunderstood and Powerlessness, and you get to experience all of them at once.

What you used to be—the real You—no longer exists in other people's memories. Your loved ones suppressed every good time they had with you, and replaced any fond recollection of you by fearing what you are now. You must be left behind, because now you're **It**, and **It** is evil.

You try to explain **It** is not you, but your body won't obey you. You're finally kicked out of your shell, and now you're just a disembodied shadow, living under some kid's bed.

***

I don't know for sure how I ended up there. Everything was foggy and felt like nothingness. I was a shadow, could only move across the shadows, so I stayed under the bed or in the closet a lot. Despite having lost everything, at least I felt safe for the first time in a while.

My mind—what little was left of it—was free, finally mine and mine along again, so the lack of a body was secondary.

I have no idea how long it took for me to be noticed. I tried to keep track of the time based on how many times the boy came to sleep above me, but I kept forgetting. I wanted to retain whatever information I could, but a shadow has no memory. So I don't really know.

"Is anyone there?" he asked. I don't know if I had seen him before that day or not, whether he was thin or chubby, or the color of his hair. I just remember thinking that judging by his voice he wasn't older than 8.

He noticed me.

Amazed by having my existence acknowledge, I tried to talk. To tell him it was lonely and dusty and maddening to be what I was—something next to nothing. I was like a phantom limb of a mind, so even though it couldn't technically ache, it did. And it was excruciating.

I wanted and desperately needed to tell someone about it.

Of course I had no vocal chords. Hell, I didn't even have a body, or an entire mind. Everything came out as a terrifying growl, and kids can hear it.

The boy screamed for his mom. I cowered in the darkest shadows as she came, sleepy and grumpy, as she turned on the light.

"I heard something under the bed," he whimpered.

She checked on me. Even though I didn't have eyes, I could somehow see her with my battered half-mind. She was older, probably in her mid-40s. She wasn't mad or unkind, just exhausted.

"There's nothing here, sweetie. Wanna come to my room? Mom is really tired today."

The boy agreed.

I envied him. I wish more than anything that I had comforting arms to fall on and rest.

**

I didn't have a lot of story with this boy, or at least I can't remember. He frightened easily so, no matter how much I wanted to communicate with someone, I refrained from scaring him. I guess I'm just bad at everything, including at being a boogeyman.

I heard conversation around the house, but for a long time, it was just the boy and his mother. I rarely ventured outside the bedroom, afraid there wouldn't be enough shadows for me to come back before morning. I was completely sure that I was going to disappear if I stepped (and I use this word very loosely) into the light.

And even though everything was bad and hopeless I wanted to exist, so I was afraid and cautious.

The house was too big for only two people. I eventually learned that the mother had an older daughter—she apparently was in college and was the most frequent visitor. The daughter was a joyous young woman, I really liked when she was around. Maybe because once, in a distant past, I had been young and cheerful like her.

I wish she was younger so she could hear me. She felt like she could bear to listen to my awful cries and not be scared, even when she was small.

As the boy aged, I understood that he couldn't hear me anymore. So sometimes I would talk aloud and make those awful noises just because I could. Just to remind myself that I was still clinging to existence.

The zenith of my life with the boy was when I learned I could manipulate objects to some extent if I was really focused, right before he decided to move to the larger bedroom his sister used to occupy. He was a pre-teen by that time, and I heard him pacing around the room looking for something.

I didn't really understand what it was, but it was some sort of memento of his late father. It was important.

Then I saw—once again, I use this term very loosely—something shiny close to me, under the bed. It was a reliquary, one of those you wear around your neck.

I really wished that I could give it to him in that moment. Really, really wished.

Then it happened. Slowly but surely, the thing moved. The boy sounded so relieved and happy when he finally found it.

I felt accomplished for the first time in my life as a boogeyman.

***

The next few years are a blur of waiting and lurking around cautiously. We boogeymen can only move on shadows, but we can't squeeze through the cracks of windows or under doors. If I'm being scientific, we're more like a slime made of shadow.

That's why, no matter how much I considered relocating to another house and trying to talk to other children, it wasn't easy. I was stuck with a teenager and a middle-aged woman who couldn't hear me.

Then the boy went to college too and it was only me and the mother for a while. Not even the older daughter would come. It was boring and lonely.

After making a painstaking effort to remember, I finally recalled the daughter and the mother having a huge fight over the character of her boyfriend; I just don't know when it was.

I was almost making up my mind about going through the risks to find another place when the mother started renovating the bedroom I lived in. the bed above me, now painted white and with pink sheets, was going to have a new occupant.

The day the daughter came back was full of tears. She cried, apologizing to her mother, while the older woman kept telling her that there was nothing to worry, and that despite everything, she was really happy.

She was now a grandmother.

***

I, too, could barely contain my excitement. Lisbeth, the granddaughter, was a cute little thing; I think she was around 4 when they arrived, and she sounded delighted with her new bedroom.

Both her mother and grandmother put her to bed that night. She probably felt warm and loved, and asked to sleep with all the lights turned off like a big girl. Chuckling, they complied, and closed the door, in total darkness. Of course the two adults had a lot of talk after all these—I suppose—years.

"Hey, little monster! I know you're in there. I'm not afraid of you," she stated. If I could smile, that's what I would have done. But I said nothing; I was unsure whether she really felt my presence or just assumed there would be a monster.

This was an opportunity too precious to be ruined. I didn't want to scare her off on the first day and lose her company.

"Seriously, little monster! Knock if you're in there!"

I made whatever sound I could. She laughed in delight; little Lisbeth wasn't scared of me.

After that, we developed our system to communicate. I would make one noise for yes and two noises for no.

Lisbeth asked me all sorts of things. Silly things, from her little kid universe, like if I thought her doll was pretty, or if she should wear blue socks instead of white. Things about her family—if I knew her uncle who lived in this room before, if her mother was beautiful, if I could go to her dad's house and hunt him. I replied to everything, overjoyed to feel important and heard.

"Do you have big, scary eyes?"

No.

"Do you have nice eyes, then?"

No.

"Are you eyeless?"

Yes.

"Oooh, that's scary! But not for me. Don't worry, Poggy."

Yes. And I still don't know why she nicknamed me Poggy.

"Do you have hands?"

No.

"That must be hard, Poggy. So you have paws?"

No.

"It's really hard to imagine you! Can I see you pretty please? I swear I won't tell mom or nana."

No.

"Aw. Are you ashamed?"

No.

She was deep in thought for a long time.

"Oooh, so are you invisible?"

Yes.

"That's so cool!"

Once again, she was quiet. I thought she was asleep.

"Can you move things??"

***

After learning that I could move things, Lisbeth came up with more ways to communicate. She would put many small objects (little balls, a Barbie shoe, etc.) under the bed, and depending on what I moved, I could answer things like "probably," "I don't know," etc. That improved our communication a lot.

We talked for hours and hours every day. Despite being limited by her youth, she was a very clever girl. She was able to ask me a chain of questions that led her to conclude that I had been human before.

This fact seemed to scare her. She then asked if her mother or grandmother could become boogeymen too.

I don't think so, I replied, moving a little replica of a racing car.

When she ran out of questions to ask me, she would ask her mom and nana: *what do you ask someone when you want to know them better?*

Luckily, they thought it was cute. They thought I was Lisbeth's imaginary friend—and, well, I was. I never meant to harm or scare her.

"Ask their profession and if they have kids," her mother replied. Lisbeth came back happily, and for a long time, she tried to guess what I worked with.

Fireman? Policeman? Teacher? Scientist? Astronaut? Doctor? Lawyer? Nurse? Actor? The person who gives you a Happy Meal in the mall? Gardener? Cleaning lady? Lunch lady?

To all of them, I replied no. she wasn't disappointed, though, just more fired up. I was a mere office worker, something kids never think of because it's not glamorous or close to their reality.

"Mom, tell me a profession!" "Uh, teacher." "No, I already asked if Poggy is a teacher!"

When Lisbeth asked "secretary" I finally said yes. Close enough.

"Do you have kids?"

Yes.

"Are they like you?"

No.

"Do you love them?"

Yes.

"And they love you?"

I don't know.

"I'm sorry about that, Poggy. You're my friend and I love you!"

***

I think I spent a year or so with Lisbeth. She healed my soul, if I had a soul to heal. No one had ever been that kind to me.

I know it's my fault that I let **It** in and corrupt my very being. But I felt that if I had been treated so well before I would have never allowed it to happen.

For the people in the house, life went on. Lisbeth's mother started dating another guy, someone the grandmother adored, so he was always there. The place was lively. It almost felt like we were all one big, happy family.

I didn't exactly sleep, but I had some sort of dormancy period daily.

I was abruptly awakened by the sound of someone entering the bedroom; I think they came from the window. A tall figure violently took Lisbeth from her bed, making her whimper, still in her sleep. It then moved to another room, Lisbeth in their arms, not turning on the lights.

Distressed, I followed. We entered the third bedroom, and I immediately moved to under the bed.

"You fucking bitch!" the person barked, turning on the lights. Lisbeth's mother and her boyfriend were jerked awake.

"Luke! For Christ's sake, what you're doing?"

"Dad!"

Both sounded incredibly scared.

Lisbeth had told me a lot about her father. Even in her childish words, I was able to imagine a world of pain and fear. Lisbeth's mother put up with a lot of verbal and physical violence, ashamed to admit that her marriage was a huge mistake.

I heard Dad screaming to Mom a lot and breaking things, but he was nice to me. He told me she had been naughty so he had to ground her. I believed him at first, but Mom wasn't naughty. She was good. She brought me here the day Dad hurt me; I didn't even know I had a nana, because Dad never let us talk to her.

Lisbeth's mother sobbed. Luke was pointing a gun at his own daughter's head.

"How dare you sleep with another man, you fucking tramp! You're my wife, I'll never give you up," he yelled. "We're coming back home now."

Lisbeth's mother started moving meekly towards him, crestfallen and humiliated. Her boyfriend motioned to stop her, but Luke spoke again.

"Come on, you horny bitch! You'll either obey your husband and be punished for your unfaithfulness, or your life will be a living hell knowing that your daughter died because of you!"

"Dad! Please! It hurts!" Lisbeth pleaded, the metal barrel glued to her little forehead.

My heart ached to know that my only friend in the world, an innocent and lovely child, was on the verge of being killed by her own father. Everyone was so scared, the room was so bright.

I'd try to help anyone in that situation. Anyone.

But the sweet little girl who made me feel someone again, who healed me, who gave me hope and reason to exist? You can bet I'd give everything to save her, including what little of me still hadn't evaporated.

So I wished with all my might that I moved the gun. And my non-body, the slime of darkness that I was, jumped towards the light.

It felt like I was a sieve, with light perforating every pore that I didn't have, permeating all my non-existent cells. It hurt. It hurt, but it also felt liberating, like I had finally atoned for my sins and was free, choosing to sacrifice happily for someone that was worth all that I had.

I was fast, a flash of dark in the light. I was able to move the pistol from his hand, causing it to pirouette e hit him in the head with the butt of the gun.

Before disappearing I saw his body starting to fall unconscious, almost in slow-motion, and I heard Lisbeth's shouting, happily: "Poggy saved us!"

***

I abruptly woke up back in my own body, like when you dream of falling.

It was gone, or at least I couldn't hear **Its** malicious thoughts anymore.

I tried moving my hands. Slowly, finger by finger, everything worked.

I laughed with joy. I almost couldn't believe my luck. I thought I was gone forever.

I opened my eyes and saw my husband by my side. I smiled happily, opening my arms to hug him. Instead, he looked scared and twitched, moving to the farther side of the bed.

"I'm so, so sorry. Did I snort? I should sleep in the guest's room, but you insist…"

"Babe, it's fine. It's me," I tried to explain, with the softest voice I could. But his eyes were full of panic. He was so washed-out, pale, thin and with swollen eyes, like he spent most of his life crying.

He probably did, considering what **It** kept talking about doing—to him, to the kids, to everyone around us.

And he looked old. Really, really old. I was ready to dismiss everything as some sort of drug-induced dream, but clearly years had passed—based on Lisbeth's uncle, at least a decade. I instinctively looked at the corner of our room where the crib of our newborn used to be, but there was nothing. The room was arranged somewhat differently, too.

"Where are the kids?" I asked. Still looking terrified, he guided me to their rooms.

"Please don't be so harsh, Rachel. I know they didn't mean to say your cooking was bad," he begged me.

My newborn was now a handsome 12-year-old little man. I cried as I hugged him for the first time in so long, and he accepted me. Somehow, he seemed to realize the difference between **It** and me.

Being a boogeyman was so scary. But nothing is scarier than being back and having to pick up the pieces that **It** left. Nothing is scarier than knowing how hard it will be to be trusted and loved again, to make it up for all the hurt that I've caused. Still, I'm grateful I'm here. I want to spend the rest of my days redeeming myself with the ones I love for everything **It** did through my body while I was almost too far gone in a dark, dark place.

Until the love of a girl shed love on my corrupted, nearly hopeless self.

TELOMERASE

Bryan was *that* friend: the guy who was always getting himself in trouble, and me by proxy—he always came up with the worst ideas, and they almost always involved scams, MLM or owing money to some dangerous individuals. I should have known that one day it would be the death of us or, in this case… worse than death.

But we were best friends, almost brothers, and that meant I could never let him go through the horrible consequences of his reckless actions alone. I promised his mother on her deathbed I'd take care of him so, no matter how many bar fights we had to go through, how many times I had to carry Bryan passed out drunk back to safety, or how many nights I had to let him stay on my couch because he was scammed and lost all his money, I felt accomplished. I was nothing but a loyal friend to a good but misguided soul.

Now, there's no one to take care of him; no one to take care of *us*. I should have known that I was not looking after him, but merely enabling his self-destructive behavior.

It all started with him owing a lot of money to a dealer. Bryan wasn't a junkie, but he was definitely close to it, and the fact that the world always seemed to conspire against him pushed him more and more towards this abyss.

After a lot of threats and countless poorly slept nights, the man came to settle the score—he was not alone, and it was clear that his entourage was not only carrying guns, but could snap both our necks with their bare hands. Hell, the guy himself was more than enough to send us to the morgue. I thought Bryan was a goner but, as he cried and promised to do anything, the dealer miraculously seemed to consider it.

"I got some new shit from my supplier, it's called Eternal Life. Cheesy as fuck. It's something never-before-seen, and she did her tests, but I have to see it for myself." I'll never forget his raspy voice, his ugly neck tattoo, his knife slightly closer as Bryan's heart audibly thumped. "You and Suits come to use it, and your whole debt is gone."

Bryan looked at me pleadingly. He knew that I had never used any illegal drug, let alone something new and barely tested, but it if was just once, maybe…

I agreed, and Bryan took the offer; the man quickly took us to his place, an abandoned storehouse near the port. I was put in a nearly empty room with a few surveillance cameras and, I assume, Bryan was in another.

The dealer's henchmen then made sure that I injected the unknown lime green substance into my veins—it was jelly-like but lumpy, and incredibly fluorescent.

At first, I felt nothing, just a little light-headed, like I was very sleepy and my brain was turning on and off in quick succession.

Then my arms started to feel longer and longer, stretching impossibly towards the infinity—they seemed to break the ceiling, rise above the tallest buildings, and then keep going up and up, until they were cold and surrounded by the stars.

It was nothing like an out-of-body experience; if something, I never felt more *in* my body. Then came the cold sweat and the burning sensation at once, but they felt… incredibly good. Like somehow combining two bad things had resulted in a delicate balance, a strange *pas de deux* that gave me the best sensation I had ever felt.

I later asked other users if they felt the same and if it was similar to taking other drugs, but they all assured me that nothing else ever felt like it, not even close.

After what felt like centuries of pure elation, came the strange part: I felt that my skin was shedding; it wasn't hurtful per se, but it was incredibly weird.

After the skin was gone, so were my bones, but they were quickly replaced by an exoskeleton—the sensation was, there's no better way to explain it, of a big shell growing out of my body, changing my entire physical structure.

And then, in my awkward and insane shell, I watched the air around me for hours, as chartreuse-colored ribbons unfolded and unveiled around me, like a peaceful and endless dance; I never felt more alive, more connected to the world in a sense that's almost impossible to put into words… that I belonged to this world more than any other living being ever belonged is the best I can explain.

The shell then receded, putting every single one of my bones back in its place, and it all was over. Tired, I went to the sleeping bag in the corner of the room and tried to sleep, but I was suddenly too hungry and thirsty.

"Man? Have you snapped out of it?" One of the strong guys knocked lightly on the glass door; he sounded almost gentle, and certainly worried.

"Um… yeah," I replied. "Something happened?"

"You just spent the last two-and-a-half days on the floor, rolling and drooling and laughing like a madman," he replied. "I'm going in, boss said I should give you a sandwich and some water when you were done."

After that, things were surprisingly normal; I gladly accepted the drink and the food, then the same guy drove me back in an unassuming car. At the time, Bryan was living with a cousin, not with me so, when I asked about my friend and the man informed me someone else was supposed to oversee him, I didn't worry too much.

As soon as I arrived home, I collapsed on my bed, and it was almost midnight when I woke up again. I had slept for no less than 11 hours.

I reached out for my phone, worried, but I had no missed calls, and the only notification was a text from an unknown number.

"Your friend's debt is forgiven. Have him stay out of trouble, he won't be so lucky the next time."

***

I tried to call Bryan over and over, but he never picked up—and by never, I mean *never again*. I talked to his cousin, who nonchalantly said he usually disappears for a few days from time to time, then to the police, to no use. Everyone who knew Bryan knew he was "just like that."

A week later, I contacted the number from the text, begging them to tell me if they knew anything, and asking if my friend got in trouble with them again.

The very same night, the somewhat nice henchman came to pick me up, and the dealer himself talked to me, after making sure to check that I wasn't wired or recording anything. He did it way less violently than I expected.

"Look, man, you were caught in this without crossing me, so I feel kinda bad," he stated. But not bad enough to not blow the smoke of his cigarette on my face, I reckoned. "You deserve to know the truth, but help me God if you go to the police with it."

"Did you do something to Bryan? Did he even leave this place?"

"He didn't... tolerate the drug as well as you did. Don't worry, he's alive but... I guess he'd rather be dead," the man who seemed physically unable to hesitate hesitated.

"What happened?"

"I guess it's easier if I show you the footage, but first, do you know what telomerase is?"

I shook my head no. The word seemed vaguely familiar from high school, but I couldn't grasp what it was, so the drug dealer grabbed his phone and showed me a short video where a science teacher-looking guy explained it in layman's terms.

A telomere is, to put it simply, an unimportant bit of DNA information in our chromosomes, at the very tip of the structures.

As you must know from school, cellular replication is happening the whole time, to a variable rate that decreases as we get older; each replication wears out the chromosomes slightly, so the telomeres are there like a protective brim or the cover of a book to make sure the actually important DNA sequences don't get damaged.

The only consequence of having your telomeres get shorter is senescence.

The telomerase is a specific enzyme that repairs the telomeres, but the human body barely produces it; that's the reason the telomeres are not constantly being replaced, and it eventually leads to death by old age.

So, if you could replenish your telomerase *properly*, you'd be technically immortal. If you produce too much of it, however, it's an abnormality in your cells and you end up with cancer.

"So far so good?" he asked, as the first video ended. I'm not the smartest guy, but I was able to keep up with the perfectly clear explanation meant for 14-years-olds. I nodded, and he played a second one.

The second video explained that, when you're born, your telomeres are around 11,000 bases long (bases are the little "letters"). And when you're old, they're only around 4,000.

Every time your cells replicate, the telomere loses a little bit of its bases, which causes it to get shorter and shorter, until it reaches a critical length; then you die because the cells can no longer divide and replenish the dying ones—so is the cycle of life.

But there is one species on the planet with endless telomerase, whose organism is coded to continue the cell replication indefinitely instead of creating abnormal, cancerous cells: the lobster.

Lobsters never die of old age, they just keep getting bigger and bigger because they are (properly) producing new cells at a higher rate than their cells are dying.

Instead, lobsters get so big that they need to molt over and over as they outgrow their shells, but molting gets harder as the body gets bigger. It takes a lot of energy, until the point where the lobster ends up stuck inside a dead shell, and bacteria start to take over.

To sum it up, lobsters are not programmed for senescence, but death catches them anyway. It's called biological immortality.

And it sounds even more painful than getting old and debilitated.

"Why are you showing me all this?" I asked, fearing that I already knew the answer.

"Because the new drug my supplier created is the telomerase extracted from the lobsters."

***

It took me a long time to process his words. Was that the reason I felt that my body was getting bigger and bigger, that I was growing a shell and that I ecstatically thought that I truly, completely belonged to the world of the living? Was I living the life of a lobster? Was it happening, and not only in my head?

After making sure I understood the important concepts, the dealer showed me Bryan's footage; he was in an identical room as mine but, while I had been there for no less than 60 hours, my best friend barely spent half an hour inside.

From the moment the substance entered his bloodstream, his body literally became an aberration, a Lovecraftian being that I can only describe because I'd rather endure this sight and go crazy than not know what my friend had to endure.

Bryan screamed in agony as his hands grew to an impossible proportion and his fingers disappeared, giving place to sharp, deadly chelicerae. Enormous antennae sprouted from his temples and literally reached the ceiling; his legs were melted together, and appendages appeared on his sides all over his body—the horrible, thin and segmented five pairs of crustacean legs, all of them still covered in human skin.

I realized the worst was yet to come when wet crunching sounds started coming from his dorse. After a few seconds, the carapace violently emerged from Bryan's back, also covered by skin, splashing clear bluish lobster blood all over the room. He roared in pain and horror and begged that someone made it stop; I then realized that my best friend's self-awareness had been completely preserved, unlike me, who simply had a bizarre but pleasant lobster dream.

His face and the frontal part of his torso remained human: he had become an anthropomorphized nephropidae or, as he'd be later called, the lobster man.

***

After explaining that Bryan had been sent to his supplier for scientific purposes, the dealer offered to take me to visit; I accepted.

"Did your supplier say anything about fixing him, and when he'll be good to go?" I asked, knowing very well that trying to save Bryan was not their priority. The man just shook his head no.

The supplier was the mad scientist type, a heavily guarded woman in her late 50s who decided that going Walter White wasn't enough and started researching ways to achieve a higher high. She showed little interest in me, as I hadn't developed any lobster feature, and only made a note about my lobster hallucinations.

"All my other subjects were completely fine and experienced nothing but unmatched bliss. Not a single one felt like a lobster, not even in a *weird but good way* like he reported," she talked about me like I wasn't there. "Bryan was the only white guy to test the drug, and his friend the first Asian, so it seems undeniable that, for some reason, race plays a fundamental role in the effects."

She then proceeded to explain that studying Bryan was the key to find out whether he was a very unlucky individual, or all the other Caucasian guys would suffer from the same fate. And, that so far, she had made little progress. When I asked if I could see him, she looked at me in surprise, like she was acknowledging me for the first time, and gestured to the other room.

The other room looked like an immense vivarium, at least 10 meters tall and with lightning typical of aquaria; Bryan was the only attraction inside, right in the middle of the reinforced glass cage.

My best friend was even larger and creepier than in the footage; his face was still somewhat human, but the eyes were more lobster-like and, between the antennae, two pairs of antennules protruded.

It was clear that he had molted at least once this week, and very recently, as the gooey arthropod blood painted the floor under him, still more wet than dry. Bryan's limbs were heavily constricted, and they were connected to a bunch of machines that seemed to be scrutinizing him.

An assistant followed me, turning on the communication equipment—a pair of microphones and speakers, one inside the glass and the other outside.

"Why is he restrained?"

"He tries to hurt himself with the pliers if we let him loose," the young assistant replied, simply; this monstrosity in front of us was nothing but part of the job for him. "Please call me to turn off the equipment when you're done, or else he'll scream the whole day."

"Bryan? It's me."

"Oh, thank God!" the lobster monster cried. "At least you didn't end up like me. I'm so, so sorry."

"No, I'm the one who's sorry for you, buddy."

***

It's been a little over ten years since then. I religiously visit my best friend once a month, it seems to be the highlight of his miserable existence. That's why I never miss a month, no matter what.

He's now in a 50 meter tall cage, and his body continues to grow; the assistant explained to me he's been trapped inside the dead shell a few times, but they broke him free. "She wants to know if, when we remove the reason regular lobsters perish, he can actually live forever."

I think it's incredibly cruel to force Bryan into staying alive as this gargantuan, horrible monster, but I have no power to change it—and I know that letting him go outside would not only be a danger to the world, but the world would be a danger to him as well. At least I can be by his side sometimes and ease his pain, even if just a little.

Bryan's mind is still perfectly lucid and human so, since his body won't let him do most things humans do, he spends his days watching TV, listening to audiobooks and such. The shady scientists created a system to feed him regularly and sprinkle water inside the cage. It's not a bad life, except for everything else.

In my last few visits, I've been trying to hide it from him, but this time it's fruitless; I'm too deteriorated. I know he noticed something's wrong, so it's time to be honest.

"What happened to you, buddy?" he asked on the microphone. I took a deep breath.

"There's no easy way to say this, but this might be my last visit. Or the next. I have Stage IV cancer."

The cancer spread so fast that I barely had time to get used to it. It never felt exactly real until I said it, and the words made both of us sob.

Bryan asked if I thought it was because of the telomerase we injected, but I denied it. I knew it was a lie, I just didn't want those people prying on me and using me as a guinea pig; I wanted to come to terms with my death and enjoy my last moments on Earth, instead of becoming just another subject for science.

They are still selling the drug, with a mere warning that it was found to have "unexpected side-effects on Caucasians," which means there are probably others like Bryan somewhere.

I don't want them to invade and study my body, but I'll make sure to leave a letter. I think I might be able to save a lot of people with a similar genetic background with the truth.

And the truth is that, little by little, I'm turning into a lobster man; from time to time, my limbs grow, an exoskeleton emerges from my back, and I keep seeing immense DNA ribbons, with the telomeres longer than ever, representing both the cancer and the biological immortality—and, if I had to choose, I'd say the cancer is a blessing compared to the other option.

I know I'm not hallucinating this time, because I managed to record myself.

All these episodes come and go in milliseconds, like I'm phasing in and out lobsterness, but every time it happens it remains just a little longer, and I feel just a bit less human.

Or like I'm drowning and decaying while still alive, stuck inside my own shell.

EIGHTEEN

When my older sister turned 19, my parents started looking at me with the deepest pity and grief I have ever seen; like I was going to crumble and disappear at any moment.

I was 16 and listening to music in my bedroom when my mother came to me with a beautiful portrait in her hands. It was of my great-grandmother Eleanor.

"Pat, you know how Eleanor used to say that when she was 18, a she-devil offered her some kind of paradise if she agreed to die immediately, right?"

It was a weird question; whenever my mother had a little more to drink, she'd retell this tale over and over. She came from a long line of spiritual but pragmatic women, women who fought to study and to work in male-dominated fields. Women who also found a good man to marry, women who had everything.

But then tragedy struck in their lives and they would lose a sister, a daughter or a niece. Always.

Once every generation, one of us dies at 18—this is the curse of my family.

"Yes, mom," I replied, and we recited together: "And she said fuck off, I have 7 siblings to help raising."

And Eleanor did. She worked her ass off to send her younger brothers and sisters to good schools, became a college teacher herself, and kept teaching every new generation of women to be strong and stand up for themselves.

My mother always loved her to bits, and proudly raised her kids the way her grandmother Eleanor had taught her. Eleanor peacefully died of old age when I was a baby, and overall lived a great, accomplished, loving life.

But grief knocked on her door periodically, as she had to bury a daughter and a granddaughter, both at age 18. My aunt Cecelia died years before I was born, and that took a huge toll on my mother and my other aunt, Christa.

Eleanor didn't believe it was a tragic coincidence. No.

She thinks that the same she-devil who invited her to go live in a better place came to claim her descendants.

After Cecelia, there were no deaths.

My sister and my cousins have all crossed the line to 19, and none of them reported anything weird happening to them.

I'm the only female in my family who is still 18.

Despite the fact that I always admired Eleanor, I confess that I thought she was being superstitious, or even mocking us—she was known for her savage sense of humor. So this conversation I had with my mother had been completely brushed from my mind.

Then today a gorgeous, magnificent woman approached me.

I am a part-timer at a frozen yogurt joint. As you might expect, the small store was empty. The little bell on the door rang, and I raised my eyes to meet a stunning, elegant woman who seemed to be in her early 30s.

She was wearing a simple and unassuming dress, but the fit was flattering. It was impossible to take your eyes off of her.

"Hello, Patricia." Her voice was velvety and melodious. "I see Eleanor's granddaughter told you about me."

I forgot how to breathe for a while. She was just... God, I had considered myself straight up to this point, but then I had found a woman that I both wanted to be like and have for myself.

"Come on, get yourself some *fro-yo* on me. Mine will be salted caramel and strawberry, if you please."

I mechanically filled two little cups as she graciously sat; not even the term "fro-yo" could make her less attractive and mesmerizing.

I stared at her intently.

"When you see Christa, tell her to see a doctor about that persistent headache. Unpleasant surprise on the way," she said casually. "So tell me about you, Pat."

"D-don't you know all about me already?" I asked. She smiled kindly, but the warmth never reached her violet eyes; it wasn't like they were cold, but they were neutral. Neutral and incredibly sharp.

"I know everything there is to know about everyone on your little planet, darling. But I'd still like to hear your version."

"I'm not actually interesting, you know?" I sighed. "I am only okay at everything. My sister is brilliant and she's pretty too, while I'm too average and not even sure what I want to major in."

She smiled so brightly I thought I was gonna go blind.

"Don't you want to be part of something bigger and easier?" she asked. "I'll offer you a great deal, the same one I offered your ancestor Eleanor, her daughter Bettina, and your aunt Cecelia. You know the results."

"I'm listening," I said. I don't know the circumstances of their deaths, but I know that both Bettina and Cecelia took the offer.

"Well, take a look around the world you live in. You're young, but old enough to know. Do you feel safe walking the streets? Isn't this world rotten? Sure, you can say there are good people; people that mind their own business, at least. But the rotten apples always spoil the whole barrel, no matter how many good or average apples there are. And lately you mortals have seen that happening to a lot of people you used to deem good, huh?"

"I don't... feel safe. Two of my friends have been assaulted. I admit sometimes I'm scared to leave my bed," I replied. "Still, I'd feel so bad about how my mother would miss me."

She smiled.

"You're a good girl, Patricia. I'm Lilith, by the way." She grabbed my hands. "Let me tell you something, although I'm sure you already know this in your heart. All the women in your family are fit for this deal, but I have to choose only one. I chose you because you won't be missed as much." I recoiled, feeling hurt, but I knew Lilith wasn't lying. There was a spark of compassion in her eyes, too. "It's not that you're not loved, it's just that your cousins and your sister..."

"Are so much better than me in every sense. I know. I panic easily, I don't trust my own decisions, and I don't have any special talent. Sometimes my life feels like such a waste."

"It's not, dear. It's not. Because you were born for something greater. Greater than these girls you deem better than yourself. They are fit for this world. You are fit for the Utopia."

"What's the Utopia?"

"It's everything there is out there, the only eternal life in the universe, offered to a select few. All the great people on Earth are nothing but a heartbeat. They will fade to nothing, like all the unassuming lives. No matter if you were Thomas Edison or a bus driver, you'll disappear on the same void when you die."

"So you mean there's no heaven and hell? And what about God?"

"Oh, God exists. God created great things. Imperfect, inferior beings like you humans are just the collateral damage of his masterpieces; the residuum of the creation. He never even turned His face to you, or batted an eyelash when we told him our plan. Lucifer and I see potential in you. Well, some of you. Most are truly garbage."

I was utterly amazed. "Why do you only take young women?"

She smiled again.

"That's a great question. Lucifer likes to collect men in their 40s, so he can laugh at their moral dilemmas. How will my family live without me, the great provider?? What if Karen marries another man and Cody turns gay because he didn't have a masculine figure?" She did a great impersonation of a generic middle-aged man. "But I take my girls while they are still beautiful and not completely tired of how unfair this world is to them. I don't want the morons in your society to make you forget what Eleanor taught you. She knew there would be only nothingness out there after she died, but she opted to stay and take care of her loved ones. It was a bold, admirable choice, and I decided to reward her for it. She was the only one I ever approached knowing that I would be refused."

"So you can't both live a great life here and go to this place you call Utopia?" I asked.

"Oh, one usually can't have it all, no. But I picked two or three of those. Like Marilyn and Cleo. They were almost 40 but still young at heart and completely unfazed by how the world tried to break them. You have to admire that."

This whole conversation felt like a dream, but I was fascinated by it. Even if she was just some crazy woman trying to prank me, or just a great storyteller, I *needed* to hear everything she had to tell me.

"How is that Utopia? Will I like it?"

Lilith snapped her fingers. The walls and furniture around us, and even the street across from the door started to fold and fold and fold, like the reality was only a 3D draft, until they became minuscule pieces of cardboard, and then they fell into the infinite under us.

We were now surrounded by a stunning, futuristic place. There was no sense of feeling cold or hungry, we could move by floating around as we pleased, and there were amazing buildings everywhere, decorated with statues of pure white marble and paintings so beautiful I wanted to cry.

I could see colors I never imagined possible, and the sky was always a warm shade of blue, but dotted with stars, and an immense full moon—like day and night had been combined to create the most perfect landscape.

Everything was shiny, symmetrical and felt right; peaceful, but far from boring. A perfect, ordered chaos.

"This place is constantly expanding, so you'll always find new things to do. You'll never live another tedious day."

She snapped her fingers again, and everything unfolded and rose back into place.

"And if I accept your offer, which I will… can I choose the way I die and do something first?"

"Oh, you have a few days to deal with all your stuff. I'm not a monster, you know?" the she-devil smiled again.

"Great!" I said. "There's only one thing I need to do before I go with you. I want to kill the man who assaulted my best friend."

Lilith agreed to allow me to do it, and we talked some more before she left.

And that's all I can remember clearly. The rest of the day was a blur; knowing that I would die, I wanted to quit my dead-end job immediately, but I had no one to quit to, and I couldn't leave the store unattended. So I stayed, surrounded by weird ice cream, thinking about the bright, utopic future ahead of me.

The she-devil told me I couldn't tell anyone I was about to die, but I was allowed to discreetly say my goodbyes. My family was really nice and had taught me a lot, and I had valuable friends, but none of that was reason enough to refuse an eternal life of happiness where I could even be friends with Cleopatra and Marilyn Monroe.

I spent some quality time with my loved ones, then two days later, I took my mother's handgun and headed to see the one who hurt and destroyed my beloved friend, both physically and mentally.

I won't describe the details of the torture I put him through. I'll just say that I only stopped when it seemed to me that he went through at least ten times what he made her endure.

And then I killed him.

"Oh, shit" was my only reaction as I realized that punishing this disgusting man felt even better and even more right than living in a perfect Utopia.

It feels like I finally found my purpose. If this world is all that there is, the only thing we can do is enjoy it.

And we'll only be able to enjoy it if we cleanse it.

I decided to take this mission upon myself. Like Eleanor, I choose the mission of making Earth a better place instead of the endless excitement of the Utopia.

The problem is, I already agreed to die tomorrow.

I WAS SOLD BY MY PARENTS

Our monthly stroll by the mall was the only thing that ever gave me a sense of normalcy in my former life.

Mom would dreamily and slowly walk by every store, contemplating the lives she would never get close to live. We watched brand new toys, shiny bracelets and a world of silk and wonder—a world that would never exist for people in our social standing.

It took me a while to understand that the trips were for her own sake, not mine.

"Your daughter could be a model, you know?"

The smiling man approached us when we were having our ritualistic ice cream—we couldn't afford anything there but the once-a-month sweet treat.

I'll admit I have unique looks, and I was the most beautiful 7-years-old. My hair was always jet-black, even as a child, contrasting with pale complexion and emerald eyes. I had, indeed, fantasized about being a model when I grew up, after seeing so many advertisements in the mall, all of them containing huge images of stunning ladies, surrounded by perfume bottles and jewelry, and dressed in daydreams.

"My husband… he…" Mom started to shyly answer, but the man cut her off. He probably went through that dozens of times.

"Why don't I give you my card and you call me after Dad allows it?"

His smile grew wider. So wide you could see something creepy underneath, but as a seven-year-old, I couldn't pinpoint what.

She agreed.

That night, I pretended to sleep and overheard them.

"How much did he offer you, Janet?" dad asked, aggressively as usual.

"N-nothing" she stuttered. In his presence, she always did.

He slammed his huge hands against the counter.

"You're lying! I know how those things work!"

"I-I swear, Bradley. He just told me to call."

"So call him, dammit!"

"Just like that?"

"What do you want me to say? We can't afford it anymore. I'm not even sure the damn prick is mine. You used to be quite the whore."

"I-I just had one other boyfriend before you, Brad," her voice now sounded teary and hurt.

It took me a few years to understand what he meant. The bastard. I looked exactly like him, he just wanted an excuse to hurt her. To hurt me.

The two of them fell silent, so silent that I could hear dad sipping from his bottle. Mom dared to speak.

"So you want to give her away?"

Another slam.

"Don't be dumb. Who's talking about giving? We're selling it."

"But you know they probably will…"

"That's none of my fucking business, Janet."

***

The next morning, Mom asked me to wear my favorite dress and pack my best clothes. It was easy because I didn't have many that could be considered good.

"Where are we going, mom?"

"Modeling," she answered in a rushed tone, her smile faltering. "We'll see that nice gentleman from yesterday."

We took the bus because dad didn't let her drive—said she was too dumb for it. He, on the other hand, was almost always too wasted to control a wheel. Our decadent Chevrolet Vega sat in the garage collecting dust.

Dad made sure to be there to see that mom didn't hide any money from him. He didn't let her work, so he knew that if she handled the transaction alone, he would probably never see her again.

Everything was quick. The gentleman was named Mr. Carson, and his slightly chubby hand gave my parents a firm handshake, then handed me a lollipop. He took a few pictures of me, said everything was good, and gave my parents the money; it seemed to be more than they expected.

"Damn, if that's the price we should make a new one," dad exclaimed, his yellowed fangs opening up in a smile for the first time in years.

Mom bit her lip and buried her face in her only coat, a beaten-up pinkish parka.

She stroked my hair, tearing up silently, and we parted ways.

Mr. Carson took me to his house. His car was brand new and he let me pick the song. The drive was so different from the ones with my parents; the songs were always filled with screams: dad cursing at the other drivers, Mom begging him to not pick a fight, him telling her to shut up. If he was in a really bad mood, he would lock me in my room and leave me without dinner because I was breathing too loud or couldn't hold back my tears while they fought.

The place was a suburban, generic middle-class house, white picket-fence style. It was gorgeous for a humble girl like me. He parked.

"What we'll do now, Mr. Carson?" I asked, afraid he would hit me for being snoopy.

"Please, call me Ted. I'm taking you to your room. Soon it will be lunchtime, but I have a task for you first." I looked at him obediently. "I left a videotape in your room's TV. Please watch it and, during lunch, act like the girl you'll see. Got it?"

"Sure, Ted!" I was overjoyed my room had a TV.

I diligently watched the tape, then after around two hours Ted took me downstairs to have a light lunch, consisting of sandwiches and soda. I did my best to imitate the girl.

"You've done well, Delilah. This is your name now, got it?"

I nodded. I don't remember the name I had before.

"I'll put on another tape for you, but you can use the afternoon to relax, too. Take a nap if you want. You'll have a lot of tasks tonight," he said, taking me back upstairs.

That night, while I prepared for dinner, I was confident in my skills. Ted left me a brand new change of clothes and told me to dress up nicely; it was a special occasion.

In the dining room stood an older woman. She was beautiful and looked remarkably like me. Her eyes sparked up when she saw me, wearing a pretty tutu dress.

"Delilah!" she hugged me tightly then, still not letting go, stared at Ted. "How did you do it? They're almost identical."

"I was lucky."

Over dinner, they explained to me why I was there.

Ted and Laura had a daughter named Delilah who died at 15. It was a painfully silly death; she insisted to go to a pool party and drowned. Most people around were drunk teenagers—too drunk to help.

Their world was destroyed; they couldn't accept losing their only child, the light of their life. She was such a good girl, and now she was gone for such a stupid reason. So they decided to look for a new one—a girl that looked like the original Delilah and could mimic her demeanor.

They were so good to me. Laura loved me to bits, and Ted spoiled me rotten. I was a true princess, living a make-believe life. I went to a great school, we had amazing family trips together, my toys and clothes were always the best, the trendiest, the coolest. I never missed the life I had before, neither my horrible dad nor my weak and weepy mother.

It was easy to become their perfect daughter once I practiced a little. Delilah never had to beg for a cup of water or be trapped inside a dark closet because she was listening to the TV too loud. As long as I learned everything about the original Delilah and could act like I was her, the world was mine.

Until I turned 12.

Ted and Laura came to my room together and said we needed to talk. I was ready to be sent back home, to the horrible, hopeless life I had before—but at least I had a good run as their substitute daughter.

"You know, Delilah… our other Delilah was perfect, but she had a serious problem," Laura started.

"She grew up. She grew apart from us. If she never insisted on making her own decisions, on going to that damn party, she would still be here with us" Ted was grinding his teeth. "We can't let that happen to you."

"I'm so sorry, Mom, Dad. I promise I'll never grow apart, I want to stay with you forever," I muttered. I admit I thought they would kill me to preserve my youth and innocence.

But Ted had other plans.

"Your father is a very good scientist. He can fix you."

"Delilah, do you want to be fixed?" Ted asked.

I said I did, still unsure of what needed to be repaired in me. But I wanted to be with them, and I want them to be happy.

The three of us went to the basement and Ted wired me to some strange machines.

"You'll be young forever, my Delilah."

"Let's hope it works this time," Laura added, uneasily.

The last thing I remember before being hit by a bolt of endless pain was understanding that there were other surrogate Delilahs before me.

***

I thought I would never speak again from the pain.

I felt my bones shattering into a million pieces and reforming back all wrong; rinse and repeat.

My body was an endless puzzle consisting of a billion pieces that nothing could put back together. My limbs literally swam in a pool of despair—metallic despair. It was my own blood.

I was nothing but a pile of organic matter for days. I was as much a daughter as I was a guinea pig. Floating, infinitely floating in his lab fluids.

Until somehow everything was assembled again.

I woke up in my bed. Both Laura and Ted were by my side.

There was a sharp pain in the back of my neck, but other than that, nothing at all. They kissed my hair, begged that I forgave them for putting me through so much pain, and asked how I was.

I was, as crazy as it sounds, fine. The hours of infinite aching were distant now, almost like they happened to someone else.

I ran my fingers through my neck and felt something different there. I asked if they could see anything. Ted gasped.

"It's a new bone."

The new bone was small, but shaped like a thorn. It prickled my finger, but didn't really hurt me; other than that, I was perfectly okay. I still looked like a person, and I looked more than ever like their Delilah—at least that's what I assumed from seeing their eyes so filled with devotion for me, even more than before.

Two years went by. While the other girls my age were quickly growing in height and shape, I never fully developed into a teenager. It was clear that something was different with me.

Ted and Laura were overjoyed to notice I was still childish in mindset and looks. It had worked, after all; they achieved a daughter that would be forever 12, forever docile and dependent on them.

I didn't mind it. Maybe puberty was nice to others, but not to most; a lot of my classmates had awful breaks of acne, and talked in irregular, weird tones of voice. One girl even had a boob way bigger than the other. I was happy being a child instead of a train wreck.

Others weren't so happy.

"Why the hell your looks don't change? Are you a fucking witch?"

It was Sandy, the tallest girl in class. She was a troublemaker, and she had picked me as a target because I was too short and my skin was too clear.

I just tried to unleash my arm from her, I swear. I don't like fighting. But I ended up crumbling her ulna and radius with my grip.

It happened in an instant; something crazy and impossible. I merely grabbed her wrist and felt everything inside her skin collapsing.

Sandy cried desperately, her arm swelling and looking like rubber, while shards of bones erupted from the skin. It was nauseating to see what was left of her bloody mass of bones. Not even someone as mean as her deserved to feel so much pain.

Nobody understood what happened, and everyone ruled out as impossible that a small girl like me could cause this damage to a strong and tall bully. The school nurse called the hospital while saying that Sandy must have fallen in a weird way.

That day, I felt the thorn-like structure in my neck burning like crazy. When I told Ted, he took me to the lab to perform a few tests.

"It appears that, as a side-effect, you became extremely strong," he said, after a few hours.

"But why I didn't crumble anything else before?" I asked.

"How did you feel when this girl Sandy tried to pick a fight with you?"

"Very annoyed."

"Well, then your strength is probably triggered by negative emotions."

I considered the information for a few seconds. It made sense; my life was so perfect that, ever since I underwent the procedure to stay young forever, I never had a bad experience—or, at least, not the kind that would make me easily break something as sturdy as a human bone.

A few weeks after we discovered my superhuman-angry-strength, I finally understood that Dad thought he was selling me to prostitution—and he was totally okay with it.

After hurting my mother in ways I'll never know and understand, after hitting me and starving me over nothing, he thought that handing a seven-year-old—his only daughter—to an unknown man was perfectly normal; if she was going to be sexually enslaved, it was none of his business.

This thought made me feel very annoyed—annoyed enough to look for my old home and pay Dad a visit.

Who would believe that a teenager too small for her age could turn all the limbs of a grown man to dust?

I WAS HIRED TO MURDER MYSELF

I have always enjoyed killing, and I blame it on my farm childhood.

Calling it a farm is a big stretch. I grew up in a shack in a rural area, having only my father and sister around. He never mistreated us, but he was stiff and relentless in his beliefs. For him, there was no such thing as male or female; everyone under his roof was, by default, a hunter.

Back when we were really young, he would leave us home alone for hours and hours. He first took me hunting when I was 3. I never thought rabbits and squirrels were cute—to me, they were simply prey.

I first hunted a deer when I was 10. I was limber and my body was stronger than an average adult's by then, which seemed to be the only thing that made Dad proud.

My sister Danna was never a huntress, but she was great at hiding. So she hid; at first, Dad was angry, but I was so good that whatever I hunted was more than enough for both of us. Besides, Danna was good enough to manage herself, catching smaller animals. She was outstanding at fishing with her own hands due to her quietness.

Killing fish made her less uneasy than killing other animals, but she never enjoyed any of it. Despite being raised exactly the same way as me, she took no pleasure in hurting other creatures.

Our father died when I was 13. The two of us went deeper into the woods and he was caught by a bear; it all happened so fast that both he and I were completely taken by surprise. What I remember more vividly is that he kept screaming, "shoot it! Shoot it, you little bitch!" as his body was mauled and torn apart.

I only had 2 bullets left, and I was too worried, so the first missed and the second wasn't enough to take down the bear—by then, he was not much more than a bloody mass of skin and broken bones. Alarmed by the screams and shots, Danna came to the rescue; she grabbed my hand and we ran like the wind.

I'm honestly not sad that my father's last words were verbal abuse; he was desperate and scared, literally being eaten alive, after all.

I forgave him in a heartbeat—the problem was forgiving myself for failing him in such a crucial moment, leaving him to die one of the most gruesome deaths I can think of. It's been a long time and I still can't stop hating myself for that.

My sister and I were more than equipped to fend for ourselves, but ended up being taken to a foster family anyway—the police said it was too dangerous to leave us where we could have a horrible fate like our father's.

Danna soon adapted to having a normal life, and she clearly was held dear by the couple. I am grateful to them for having a comfy bed and finally learning how to write and read, but I kept to myself at home. I missed Dad and, most of all, killing things.

I went hunting alone every day. The first time, the new family was impressed by my ability. The second time, my foster mother muffle-cried "the poor ducky"; the third, my foster father begged me to give what I hunted to someone else, instead of cooking it in their yard.

I started selling it. I made some nice cash, and gave everything to my sister's college fund. She was smart and needed the money after all. I just needed to smell the delicious bitterness of fresh blood.

By the time I was 18, I married the sweetest man. It was crazy how we balanced each other's personality, him being always so calm and gleeful. Thom was 15 years older than me but a kid at heart, while I was experienced beyond my years—probably the reason why we were such a good match.

My husband, a well-known merchant who sold a myriad of things in our small town. He sometimes sold parts of my hunting; the meat, the fur, the heads as prizes.

We were happy. We lived 5 great years until he was shot in a robbery.

It was so much worse than losing my father; while the old man had been claimed by the laws of nature, murder over a petty amount of money was disgusting and despicable beyond words. Besides, when Dad died I had Danna, but now she was far from me and I had no one.

From that moment on, a burning rage lived inside of me. The eagerness to kill took over. I didn't know how to manage a shop, so I asked my husband's brother Stu to take his place in management, but Stu was a drunk and a buffoon, and soon the shop bankrupted. I was left with nothing.

When I learned about a certain shady part of the internet, I finally realized I could sell my services and satiate my ever-growing bloodlust.

At first, I was hired to hunt beasts, to take down predators so people's chickens and other farm animals could be saved. Then, I expanded my business.

I'm famous now—I mean, my work name is. Nobody knows my face, nobody knows I'm even a woman. My body is small and strong, perfect for sneaking in. I look trustworthy enough to have my target take me to dinner. Sometimes it's too easy.

I have built a name between politicians, and rich cheated wives love me. Of course, my clients are not always from the highest social standings, and they try to bargain a lot. It's not unusual that some broken-ass guy asks me to murder his rich father/uncle and get paid after I do the job, when he gets his inheritance. I just laugh at their faces and tell them to fuck off or else I'll murder them instead.

I had fun dismissing the miser non-clients, until the day my intuition—no, my *instincts*—told me to keep talking to the guy after he told me his conditions of payment.

"I will inherit some money," he wrote, "but the thing is, I used to have a brother. He's dead now. No kids. But I talked to my attorney and he told me his widow will get half of my money. So I want to eliminate her."

"Sure, just send me her info," I replied, for the first time. Because I knew this story. I didn't want to be paranoid and think it was me; I just felt sorry for the poor woman and maybe would fuck up with the guy.

But it was me. My brother-in-law, who was constantly helped by me and my husband after losing everything in gambling over and over, who ruined our store and I never said a thing, wanted to kill me. No, worse than that, he wanted to hire someone else to kill me, because his coward ass couldn't even do it.

I took the job. The next day, I went to see my sister Danna, and asked her something no twin sister should ask the other—can you die in my place?

***

When I take a job, I will finish it, no matter what it takes. So I sent my client a picture of my dead victim, my sister. I was famous for this particular modus operandi, so he was positive that the job had been done.

As I said, Danna ain't a huntress. She's a great hider. So, after I forged her death and gave Stu a false sense of safeness, he found my sister, disguised as me, in his dirty apartment.

"D-D-Dora, what are you doing here?" he was stuttering and sweating.

"Just came by to talk a little about the inheritance we're about to get," my sister calmly said, perfectly mimicking my voice and intonation.

Stu never knew I had a sister because she lived far away during her graduation. Both I and my husband always kept to ourselves and never had a wedding party, so our families didn't know each other very well.

"Inheritance? I don't know what you're talking about," he made a poor attempt at lying.

"Why don't you ask the hitman you hired, Stu?" she asked, as I came from behind him, wearing the exact same clothes as her. I gotta admit it was so much fun to stage this.

When he turned to look at me, Stu was pale, and I'm pretty sure he pissed himself.

"W-w-what is going on? What kind of joke is this?"

That's all he could say before I gagged him.

"It's your fault that my husband was shot, isn't it?" I stabbed him once.

I knew very well how to lethally stab someone only once, making a cleaner death, but it wouldn't happen this time. "You fucking deadbeat. Your damn loan sharks broke in the store and killed him. You let the store go bankrupt because you were fucking terrified of staying there."

He shook his head desperately, trying to deny it, but his eyes told the truth. I never fully realized it until that instant. It was a moment of clarity and I hated his guts even more: not only did he see my existence as a mere inconvenience between him and some money, but he sold his own brother's life for pennies, the coward fuck.

After Danna played her part, she did what she was best at: she hid, not wanting to see the bloodbath I was about to cause. I did what I was best at too: I stabbed and stabbed and stabbed.

When the body was found, the police immediately arrested Stu's loan shark. They were investigating him for a long time and just needed one more move to make theirs. My theory about the loan shark killing my husband was right.

I noticed that the revenge brought me some closure, and it made my bloodlust diminish. I still go hunting most weekends, but I'm done with killing people.

Nothing can bring Thom back, but I can move forward, learn new things, work with something else. I'm still young and have a lot to live, and I know that he would hate to know I spent my whole life sulking because he's gone.

So let me give you an advice: if you're thinking about hiring a hitman, don't. The best one went out of business.

But if you do, don't be cheap.

FORGOTTEN PICKUP

"Oh my fucking God!" I screamed suddenly, looking at the clock. James and I had agreed that having me work from home would be the best way for me to keep track of our children's activities.

Now there I was, failing at it.

I hurriedly threw a jacket over my pitiful working pajamas and grabbed the car keys. I'll admit having driven slightly recklessly, the thought of my poor boy sitting all alone in the playground too hard to bear.

Literally one second after I parked the car, the backdoor was opened, and a little blonde boy materialized on his usual seat.

"Hey, mommy!" he greeted me, cheerfully. His golden hair was covered in sweat, despite the cool weather.

"Hello, Tommy!" I smiled back. At least his clothes weren't muddied. "Too much running around today?"

"Just a little!" he replied, and started drawing furiously on a coloring book. When I say furiously, I mean it literally; Tommy was making holes with the crayon across the pages.

Is five supposed to be a strange age? His older sister was the most quiet, easy-going girl during kindergarten. I can't believe it's been over five years ago.

Maybe it's because he's a boy. Boys are always difficult, I thought to myself.

"Mum, I'm hungry. What's for dinner today?"

Shit. James used his day off today to spend the day with our six-month-old at his mother's house so I could get some work done. Making dinner was the last thing on my mind.

I texted my husband as we stopped at a red light. Tommy was still using his crayon to destroy the coloring book, but at least he was quiet.

"Don't worry, baby, I'll bring food from Mom," was his reply. Great. Now my delightful mother-in-law knew I'm not able to simultaneously work, take care of my children, and feed my family properly.

A horrible thought crossed my mind. Why did we even have 3? I always said I wanted only two kids.

"Mum, I'm so hungry," Tommy said again. We still had a while before dinner, so I stopped by a famous fast-food drive-thru and got him a burger, absent mindedly.

When we finally got home, I unpacked the car and noticed Timmy had only eaten the meat, leaving bread, pickles, and cheese behind. Ugh. The picky eater phase.

I left Tommy playing downstairs and headed back to my office. If I hurried, I could get all my work done before James and our baby girl were back. My oldest was at our neighbor's, getting some school projects done. God bless the Davidsons and their well-behaved daughter who's good friends with mine.

Just one more hour. You can do it, I psyched myself. After putting on some classical music on the headphones, I immersed myself in work.

My hungry stomach hurting was the only thing that made me realize that way more than one hour had passed. For the second time that day, I cursed out loud because I lost track of time.

It was 10 PM.

Why the fuck James didn't come fetch me for dinner when he got home?

I went downstairs angrily, but stopped dead in my tracks as soon as I realized the smell.

But despite the metallic and bitter scent, nothing could prepare me for the carnage in my very living room.

James and my two daughters were completely mangled, their blood and guts all scattered. Their eyes and part of their viscera were missing. I'll never know if they screamed before being ripping apart, but I'm assuming they didn't, or the neighbors would have called the police.

Unless the neighbors were eaten, too. Tommy *said* he was hungry.

That was when I realized I don't know any Tommy. *I don't even have a son.*

THE DOORS OF THE UNIVERSE ARE CLOSED

1

Have you ever wondered why, despite its infinite vastness, we never found anything or anyone in outer space?

I always believed that people out there are hiding from us because we are hideous little beings, pathetic talking monkeys, stingy aberrations that never learned to speak the language of nature, listen to the sound of the planets and understand the smart way to use the resources, both inside and outside our bodies.

In my understanding, each and every one of us is an unfulfilled god, wasting our potential for so much by becoming so little. Our lives are too short and we crave immortality, pathetically multiplying ourselves simply to spread our genes like animals—so no actual smart form of life would want to get close to us.

In other words, we won't find extraterrestrials because they won't let us: we are not welcome.

But, when I was involved in a discovery that defied everything that I knew, I realized I was still thinking too highly of humans. Our importance is much, much smaller than I believed.

Now I'm haunted by this knowledge forever; the more I know, the less I want to know, and the more I wish I could be a happy simpleton believing that some god created an entire universe just to decorate our night sky with distant planets and stars.

***

"And lastly, let me tell you the main reason why you should consider microbiology: it's estimated that we have discovered and cataloged no more than 1% of the microorganisms living inside our body. We know a very, very small fraction of everything there is to know, so the possibilities of our work are endless. It's a field of constant discover and wonder, and I would be very happy to call some of you my peers in this journey," I finished my speech, and was met with enthusiastic applauses; colleges invited me yearly to explain my profession to freshmen, and hopefully claim a few promising ones as my underlings.

As the students left the auditorium, and I started to grab my things, a tall man in dark glasses and a casual raincoat approached me.

"Amazing speech as usual, Dr. White," he congratulated me, but I knew that a man with those looks wasn't there just to compliment me and leave.

"Thank you! Have we met?" I replied, extending my hand for a handshake that never came.

"No, no, don't mind me. I just came to escort you to an important conversation," he replied. "Shall we?"

"Am I in trouble?" I asked, with a nervous laugh.

"Quite the opposite, Dr. White. It seems that one of your studies has become a matter of utmost importance to humanity itself."

With those puzzling words, the man guided me to an official-looking car; by *humanity itself* he meant, as expected, the government of the United States.

The drive took no longer than 40 minutes, going farther and farther from the city. The man was quiet and polite, and our only other interaction was him asking for my computer so he could copy a few files from my work. I fidgeted nervously, knowing very well that I had to be compliant because, if things went south, a taser and some fight training in high school wouldn't mean anything.

But, luckily for me, they only wanted my knowledge—although, looking back now, I'd rather die than help unfold the horrifying truth.

The car parked in a large, unassuming lot, and Mr. Raincoat escorted me to a modern, sterile building. After going through long, empty corridors, he opened the door to a conference room. I entered.

There were only four more people, and one of them was a vaguely familiar face—but the first to speak was another one.

"Thank you so much for coming, Dr. Caroline White," the only other woman in the room got up and gave me a firm handshake. Despite her clothes being topped with a spotless lab coat, it was evident that she was finely dressed; clearly someone very important.

After saying that I could call her Councilwoman Diana Smith, she introduced me to the three men in the room—a NASA scientist, an anthropologist and the familiar face: an older gentleman that was one of the top gastroenterologists in the country, whom I'll call Dr. Davis.

I had no clue why such a diverse group of people like ourselves were reunited.

"Let's do it step by step, and it will become abundantly clear why each of you are here," the councilwoman said, and projected an image on a large screen. It looked like some sort of mammal seen from the inside, and there was a tiny object on it.

"Dr. Davis, can you tell us what this image is?"

"This is unmistakably a human intestine with an endoscope in it. Although I suppose the image was manipulated, because not only the quality is too high for normal equipment, but also because it would be... inadvisable at least... to insert a second camera," he replied, on a calm, confident medical tone.

"Interesting how you immediately mention that it's *human*. Could you please enlighten us as to why it's not an endoscopy on another species?"

"If you require me to be fully technical, I'm going to need to talk to a veterinarian. But, if we're thinking simply, the equipment used for pets has another proportion, and their insides are fundamentally different. Besides, while endoscopies of the upper gastrointestinal tract are common for animals, colonoscopies are not."

"Very well, very well," Smith nodded. "Now, to the second image."

The second image was one of mine: a bacterium that my team recently discovered in the stomach of a man who lived in an isolated indigenous community; our latest project involved comparing the gut microbiota of people with different ethnicities, eating habits, etc.

The bacteria had a very peculiar shape that immediately caught our eye, and I was working on a paper to first introduce it to the scientific community.

Before I could say anything, Smith turned to the anthropologist.

"Dr. Renner? Could you please tell us what this is?"

His face was full of the most intense, genuine wonder I have ever seen. The only way I can describe it is that he looked like God right after creating Adam.

"How? How did anyone do it?" he asked, his eyes watering. "It's impossible… impossible and yet…"

"Please explain to us what's so surprising to you, Dr. Renner."

"Due to the nature of amber, it's always been considered impossible, but we ran the simulations. This is very similar, if not exactly, what a human fossil would look like if it could be entirely caught on amber," he replied.

"Is this your simulation?" the councilwoman showed us a third image, similar to the second, but that I could perfectly tell apart from my research. It made sense that they were alike since the bacterium was almost perfectly shaped like a microscopic human body.

Dr. Renner confirmed it.

"Now," she returned to the first image, "what would you say if I told you that the endoscopic image is not a human stomach, but a picture taken by one of NASA's very own rovers, Dr. Davis?"

He looked astounded. "Well, I'd say I didn't know planets looked like that. I thought rocks couldn't possibly look like guts."

"*Human* guts," she highlighted.

"I am here to confirm that this image is legit from NASA," remarked the other man, who was quiet until now.

"And Dr. Renner, what would you think if I told you that the second image is actually a newly discovered bacterium on Dr. White's research?"

"I suppose I'd say that I didn't know that bacteria could come in such shapes."

"So now that each of you, the top experts on your field, gave me your precious input, let me put two and two together: This is the ultimate evidence that the universe we live in is nothing more than the guts of a larger being. Each of us is, in a sense, the god of the microbiota living in our body. The larger being. Well, everything we know—and everything we don't know—is, too, contained in an intestine. And, with your help, I can prove it. Do you want to be part of the biggest scientific breakthrough ever made?"

"Do you have a plan?" I asked.

"I have most of it, and I'm pretty sure your brilliant minds will easily fill in the rest," she sounded as honest as it gets. "Are you in?"

The glory of knowing, the thrill of a new discovery, made us agree immediately. And, regretfully, we all started helping develop the plan that would ruin our sanity forever.

2

"So, the first thing we should do if we want to understand what we are is remembering where we actually came from. If we live inside something's digestive tract, it's extremely likely that there's a *before* for us, a time before being born into this world, when we were outside. But it is a dormant memory," said Dr. Davis; not only he was brilliant in his field, but he also had great inputs regarding other medical subjects. "There are methods to unlock people's memories from both the intrauterine life and past lives, but we'll have to step up a notch here."

Councilwoman Smith had a larger team, which she consulted about our ideas to make sure we weren't making any fundamental mistakes. She seemed pleased by Dr. Davis' words.

"It makes sense," Dr. Renner agreed. "We'd have to awaken a deeper part of our mind, but wouldn't that involve drugs that can cloud our judgment?"

"Don't worry, Dr. Renner, I can provide the most safe and modern nootropic we have today. The dose is too small to do anything but the desired effect: enhance your cognition," Smith replied. "I just needed you to come up with the *how*, we have the resources for anything."

The anthropologist nodded.

"After taking it, we'll undergo a virtual reality experience that should trigger some memories of familiarity," Dr. Davis explained. "Any questions?"

Dr. Martinez—the NASA guy—raised his hand.

"I have a question for Dr. White, if you don't mind."

"Go ahead," I replied.

"This bacterium you discovered… is it a good one or a parasite?"

"It's not that simple to determine, but I can say that, like most microbes on your gastric tract, small amounts of it are either beneficial or harmless, and cause no imbalance to your health. But it's likely that large amounts can be detrimental, as it kills some other microorganisms your body needs."

"Sounds like us human indeed," Dr. Renner remarked; I refrained from telling him that this is usually true to all species, except for the ones that are completely parasitic.

After a few more questions and clarifications, we were good to go. Each of us scientists were put on a reclining chair and, while having our vitals monitored by Smith's team, a virtual reality headset was put on us, and we were given a small pill.

After a few moments, the same images started to surround each of us.

The best way I can describe the sensorial maelstrom that I went through is that my mind was forcefully, unkindly expanded, while simultaneously bombed with ridiculous pieces of knowledge that made sense for me to have, but that I never had grasped until now—in other words, a never-before-seen corner of my brain was unlocked.

I had ayahuasca tea a couple of times, but the way it expanded my mind was gentle and mystical; now, the smart drug paired with strangely familiar images of going through a tunnel seemed to be tearing my mind apart to make more things fit inside it, like it stretched my very being into expanding irreversibly and beyond repair.

And then I remembered.

Before I was born, I went through a very, very similar tunnel; it's a raw memory, more a feeling than anything else, because back then I didn't know any words to express concepts—but I know, deep in my gut, that it has happened to me.

It's unexplainable, and yet, viscerally comprehensible.

I don't know how long the whole experience took but, when we were done, every single one of us was a mess. I didn't realize that I was trembling before I saw Dr. Renner uncontrollably crying, the mild-mannered Dr. Davis squeezing his head between his hands with perplexity, and Dr. Martinez violently pinching himself to make sure everything was real.

"Does anyone know what you saw?" Smith asked, composed as always.

"I just know that it's forbidden knowledge," Dr. Martinez replied. It surely felt like it; like something my mind had been purposely making sure to not acknowledge in order to protect itself.

"It was a tunnel that felt incredibly familiar, like an inexpressible déjà vu," I remarked.

"I saw my body from the womb into life, I felt it developing and changing," Dr. Renner added, still sobbing. "It was beautiful and terrifying."

"You're all right in your perceptions, but failing to grasp something bigger," Dr. Davis got up, and Diana Smith grinned. "This tunnel, this forbidden knowledge, the route we made before being born... it's nothing but the life of a lactobacillus. Being swallowed, going through the esophagus, the stomach. We humans are, on a larger scale, lactobacilli. It's likely that not only the ones inside us are sentient beings in their own universe, but the one we're inside and the others around it are inside an even larger being."

"So existence is eternal and infinite because it's like an endless matryoshka," I remarked.

"Something like that. Now, do you feel any different?" Dr. Davis responded, still squeezing his head.

After the initial shock of unlocking this large-than-life knowledge, I realized that my head was overwhelmingly strange.

"My perception is ridiculously enhanced," Dr. Martinez replied, and I knew exactly what he meant.

I could hear the buzzing of a fly three rooms away—and discern it from any other fly in my hearing range, which was suddenly enlarged to unimaginable proportions.

I could see every single pore in everyone's skin: a pimple that was about to erupt, the tiniest scars, every single baby hair in their faces.

I looked at our glasses of water resting over the table, and I could precisely tell you how many milliliters were in each of them. I could feel the slow but never-stopping movement of the world, both around the sun and itself.

I could even hear plants communicating, although I didn't know their language.

All my senses were violated and overloaded by all the new information that my brain used to either be unable to grasp or ignore.

That meant that sounds were so amplified that even the slightest tapping of someone walking was enough to trigger a migraine. That meant that our eyes could let in so much more light and that our brain could process so much more information, that we were able to understand all the unperceivable colors, telling them apart from the normal ones, and we could see in the dark.

I think Dr. Davis's words, paired with the unbearable sensorial overload, broke Dr. Renner, because that night he went home and overdosed on sleeping pills.

3

Mr. Raincoat was the one to give us the tragic news. Despite only knowing him for a day, his demise left us dispirited to say the least. It was the loss of a human life, of a clever colleague, of one of the only people in the world who shared with us something so crude and transcendental; someone who could *understand*.

Not only we were a man down to shoulder our disturbing experience with, thus making it heavier, but we also knew that eventually each of us would break in a definitive, unfixable way too.

It was a matter of time before both the forbidden knowledge and the unlocked perceptions of the world drove us all mad.

"So, have we proved anything?" the usually quiet, stoic Dr. Martinez asked Smith accusatorily.

"First of all, it was his choice. I don't see any of you doing the same because your mind is stronger than his," she replied dryly. "I'm as sorry as the next guy, and I'll make sure that Renner's contributions won't be forgotten and the world will sing praises to him as much as to the rest of us. He died honorably, due to his greatest discovery, just like Marie Curie. And secondly, now that you have unlocked perception beyond the average human, we just have to coax our... host... into doing something that proves its existence."

"And how exactly are we doing that?" I asked.

"This doesn't concern the three of you. It's taken care of."

"I'm not going to be a part of this murderous farce anymore," Dr. Davis got up and tried to leave, but Mr. Raincoat blocked his path menacingly, hand on holster, and tapping his feet unbearably loudly.

Neither Raincoat nor Smith had to say anything, but the three of us knew that we were too far gone to give up. We were in this together until the end, whether we liked it or not.

"How are we supposed to know what to expect if you don't tell us?" I pressed.

Smith ended up telling us her plan: she had access to multiple nukes—including new, experimental ones—and they had been released into the outer space, a decision she made single-handedly, and long before she had us join her; apparently, our role was just to be guinea pigs that could deal with the only part that she couldn't: how to unlock enhanced human perception.

The building was now swarmed with telescopes and equipment I couldn't even understand, but I knew they were meant to monitor any changes—meant for us.

Dr. Davis, Dr. Martinez and I exchanged a look, and I knew verbatim what the two of them were thinking; it was when I realized that the three of us now could communicate telepathically.

"Am I crazy or can you two hear my thoughts if I focus on you?" I asked. The two of them replied positively.

"Let's not talk with our mouths anymore. She's dangerous, and honestly, listening to my own voice is horribly loud now," Dr. Davis remarked. We agreed.

"What do we do? How do we stop her?" Dr. Martinez asked.

"I think nothing can stop the nukes she already fired," I replied.

"But who knows what she'll do next if no one stops her. I think we have to kill her," said Dr. Davis.

"Don't you want to find out if the theory of us being just microbiota in someone else's body is true?" I asked.

"After what we experienced with the VR? I know it's true already. And I don't want to find out anything even worse," Dr. Martinez replied.

"I agree. My mind can't take much more. I know I'll soon perish like poor Renner," Dr. Davis added.

Knowing that our hands were tied and we could do nothing but wait for some reaction—that likely only the three of us could perceive—we sat in the room with the woman who promised us glory but handed us only unbearable madness.

And we waited.

4

For a whole week, nothing new happened; time probably had a different flow outside of our little universe.

Our senses expanded more and more, and now a mere pencil being dropped ten stories below was enough to give me horrible headaches.

Mr. Raincoat put me and my two remaining colleagues in a soundproof room where we were being monitored 24/7; they didn't want us to go home and end up like poor Renner.

It was on the 8th day that something happened—something that's still unbelievable, and yet, undeniable.

The three of us were making plans to kill her, when suddenly something sent us off our tracks, like we were in a freak train accident.

Instead of feeling the planet lazily turning, it jolted violently. And then we heard it—something like a voice, but like it was speaking from deep inside our cells.

"Send the sample to the lab."

It took us some time to realize what it meant, although it seems obvious now.

***

Noticing our pained faces, Smith entered the room to talk to us. She knew for sure that, from the way we reacted, something had changed; the sly fox.

"Distract her and don't worry about me. The two of you will be fine," Dr. Davis said inside our minds.

"What happened?" she asked us, very softly.

"The Earth is moving too fast," Dr. Martinez replied; it wasn't a lie, but more like a half-truth. "Something different is definitely happening."

She simply gestured to Raincoat right outside the glass window; he probably started sending other people in the building to the observatory.

And I could see the councilwoman was barely holding a satisfied smile.

"How do you feel? Tinnitus? Some sort of condition? You need a nurse?"

"Nothing worse than we already had, just the world making a crazy movement," I replied. "It doesn't feel like spinning—the spinning is still there. It's more like half of a pendulum."

She took notes, looking very interested; All the while, Dr. Davis was moving carefully and slowly towards her, so much that she could barely notice it.

"Keep going," he told us.

"White and I have a few theories related to that," Dr. Martinez said. "We always wondered why, despite the vastness of the universe, no one has ever contacted us."

"We both used to think humans were inferior to alien races, but now, with your discovery, we have a few conclusions," I replied.

"Oh, is that so?" she asked, a sharp look on her face. "When have you two discussed this? You've spent this whole week quietly."

Shit.

"We actually have some sort of voice of wisdom speaking inside. It told us the same things, it said so," I quickly managed to lie; I have been a decent liar my whole life, and I just needed her to believe it long enough for Dr. Davis to do whatever he was planning to do.

"The first conclusion is that what's the observable universe for us is still nothingness compared to what's out there and we can't possibly know," Martinez intervened; she seemed less alarmed.

"The second is that, if we are akin to the microbes living in our body, then the other living beings 'near' us are too, so they might not have the means—or even the intelligence—to contact us. Hell, chances are they are blissfully unaware of themselves," I added. "And obviously, we might have seen them but not have what it takes to understand it. Does a bacillus always recognize a streptococcus? It's unlikely."

She lightly nodded, intrigued—the last thing that she'd ever do, because Dr. Davis had stealthily reached out to her gun, cocked it, and shot her.

Before any of us could react, he then shot his own carotid, with a big smile on his face.

***

Martinez and I went deaf with the horrible noise of the two shots. The two of us were eventually released, since no one could prove that our claims about the Earth moving differently were true; the ones who came after Smith died were skeptics, and they simply decided that we were under too much stress to be reliable. The study was terminated.

As it normally happens, it's better to believe in anything else than facing the truth.

My former colleague and I are both trying to live normal lives again, and we still keep in touch—no one else could even fathom the things we saw and the things we know.

But we still wondered why the telescopes and high-end astronomical equipment couldn't prove that the Earth moved abnormally, because everything is still exactly in the same place.

Send the sample to the lab.

It only hit me today.

No one noticed the Earth moving because, being the origin of the problem, it was removed from the body—and everything we know in the universe came with us. It's impossible to observe any changes if everything around equally changed, if our whole chunk of the cosmos was moved somewhere else.

We are now in the lab, living in some sort of petri dish.

MY TWIN LIVES UNDER THE BED

Mark and I are 16-years-old—or at least, I am. He died when he was a baby.

"It was a terrible accident," Dad says. "It could have happened to anyone. Please don't think poorly of your mother, she loves you so, so much."

If I'm being fair, this part I can't deny. I am my mother's pride and joy, and she'd do anything for me; well, anything *but* give my twin brother back. Or let me speak about him. Or not slap me when I beg her to let me be with him.

But that doesn't happen often because I know better. I gave up long ago, and I keep secrets from her now.

I was always curious. A nosy child. That's probably why I know everything I know.

Still, I didn't think a lot about any of it until I was around 10.

Dad explained to me that having twins is really hard. Both he and Mom are estranged from their families, so I don't have grandparents or aunts in the figure, and they didn't have any help with us. The two of them were sleep-deprived and had two noisy, poopy babies to take care of.

She was so, so tired, and her hand slipped because she drowsed. Then Mark, at only a few weeks old, was on the floor, his little head crumpled by the fall.

Of course I can't remember it, but I assume it to be true because I know babies' heads are really soft; their design is super stupid overall.

I imagine there was a lot of blood and ugly crying, and maybe his little brain was all gooey and scattered on the floor, but Dad won't tell me the gore details. The point is that he died, and my mother felt absolutely awful for letting it happen, so they took extra care of me. They wouldn't be able to survive two dead kids, I think.

"It was really scary. We don't know what we would do if we didn't have you," Dad repeated over the years, and he always patted my head or kissed my hair. "We love you so, so much, princess. I can never lose you."

I remember the first time I asked Dad directly about Mark. I think I was 11.

"Do you think you and Mom would love him so much if I was the baby who died?"

"We would love him, of course! But your mother always wanted a little girl."

"So was Mom disappointed to have Mark?"

For some reason, Dad was astounded when I asked him that. I had never experienced an uncomfortable, heavy, difficult silence before.

"What's the matter, Dad?"

"We never told you your brother's name, so how do you…"

"Oh, Dad, but he told me! He lives under my bed, don't you know? Of course you do. He said he almost died, but then you let him live there. As long as he hides from Mom, because she would be too scared!"

Dad's face was white as paper. I was young, but I felt like I had peeked through a keyhole and learned about a world I wasn't ready to find yet. "Princess, this is a secret only between you and me… and Mark, of course. Don't tell your mother about it, Martha. *Never.*"

"Why? Wouldn't she be happy to know her son is alive?"

"It's complicated, princess" I remember the way Dad bit his lip until it bled a little, then told me in a whisper: "Now go play with Mark, okay?"

Mom was a successful psychiatrist (whatever that means), so Dad was the one to quit his job and stay home with me. From that day on, he'd make me extra food to feed Mark, buy some extra toys so Mark and I could have more fun, and we even had a secret code to put Mark back under my bed when Dad heard Mom's car parking in front of our house.

She worked a lot, so our days were mostly filled with joy.

I was really happy, but I felt like Dad and I started drifting apart. He barely paid attention to the two of us. Maybe he thought that since we were almost teenagers he didn't need to watch us that much, or maybe, just like Mom, he didn't like Mark a lot.

I insistently asked him about it, but he'd always say something generic like "of course I love your brother too." or "I'm just tired."

Shortly after that, Dad started taking me to a therapist, but I didn't really understand why. And I didn't know why we had to keep that a secret from Mom, too.

But I complied. I loved being a good daughter, and being called *princess*, and not being slapped for asking questions.

Dad kept telling me that it wasn't Mom's fault that Mark died, and I believed him—at first. But as I grew up, I started learning things. I learned that parents tell convenient lies to protect your feelings, and about postpartum depression.

"Mark," I asked him once, when I was 14. "Did Mom try to kill you on purpose?"

"It took you long enough to figure out! You're really slow, Mar," he replied, nodding enthusiastically with his slightly deformed head. "Mom didn't want a son, and she didn't want to ruin her career. She was also, you know, really sad and didn't think things straight."

"Do you hate her?"

"I don't think so. But I don't love her either. She's the reason I have to pretend I don't exist and hide under your bed."

"Is it too bad?"

"I love being with you, sis. But in a few years, you'll be a grown-up and where will I go? I don't even know how to read."

In my whole life, I never felt as sad as I did that day. I started to plan something, but I didn't have the guts to do it.

That until recently.

Mom's work had an event for the employees' children, and she took me—until that day, I never heard much about her work, and barely knew what she did.

It was horrifying to find out she was the director of an asylum for the mentally ill—one with a really bad reputation. She didn't believe that the patients could improve, or even get a second chance. It was a place where fragile people in desperate need of help were sent to in order to languish to death.

Mom was evil, and she had to go.

I waited until one of the rare moments when she was home but Dad was not—it was a Sunday, and she was relaxing while he went out for groceries.

Even though I never had the courage to actually do it, I've been training for this moment for years. *My hands were now strong enough to strangle her.*

She would never have suspected me, her beloved daughter, her *princess*. She didn't even put up a fight and her body soon went numb. Then she stopped breathing.

I didn't feel good about killing her. It felt wrong and dirty, although it was a relief. I was like a soldier killing in the war with no joy, but for the greater good.

I decided to hide her body under the loose boards of my bedroom. It felt fit; she murdered Mark, and even though he somehow survived, he had to spend 16 years living under my bed.

Now she was the one who had to spend eternity down there, and way deeper.

When Dad came home that night, I pretended I didn't see her, but told him that I think I heard her leaving.

Dad seemed to believe me at first, despite Mom's car being in the garage, but he realized something was wrong because I grew happier and happier with her absence. And the smell... I'm ashamed to say I didn't plan that far ahead. I tried to use perfume, essential oils, and even bleach, but every day it was harder and harder to conceal it.

I barely had time to enjoy Mark's newfound freedom because I was so skittish the whole time, and the house literally smelled like death.

I knew I needed to burn the body, but it would be impossible for Mark and I to do it on our own. We needed to tell Dad.

So I ended up confessing, thinking that he would be able to forgive me. Thinking that maybe he hated Mom for taking away his son, too. And that the three of us would be happy now.

Instead, Dad knocked me down and I blacked out.

When I came to, my whole body was restricted by a rope. I heard his muffled voice coming from the next room. He was pacing, nervous and noisy, which meant he was talking on the phone.

"Martha has been having delusions since she was 10... she suddenly started thinking her dead twin was alive and under her bed... I know it's my fault to go along with it so I could protect her... I tried psychotherapy but she didn't improve... I never thought she would become violent... you know how Sharon thought that schizophrenia patients were unfixable... I couldn't lose my only daughter to a cold and inhuman mental ward."

I still don't know very well what he meant, but that's how I ended up here.

***

The above was written by Martha Goodwill, 16, a newly admitted patient at the Saint Alphonsus Humanized Psychiatric Hospital, when asked to write a report about her life and the reason why she was sent here.

Ms. Goodwill shows lucidity and awareness of her surroundings at all times, but is adamant about the belief that her deceased brother is alive. Due to having murdered her mother during a delusional crisis but being unimputable, Martha's father/legal guardian willingly sent her to us.

—Travis B. Wilson, head director at the Saint Alphonsus Humanized Psychiatric Hospital

THE FAMILY EXPERIMENT

1

Sociology always fascinated me, and, after decades of writing books and being a professor, I was lucky to become part of a team funded by very important corporations to create a daring experiment: we wanted to know what happens when you isolate a common family from the entire world.

The structure for the study was amazing, courtesy of a very high budget; we had an entire house built inside the facilities and did a few long, meticulous interviews to select our subjects.

The Smiths were a typical suburban family of four. The father, Regis Smith, had recently lost his job. He had two teenagers, Maya and George, and his wife Sandra had never once worked in her life, so he was pretty desperate to get in.

They were selected over a second family that met all our expectations because they had no other living relatives; both Regis and Sandra were only children, and both their parents had passed. They also had no close friends, nor did their children.

The sponsors urged us to believe we saved a family from being homeless, but every time I remember what happened, I believe it less and less. Here are the most relevant parts of the log that we researchers collectively kept.

We took turns surveilling the subjects 24 hours per day and in every room of the house. There were three 8-hour shifts, each including a sociologist, a psychiatrist, and a few assistants. I may have inserted a few extra pieces of information to help you understand better the whole story. Also, we called the subjects by numbers to avoid humanizing them too much, but I'm transcribing their real names. In time, you'll understand why.

Day 1

They are all quiet and awkward, too aware of the monitoring to do anything normal. All four of them mostly just sit around uncomfortably.

The subjects have internet access to keep a sense of normalcy, but it's very restricted; since they have to be isolated from the world, they can't post on social media or comment on sites, only use it to read news, books, and the like.

Their internet use is being remotely monitored by techs related to our team, and can be terminated forever at any time if they break the rules.

Day 2

Maya woke up screaming from a nightmare. The subjects are slowly adjusting; the monitoring is very subtle and the countless cameras and mics are very well-hidden, so it's easy to forget they are there—especially with your family around, I suppose.

Day 3

One of the cameras malfunctioned yesterday, and I had someone go and change it without being seen, but today, the image is all black again. It's a mere closet and the subjects don't know this part of the house is monitoring-free, so maybe there's no need to change a second time. At least, the microphone there still works.

To keep normalcy, we ask the adults to make a few daily tasks. Besides cleaning and cooking, they have to homeschool their kids, make grocery lists, clean a car that never leaves their garage but is constantly being dirtied by one of the assistants, and at least one of them should keep a fictional remote job.

They also have to wake up early every day like they were in the outside world; this has put a huge stress on George, who's clearly a night owl and bad sleeper in general.

Day 6

Sandra and Regis are fighting the whole time. He tried to delegate the tasks, but she called him controlling. She wants to homeschool the kids, but he says she's dumb as a door. She offers to have a job then, but he says she's only good at household chores. Sandra is pretty hurt and mad.

Day 9

Maya went to the grocery room (a separate part of the house where one of the assistants puts food and basic home supplies once a week) and spent 45 minutes talking to herself. All of them picked this habit around day 4. The house is not big enough for them to have a lot of privacy, and everyone is bothered by each other's constant presence. This is getting interesting.

Maya mumbled precisely 103 times, "it's unbearable that dad never leaves."

Day 16

George has been having more trouble than usual with sleeping. He moves too much in the bed, then wakes up tired, in a cold sweat. He loses focus while studying. Only his sister seems to notice he has a problem.

"We'll leave this place eventually, right?" the 13-years-old boy asked his older sister. "I really want to go to college one day."

She said "sure, don't be silly."

Day 23

Regis isolated himself from the family, focusing on his work; he builds furniture and wooden pieces on demand (obviously, our fake demand). His work is very noisy and it's clearly driving everyone else crazy.

He's the only one who seems to be happy, or at least not stressed all the time. He and Sandra are alternating between screaming at each other and completely ignoring each other, but despite the fight, most nights in bed he looks for her in the dark.

Her sighs suggest that she only wants the semi-consented (at best) sex to end, but it doesn't seem to bother him at all. Dr. Ivanov, my assigned fellow psychiatrist, thinks he even enjoys it; how she clearly doesn't want him to touch her, but has no will to say no. She thinks it is her job because he is better than her. And he knows it.

What a scary man is Regis. I'm excited to find out who he really is when the social persona he puts on shatters; I'm convinced that there's still something more. Something darker.

Day 38

Everything was going relatively fine (or, I should say, eventless) until George woke up once again in a sweat, and trembling. Without notice, he simply got up, went to the kitchen, and cut his wrist. The knife was too sharp, and the wound was way deeper than intended; had he used all his strength, he could have severed his own hand.

Instead, it was half-detached and dangling from the arm, skin and muscles destroyed as nothing but the bone keeps the hand from falling off.

We were ordered not to help directly; after all, we wouldn't be there to save the boy's life if it happened under normal circumstances.

Sandra was the one who found him, collapsed on the kitchen floor. She did nothing but scream, looking in a direction she thought to be a camera.

"YOU'RE KILLING US! YOU'RE PSYCHOS!"

Maya, quite the practical one, went to the grocery room, where we had already provided a good first aid kit, painkillers, and antibiotics to help deal with the trauma and relief the pain—in case someone was clever enough to find it, of course. We're not that bad.

She sedated her brother, cleaned the wound, and clumsily sewed his hand back, then bandaged the whole thing. It was a decent job for a 15 years-old with no medical training, and I was proud of her like God was proud after creating Adam.

Day 39

Once again, Sandra is screaming at a supposed camera. "You need to provide medical care for my son. He needs a psychological evaluation and antidepressants!"

Sorry, Sandra, but the point is observing your family with no contact with another human being. Besides, he's being evaluated. We just can't tell him the diagnosis.

Our silence seemed to kill her inside.

Pointing her finger in the wrong direction, she added: "You need to do something or I will!"

Day 42

Sandra tried to contact a psychiatrist online and had to be put in solitary for a week. Her internet access was terminated for life, too. No more fantasizing about ethnic males in thongs for you, my lady. Or browsing through recipes just to realize on the next grocery day that one ingredient will be always missing because, you know, life is full of inconveniences.

It keeps the normalcy.

She keeps screaming at us.

"How long will you keep us here? Six months? A whole year? I can't stand another week in this hell."

The solitary seemed to make her bolder, without her husband to complain about everything she does.

Day 48

Regis was cranky and borderline abusive to his kids the entire week. This was the first time he addressed us.

"How am I supposed to not fuck for a week, you sick fucks? Are you enjoying my misery? This crap is over. I want to give up. I'll contact my lawyer."

But he never did. He may have power over his weak-willed wife, but he can't do shit to us, and that makes me smile.

We don't particularly enjoy human misery, Regis. But we enjoy yours.

Besides, he's our most interesting subject.

Day 53

Sandra was hysterical for the week after returning, but calmed down once Maya went to the grocery room and brought a fair amount of booze. We only give them alcohol on special occasions, and Christmas was coming. Cigarettes and drugs, though, are strictly banned—another reason why Regis wants to suit us.

Sandra kept all the alcohol for herself, demanding that her daughter "keep it a secret from the boys." Her addiction made it easier to get through the next month; too bad for her that we planned a very finite stock.

Day 62

George tried to "end all this" by setting the house on fire. Our fire alarm is very good so, besides a few second-degree burns on his former good hand and a wet house, nothing happened.

He claims to miss a girl named Karina. We imagine she is a school crush.

Sandra started to change; she sent Regis to sleep in his small workshop. He slapped her in the face so hard that she was bruised for a week, but she didn't back off, and he was too surprised to do anything else before she shoved him out of the door.

You can see that this man is very used to resorting to physical punishment to get what he wants from the weaker, and the only reason why it took this long for us to see him in action was that his family already knew better, and did everything to avoid his fury.

Day 70

Sandra told Maya, "we girls gotta stay together." Maya is not interested in being anybody's ally. She seems to do better alone.

We had to change the closet camera again, because George has been spending more and more time there. Now, instead of static, all you can see is darkness; a reddish darkness, like when you close your eyes on a sunny day. We should probably put one camera out of the closet, but facing it.

Maya asked who is Karina, but George won't answer.

Day 73

George is gone.

Yesterday, all the cameras in his room malfunctioned. You could only hear sounds. He was talking alone—we're sure of it, because all the others were being seen in different rooms—but he was distressed, like someone having a heated argument.

"No! I won't kill Dr. Shantan!" were his last words before a loud series of bangs started. Maya rushed to his room and screamed.

"No, George, please! Please, stop hurting yourself. Please! PLEASE."

You could hear her loud crying as her parents approached the room. The cameras went back to normal (except the one in the closet), and whatever was left of George was a dreadful sight. His whole head was ripped open, with blood and brains staining the closet door, the floor, and his sister. He was barely recognizable as a human anymore, but looked a lot like a pumpkin ran over by a truck.

"He banged his head so strongly," Maya said, between sobs. "He killed himself in an awful way. Awful, awful way."

For the first time since the experiment started, I grabbed the only microphone that can be heard inside the house.

"Lock yourselves in other rooms immediately. We are removing George."

2

George isn't dead. To this day, he is still in a coma, living like a vegetable, which is much worse; it would have been merciful if he died, but he didn't. There's a good chance that he's enduring all these years still conscious.

After this major incident, we wanted to shut down the experiment and free the remaining subjects. The whole team wrote a manifesto containing details of the horrifying events so far, and the guys who went in to remove George reported "an unexplainable sense of misery and hatred permeating the whole house," but it only made the bigwigs want to keep the experiment going even more; they were very interested in the results.

Monsters. And I, for one, am a monster by association. I stayed. My career would be ruined if they released information about my participation in this unethical project, and I was too deep into this to not see it through to the end.

Day 80

It's fascinating to see how humans deal with mourning. Most of us need to be let alone 90% of the time we spend grieving, but the 10% of interacting with other people and feeling their support is crucial. Without it, you fall apart.

George wasn't dead, but everyone could comprehend he might as well be. There was no optimism about his recovery, and the overwhelming feeling of hopelessness tore the family apart.

Maya locked herself up even more. She spent the whole time keeping her mind busy and active, mostly reading. She used to play the piano ever since she was a little girl, but we purposely didn't put a piano in the house.

She started to compose songs using a website that emulated a piano. Back then, smartphones weren't common, so the subjects didn't have phones, only computers.

I smiled. She was strong and resourceful. It pained me to know that she was never leaving this place alive.

"*How long do you intend to keep us here? Six months? One year?*"

Sandra's words stuck on me, because I couldn't tell her an answer I knew by heart.

This is the cruelest part of our experiment: there's nothing to look forward to. We're keeping you here forever. Until every last one of you dies.

Day 83

Regis punched and smashed all his handwork. The food will be very scarce next month; unfortunately, by destroying the commission pieces, Regis didn't earn enough money to afford to feed all of his family properly. Normalcy.

Day 88

For a while, the remaining subjects tried to behave as a family. But, as soon as something didn't go as expected, they exploded in rage and tears. Regis and Sandra physically fought, and Maya had to choke her father with her bare hands until he passed out.

"I thought he was gonna kill you," she offered to her shaky mother, then locked herself in her room.

The peace had lasted mere two days.

Day 97

Just like George, Sandra has been talking to someone that's not there, and they're fighting. She doesn't eat anymore. Regis and Maya fought over what little food they could get that week. None of them seems concerned with Sandra.

"She's too weak for this. She's better gone."

Maya repeated this 103 times.

Day 104

Sandra lost a lot of weight and isn't sleeping. She just walks in circles around the room, calling for George and arguing with an invisible being. Her broken mind seems to have regressed to her son's childhood. She keeps baby-talking with him. She giggles and coos too; it's a little sad.

Maya took upon herself cleaning George's room; she had removed the extra gore earlier, but only now really took the time to go through his things. Maybe understand why he took his life in such a brutal way.

She found a whole notebook filled with the words "don't go into the closet." The writing gets more and more desperate until you can barely decipher his words.

She didn't go into the closet.

Day 106

Sandra used the last of her strength to gouge out her eyes with two spoons. Maya tried to help her, but she didn't let. The woman begged to be left to die, and neither her husband nor daughter dared to stop her. They clearly weren't against it.

I have to praise Sandra for her creativity. After George's first suicide attempt, we removed all the knives and potentially piercing objects from the house. It made everyday life a nightmare because they weren't allowed to own a single pair of scissors, and could only eat using spoons or their hands.

Speaking of eating, still not enough food. Maya is rationing hers wisely. Regis is a mess.

"I'll be joining Karina now. She was George's twin sister. You don't remember her because you were a baby too, but she died on her first days. Your father accidentally let her fall from the bed."

These were Sandra's last words for Maya.

Day 111

Maya keeps telling herself "don't go into the closet" and shivering.

She wrote it too, but not as many times as her brother, and nowhere near as desperate. Under the last time, she added, "there's a presence there. The same feeling from when we were little."

The camera inside the closet still doesn't work. The cameras pointed to the closet malfunction constantly, for no apparent reason. They get normal whenever you put them somewhere else.

Day 116

We removed Sandra's body the same way we did to George. Then today we symbolically put a cross in the garden. I'll briefly explain that the house is completely inside a building, but they have a small winter garden, with tall plexiglass to let the sun in.

Maya found it eerie to have a graveyard in her own house, but she still keeps busy; she's composed enough to learn things, and is teaching herself Japanese.

Regis keeps calling for Sandra, and he still sleeps in the workshop. During the night, he goes to their old bedroom door and knocks desperately until he falls asleep on the floor.

The thing is, the door is unlocked and open.

Day 223

Regis lost touch with reality.

Now he knocks on Maya's door and thinks it's Sandra whenever he sees his daughter. He spends the whole day screaming and banging, while she took it upon herself to work. Maya spends her days making sure that Regis is locked and crafting the wood pieces to make money and feed herself; she's been feeding her insane father with the bare minimum to survive.

Dr. Ivanov thinks she doesn't want him to survive, but still can't find the courage to let him die; having to take care of someone gives her purpose, and, while annoying and demanding, it's better than being alone.

Day 225

It's Maya's 16th birthday. We sent in a beautiful cake. She bitterly laughed and accused us of having a twisted sense of humor.

She gave Regis a small piece and he went hysterical, refusing to eat. He thinks Maya is dead and Sandra is the one who's alive, but delusional.

Day 234

Maya was doing well until today.

Regis is malnourished and his sclera is all bloody-red, protruded veins. I think he went blind.

But he still somehow had the strength to free himself from three locks and find Maya; she was in George's room, trying to analyze his computer to get some answers about his death.

We still don't know how. It all happened in a matter of seconds, like it was some unknown force.

Regis broke into the room and tried to force himself on his daughter, still thinking it was his wife. The human in me didn't want to watch. The human in me wanted to interfere.

But the sociologist, thirsty for a peek at the darkest of his mind, watched in fascination.

Maya was taken by surprise, which gave Regis the upper hand. But in a few seconds, she was able to recover. She had been eating and sleeping properly, and we knew she was strong enough to literally squeeze his neck until he died. But she didn't do it.

She shoved him in the closet and locked it.

Day 235

We keep hearing Regis's screams on the closet's microphone. It's maddening. He's begging to be killed, and you could hear faint noises of skin and hair being ripped off. Please. Please, someone, free me from this.

Please. Please.

Day 236

The screams have stopped after 45 hours. In the first five hours, Regis screamed, "I'll get Dr. Shantan for you. Let me go. Let me go. Or please just kill me. Just kill me. Just kill me, it hurts so much." It was always the same words, growing more desperate every time they were pronounced.

For the next 2.400 minutes, he could only babble incoherently and cry.

Maya locked George's room from the outside, barricaded it, took all the food to her room, locked her door, and made a second barricade. She's scared, but trying so hard to focus. So hard.

Day 237

I'm a mess.

We're not supposed to keep a personal log here, but I need to report it. It's relevant to the experiment.

Yesterday, after leaving work, Dr. Ivanov took his life.

He had been quite disturbed by Regis's screams (obviously, we all were, but he was usually the colder one in the team).

Today, shortly after hearing the terrible news, I found a brief letter in my pocket. It was signed by him.

I used to think of myself as a brilliant man that could comprehend the human mind better than pretty much anyone. Maybe I am, but you know what? Is Josef Mengele remembered for being a brilliant doctor that brought countless advances to medicine, despite it being thanks to his cruelty and willingness to perform experiments that cause awful suffering?

No. He's remembered for being a Nazi. That's what he was, above all. I, too, am in the first place a monster. I hope there's no afterlife, because I fear the punishment for eagerly watching the human mind fall apart.

You were a good man when we met, Melvin. I hope you still find this man inside you.

Andrei

Day 1.028

She's still there.

Once again, after Andrei Ivanov's suicide, we researchers begged to end this madness. But the sponsors wouldn't hear of it.

Unless, of course, we were willing to pay for every penny we spent on this project, and a substantial fine for breaking our contract.

At least Maya never does anything out of the ordinary. She never went to George's room again, and after a respectful amount of days, she moved to the master bedroom.

She's been really good with the craftwork. Her cooking skills clearly improved, she now knows conversational Japanese and German, and even started working out. It haunts me how strong her will is. If Dr. Ivanov was here, he would joke about wanting to open her brain to study.

I should feel thankful that my job now consists of watching a young woman living on her own until the end of time, but I can't stop thinking about everything that happened. I close my eyes to sleep and I see George's smashed head. I look at any woman and can perfectly picture her scooping her eyes out. I see a man and I fear he'll descend into complete madness until he ends up tortured to death by an unknown entity.

Every day.

All the time.

3

From time to time, I still think about the day I interviewed the Smiths. They were perfect for the study because they had no living relatives or friends outside their family nucleus—no one to miss them. A lower middle-class suburban family that would do anything not to fall in disgrace after the dad lost his job.

Back then, I rationalized that we'd be providing housing and a peaceful life to a family forever; but the truth was that we all knew very well the experiment would ruin their lives and, while Regis and Sandra signed up out of their own volition, their underage kids had no choice.

And none of the four knew that, once they crossed our long white corridors, they'd never come back alive.

The Smiths didn't realize that they were being recorded in the waiting room right before I asked them to come in for the interview.

"We are very happy and normal," Regis practiced in front of the mirror; it seemed that he really wanted to be chosen—maybe because he realized that we would never intervene, so he could do anything without consequences. "My kids are the best, never give me any trouble."

He clearly had made the whole family wear their good clothes, and threatened under his breath to have awful things happen at home if we didn't behave properly.

"That if we still have a home," Sandra muttered in an unpleasant tone, her mouth in a fine line. "Your dad can't find another job."

Regis's face was the only one to light up when I opened the door and invited them in; the interview started as normal as it can get.

"Does your family have some kind of secret, Regis?" I asked, half-jokingly; I didn't expect anyone to be honest about that. "Once you're there being monitored, we'll find out anyway, so you'd better tell me!"

To my surprise, the faces of both the parents went somber and tense.

"We had a baby who died," he replied, as Sandra shifted uncomfortably. "She was George's twin."

"I'm sorry! Did the baby get sick, or some sort of accident?"

"It was an accident," Sandra replied, hurriedly, and we soon resumed normal conversation.

After the group interview, I had each of them talk to me individually. The young boy and the stay-at-home mom didn't have a lot to say, but both Regis and the girl talked again about the dead baby, the man heavily implying that he did that on purpose, but not giving me a clue as to why.

I pressed him, asking questions; probably too many questions.

The daughter was the one to provide me more precious insight about the situation.

"My sister Karina was dropped by dad as a baby. And I once found a note that he wrote to mom saying something like *I'm sorry, but the baby was evil*," Maya's smart eyes nervously shifted around the room. "I was too young, so maybe I'm misremembering it, but dad wasn't like that before it happened. I mean a brute."

"The death of a child will always change a person, Maya," I replied.

"And after that, the house always felt strange. Like there was hate in the air. I thought it was because my mother hated my father for killing her daughter, but I guess it was something else."

"Why would you think that?"

"Because two years later, my mother's mom died in a freaky accident after trying to open the closet in George's room... you know, the room that he'd share with our dead sister if she was alive," she bit her lip. "After that, things went back to normal. We lived for years in the same house and nothing happened."

Could it be that, by changing houses, they brought back the vengeful ghost/demon of their deceased baby? Did it make any sense?

I'd usually say no, but it's hard to be a logical man knowing that, when the team went in to retrieve Regis's body, we found nothing. No body, no blood. The closet was spotless, like nothing ever happened there.

Day 1.092

Now that Maya is of age, and is working really hard, we decided to make her a nice surprise.

She will live on her own forever, so we thought she might as well have a little fun alone.

We left a few… female pleasure supplies in the grocery room.

I swear to God we weren't trying to be gross or watch her in a creepy way. During the experiment, we heard all the four members of the family masturbating, and the parents having sex. While part of life and the experiment, these experiences were disgusting and we were more than happy to know they always did it under the sheets.

When she went to the grocery room and saw the dildo and things of the sort, she laughed for a whole hour. A literal whole hour. Her face was red, her hair was messy, and she was tearing up. Her legs were shaking so hard that I was genuinely afraid Maya was going to burst.

"Guys!" she yelled, clearly addressing us. "You know what? I have lived all these awful days without once complaining or freaking out. I took care of my good-for-nothing parents. I fixed my brother's damn amputated hand. It was so gross. SO GROSS."

She paused to wholeheartedly laugh a little more.

"I learned fucking Japanese and fucking woodwork, and I was good at it. Things I have no interest in at all. Just to keep myself sane."

Just to keep myself sane. Just to keep myself sane. Just to keep myself sane. She repeated the last phrase 103 times.

"This is a clear dissociation episode," the new psychiatrist in my team remarked. I currently know him for way more time than I knew

Ivanov, but I refuse to learn his name. I refuse to acknowledge his existence; he's just an annoying voice to me. I can't handle feeling like shit again when he eventually jumps off a bridge.

"But you're never letting me out. Never. I'll never date someone. I'll never marry. I'll never go to college. I'll never do *anything* but be a creepy show for you guys. So you know what? Let's make it creepy. Let's make it creepy as fuck."

Day 1.093

We broke her.
We broke Maya, someone I grew to admire and even feel affection towards. And we did it by trying to be nice.
She's masturbating no-stop. She's trying to break her body too, now that her mind is shattered.

Today

Maya Smith stood motionless in her bed, still with her dress lifted and no underwear. The first thing I felt was relief, because The Family Experiment was finally over.
I said the assistants could go home, and the new guy and I decided we would go in and fetch her lifeless body. I turned off all our equipment, smiling for the first time in over 3 years.
The new guy leaned over her to check if she was actually dead. She wasn't.
You see, Maya Smith developed a bold plan to escape. She started to craft a wooden knife in plain sight to test us. If no one reprimanded her, she knew she could count on at least one of the watchers.
This watcher was me. I've been watching her alone since our new guy sucks and barely does his job, and the assistants are only required when I need to take notes or keep track of multiple screens at the same time.
Maya was counting on the fact that the researchers had to be as bored and miserable as her by now, and that we were probably being pressed into keeping the study going.
As soon as he leaned over her body, Maya quickly stabbed the new guy in the belly as he approached her body. He coughed a lot of

blood; I ran in his direction to help him, and whoops, let the subject get away.

The cameras were off and no one else from the project was in the building. The security guards didn't know her. She was free. She was free and sane after putting on a very convincing show.

This was the first time I was able to properly breathe since The Family Experiment started.

There are many reasons why I'm writing this suicide letter. First of all, I wanted to let someone know about this vicious experiment. In the second place, I know they will get me for letting her get away. They can't prove I did it on purpose, but they'll know. They'll always know.

I decided to help Maya after I made up my mind about the suicide. My sons are both adults and forgetful of their old father these days. My wife died a few years prior to the project. I'm fine knowing I'll barely be missed. She, on the other hand, is so young and determined to keep living. How could I deny her that and just let my own death go to waste?

The third reason is, as you know, I'm Dr. Shantan—the one the reddish evil presence in the closet has been claiming. Maybe if I offer myself to it, no one else will have to suffer.

I love you, son. Please don't blame yourself for not giving this old man more attention; I know you thought I was doing better than ever, and nothing you could do would avoid my death. You've been a good son, Saul. You and David were the best children I could ask for.

I wrote a whole different letter for your brother, because I think he's better off not knowing. For your own safety, please keep everything a secret. I'm sorry to burden you with the truth about the last years of my life.

I just have one last favor to ask you: if a woman named Maya Smith ever looks for you, please help her with whatever she needs. You'll be helping your old father.

Love,
Melvin Shantan, a.k.a. Dad.
November 20, 2013

***

This week, my older brother Saul was diagnosed with terminal cancer. He asked to talk privately to me, and decided to tell me his last secret: he got a very different suicide letter from our father back in 2013, entirely transcribed above.

I'm David, and I've been married to a woman I love with all my heart since 2015. Her maiden name is Maya Smith.

ARE YOU FINE?

If mommy asks if you're fine, you say yes… even if you're not—that's the mantra that she had me and my sibling repeat whenever we had a problem that required her attention, even since we were little more than toddlers.

I know I should blame my mother for all the tragedies in our lives, but I don't—not after what happened to her. She truly atoned for her mistakes. Being a single parent is hard, living in poverty is hard.

My brother Jacob and I were only a year apart, me being the older.

I had to take care of him pretty much alone when I was barely able to take care of myself. Our father was gone and Mommy's boyfriend, Frank—the only one that didn't hit us—had died in a freaky accident. We had no other relatives, at least none willing to help, and she couldn't afford a nanny; hell, she could barely afford food and thrift store clothes for us.

"Mommy is so tired," she'd repeat, kissing my forehead before she locked herself in her bedroom, while Jacob cried. "I'm sorry, Stella. I'm so sorry."

I was the one that had to handle him, even if I was afraid of the dark too. She stole my childhood and parentified me, and that wasn't even the worst thing that she's done.

I wonder now if we would be better off in foster care, but I know awful stories about that. At least I know she loved us—she never mistreated us or hit us, and she always got rid of her boyfriends when they were mean to us, even if their lazy asses helped pay the bills; only people who lived in poverty know how little choice economically vulnerable women have when it comes to their relationships, because their income usually is not enough to house and feed their children.

And yet, she stood up for us against the world. Mostly.

I had my first period at only 10. I came home crying, confused about what had happened. I knew nothing about pads, cramps, or blood coming out of your secret parts.

Jacob was really worried about me. I took a bath and we both sat in silence until Mommy came home; back then, calling her wasn't an option—and wouldn't be even if we had phones at home.

By the time she arrived, I was bleeding on my clothes again. It was so late and I was so hungry, but I was afraid of moving and suddenly dying.

"What happened here, Stella?" she asked in a severe tone.

"I started bleeding out of nowhere today. Am I sick?" I got up, showing the huge stain in my beaten-up shorts, and now on our old couch.

"No, darling, just…" she scraped together a few coins, her eyebrow twitching a little. "Here, go to the grocery store tomorrow and buy something called *modess*. Ask the cashier lady to help you if you need, ok? Buy some bleach too."

"Mom, I'm scared," my voice came out more high-pitched than I had intended. I wanted to be a good girl, but I also wanted to feel like I had someone to be there for me for once—just once.

She sighed.

"If Mommy asks if you're fine, what do you say?"

"I say yes, even if I'm not," I recited, like she taught us many times, holding back my tears.

I want to think Mommy just wanted us to be strong, but it was really, really oppressing. I cried myself to sleep, hungry, confused, still oblivious to the nature of my condition.

On the next day, the grocery lady was really, really nice to me. I'll never forget how much she helped me, and how a complete stranger was the one to explain everything I was going through as a girl and a future woman.

I went home and told Jacob about it while he helped me bleach the sofa.

"That's so crazy! Will this happen to me too?"

"Of course not, dum-dum. It only happens to girls," I said, with an air of superiority, even though I had learned all that stuff mere 15 minutes earlier.

It wasn't easy, but we grew up. Jacob used to be a cheerful kid, but as the years went by, he locked himself in; he even became one of those weird kids that are always wearing a hoodie to cover their faces, regardless of the weather. Whenever I asked if he was fine, he would drily say yes. I thought it was simply puberty hitting my little brother the wrong way.

I was simple-minded, and I had so many other things to worry about. I even had to get a part-time job to help Mom.

At school, I did my best not to stand off, so I wasn't particularly bullied; my class had another target, so I didn't know what true suffering in the hands of evil kids was.

Even when I heard younger kids making mean comments about my brother, I was confident Jacob was strong enough not to care about random offenses.

I know he would be, if it was the case; that's what mom taught us, after all.

But it wasn't the case; I wish I knew better.

But I didn't. And, on a Friday afternoon, I was the one to find him.

At 13, my little beloved Jacob was living through hell at school because of who he was, and he couldn't take anymore.

He—I don't know if that would be the right pronoun now—was too feminine.

It was the 90s, and a bad public school. Boys that weren't traditionally masculine were bullied. Being effeminate was reason enough to be heavily harassed every day, being a gay kid was hell. Can you imagine what Jacob had to endure for feeling like he didn't belong in his male body?

Jacob had been beaten by the boys at school that day, and you could see the purple bruises all over his feeble body. He came home earlier knowing what to do.

They told him to.

They said he was an aberration and he should die, and Jacob had no one to tell him otherwise; both mom and I were busy working and we failed him.

His goodbye letter to me was the most heart-wrenching thing I ever read. He knew I would accept and understand him, but the pain made it impossible for him to accept himself, and all these years having to pretend everything was fine didn't allow him to speak up or ask for help. The way we were raised made him believe he had to just endure it all, and when he couldn't anymore, there was only one answer.

I knew he was gone from the moment I saw a limp, pale figure, but I still ran to our neighbor's house to beg for help, and to have someone dial the emergency number. As I did it, I felt the cold breeze in my face, thinking how cold afternoons with a pale sun like these were his favorites. And now my little beloved brother would never see or feel that again.

Or anything at all.

After knowing the pain Jacob was going through, the thought of him never feeling anything again was soothing.

But I still feel like half my mind, soul and body died that day.

People pretended to feel sympathy during the funeral. The school spit the same victim-blaming bullshit every school does when that happens; Jacob should have talked to them. They cared about the students' well-being. They would never allow bullying, *if only they knew*.

For a week, all our neighbors wanted to cook for us, to clean our house, to go grocery shopping for us, to help us in general—even the parents of his perpetrators. After that, the community forgot about our existence once again.

While I had other people to relieve me from the household chores, I cried until I felt numb, then stood motionless, then cried again. Sleep came in small waves, always washing ashore bad dreams.

I don't remember if it was on the third or fourth night that I heard Mom's horrible scream, but her room was always locked from the inside, so all I could do was listen close to the door.

"Jacob…" she muttered, in shock and fear.

"Hello, Mom. Do you feel alright?"

"Jacob, my love, you know I feel awful—" she was interrupted by a noise that sounded like a slap.

"Wrong answer. You have to say you're fine. Remember? Say it. SAY IT."

"I-I'm fine."

"I am not, Mom. I am not fine. People told me I'm an aberration and I should die. And you know why I believed them, Mom? You know why I couldn't deal with the pain they caused, Mom? Because of you. I hate you for forcing us to always tell you everything was fine. *Nothing* was ever fine. You forced Stella to be my mother when she was a child, too. Why did you even check on us if you didn't want to know that we weren't fine? Answer me, Mom. I'm talking to you. *We're* talking. Do you know this is the first time? I had to die to actually talk to you for once."

"I… I am so sorry, Jacob. I love you so much, so much," she cried.

"That's not what I asked. It's a little too late now."

"I… I thought I had to. To ask. Even if I couldn't handle to hear anything else, to hear your problems. I'm sorry for being bad for you. I'm so sorry. I had so many problems of my own I didn't have time for yours. I'm so sorry."

On the next morning, Mom had a few bruises covering her body. This would be a constant sight for months.

When I had to go back to school, I noticed five boys from Jacob's class were completely covered in purple, greenish and black bruises, way worse than mom's. They apparently weren't so sorry.

As I passed them on the hall, I grinned in satisfaction and couldn't resist the urge to ask if they were fine. As I suspected, they had learned a new lesson on the last few nights: they said yes—even if they were not.

THE LOST PLANET

It was a cold, rainy and eerie night when the blissful veil of ignorance was lifted from my eyes. This is not a story about astronomy—I am a mere college professor, teaching subjects seldom related to the cosmos. This is a story about how easy it is for unknown forces to manipulate the whole of mankind.

Now I'm one of the few people who remember Orcus—the fourth planet in our solar system, back when Mars was the fifth.

If memory serves, Orcus had been one of the first planets to be discovered through modern telescopes; despite its proximity to the Earth, in ancient times, astronomers were unable to see it due to its color that made it blend in almost perfectly with the surrounding void—thus the name.

I never gave Orcus a lot of thought, other than when I had to talk about it in my classes—Orcus had a unique, black atmosphere, which had been speculated to be compounded by crude oil decades ago.

Needless to say, a certain country took an obsessive interest in it.

I remember that the exploration of Orcus, initiated no more than a decade after the successful landing on the moon, was very low key for something this big. You would eventually read an article on new evidence that its atmosphere could actually be a (figurative) gold mine, and how that certain government was making heavy investments towards sending a manned expedition to it, but back then a lot of other discoveries were being made, from infrared satellites being released to exoplanets being found.

It was a subject of interest for chemistry, but not enough to come up more often than once a year; and every year I showed my first-term students the same PowerPoint presentation about the chemical composition of all planets, focusing on Orcus, unanimously considered the coolest of all by my classes.

Up until 2012, everything went smoothly.

Then 2013 came, and the faces in the classroom were either confused or amused, but in a way that showed I was the butt of the joke.

"What's the problem?" I asked, truly ignorant. I looked at the current slide half-expecting it to show me in my underwear dancing with my dog. But there was nothing wrong with it—it was about Orcus.

"Did you just made up a planet, professor?" one of my most competent students asked.

"Don't be silly, all of you know very well the planets in the solar system. Everyone's been in elementary school, right?"

"How many planets are there in the solar system, sir?" another student asked with a tone almost too benevolent, like I was some decrepit old man who forgot his own name.

"Ten. Or nine? Pluto comes and goes, but other than that it's Mercury, Venus, Earth, Orcus, Mars-"

"Sir, why not try googling this planet Orcus?" a third student carefully suggested. I complied, still half thinking they had organized an elaborated prank, but slightly nervous.

No results.

They weren't hilariously gaslighting me into believing a whole planet—the closest one to Earth—suddenly didn't exist. It was true.

Every single student in the room looked at me with such pity that I dismissed the class and spent most of my morning crying in the parking lot. I *was* getting old and mad.

The next day, I was summoned to the dean's office. The university—almost too generously—offered to send me to an isolated research facility where I could develop my studies full time and still get 70% of my teacher salary.

Twice divorced with no kids and rarely visited by my few living relatives, I gladly accepted it, and in a matter of days I was renting my house while moving halfway across the country to work alone.

Besides, I was too embarrassed to return to the classroom.

My lodging was a pleasant cottage, with a great lab for one behind it. My bedroom had a nice view of distant, deep-blue mountains and the university sent me a housekeeper once a week; she even brought me groceries, so I didn't have a worry in the world.

From 2013 to 2020, life was a blur of immersing myself in my work, improving my baking abilities and talking to no one—the housekeeper was Russian, and when she showed signs of learning English, she was replaced by a Brazilian one.

It was early February when Sarah knocked on my door; a former student of mine who had become a brilliant astronomer.

"I finally found you. You remember Orcus too, right?"

***

I gladly let her in, the first visit I had in almost a decade, and made us some good tea from the herbs I've been growing myself.

"You sleep with noise-canceling headphones playing white noise, right?" she asked. I shook my head no, then remembered that I used to before I lived among all this peace and quiet.

Her face switched from determination to a shard of panic, then confidence.

"I know it had to be it. That's how they didn't catch our memory, then," she observed.

She then proceeded to tell me everything she knew about the fourth planet of the Solar System—and it was *a lot*. The night came, cold and wet, and I said she should stay for the night instead of leaving in the storm. Sarah didn't protest, in fact it seemed to be her plan all along. Then, although I was over twice her age, I became her apprentice for the next two weeks.

"When I realized Orcus was no more, I kept my mouth shut. *They* made the university send you on a retreat and that was clever. People wouldn't believe an older chemistry teacher was the only one to know something they didn't remember, no offense. It was easy to get you neutralized. But being an astronomer, I'm a different story. People will start to believe the truth if it comes from me. So promise me that if I ever disappear you'll make public everything I told you."

I promised.

"*No matter what they do to me,*" she added, under her breath.

It didn't take long.

We didn't realize that the housekeeper was probably forced to report anything different in the house. On the first week, Sarah managed to hide, but the maid—probably suspicious that things were a lot different in the house, and afraid to be punished—rummaged through the lab until she found my partner in "crime."

It was another cold and rainy night when *they* came. First, the lights all went out. Then the shadows surrounding us became solid. Sarah let out a pained scream.

An unnaturally raspy and robotic voice, so emotionless that it felt evil.

"Stop pursuing Orcus."

I passed out, and when I woke up in the morning, Sarah was gone. The signs of struggle were everywhere.

Slowly, I started putting back together the damaged furniture.

The next day, as to leave no doubts that *they* were serious, they sent me Sarah's index finger inside a Tiffany-blue box.

I thought that maybe if I actually made a conscious effort to forget it all, she would be released. I kept my mouth shut and focused my whole mind on my research, although it felt pointless now.

But over the next weeks, I received more boxes with her body parts.

So here's my story—for Sarah.

I don't have a lot of time, as I noticed solid shadows moving around, just waiting until nightfall to catch me, but I'll summarize what I learned from her.

Between the years 2005 and 2011, NASA discovered that Orcus' blackness wasn't due to its atmosphere, but due to the singular nature of the planet and the living things on it. It's hard to explain, but basically the beings and the planet are one. A black, sentient mass that can shape-shift into virtually anything; of course, *this* information was a secret.

By 2012, Sarah herself had discovered a groundbreaking information: the orclings fed on thoughts and knowledge—they phagocyted all the space probes that NASA sent to Orcus, right after the information was transmitted, indicating that they wanted to be found out.

Knowing that a disaster was on its way to wipe away mankind, a selected group of plutocrats requested a deal with Orcus. They complied.

On December 21, 2012, there was a worldwide blackout, although this knowledge was wiped out too. When we woke up, things were strange and felt somewhat wrong, but they were still similar enough to our old reality for us to go on about our lives.

Not even Sarah knows how they did *that*, but we know how they wiped people's memories: low-frequency radio waves. People whose ears were completely protected that night, like Sarah and I, were unaffected by it.

Although there's a lot we'll never know about it, what we do know leaves no doubt.

Take a good look at everything around you. Are things *actually* normal? When you turn off the lights and stay very still, don't you feel something solid and quiet moving in the shadows? Something dark and always watching?

I know that your memory was eaten, but if you really put your mind on it, you'll realize that the world you're seeing now is nothing but a simulacrum of how life on Earth used to be.

Because the planet that disappeared without a trace in 2012 wasn't Orcus.

It was the Earth.

THE DOMINO THAT DOESN'T FALL

1

I used to think that life was cruel, but that's not entirely true. It's uncaring and unconcerned.

No matter how you feel, the world still turns, taking you with it whether you like it or not—not out of some form of sadism, but simply because that's the way things are. Those are the rules, usually unfair and forever unchanging. Trying to defy them, trying to come up with something new, is both frowned upon and laughed at. It's frustrating to no end. It's fruitless.

Sometimes you think you can't go on, you think you need a break, but few of us can afford the consequences of these luxuries. You can be the most miserable person on Earth, but you'll still have to wake up tomorrow and do your job and pay your bills. You won't stop being a cog in the wheel just because you feel like it. You have to play your part, no exceptions—because no matter how irrelevant is the information contained in a puzzle piece, the big picture will still be incomplete if it is lost.

Out of duty, out of pride, out of necessity: you can't let yourself be the weakest link in the chain.

But what if you could manipulate those odds? What if you could be the domino that doesn't fall? Would you take the opportunity despite not knowing what cosmic imbalances might result from your actions? Would you be willing to risk more than you could possibly comprehend just to gamble on subverting the very rules of existence?

This is the story of a woman who said yes to that.

***

I don't remember how the small apparatus ended up in my hands—it felt like it has always been mine. I know I had it as a kid, but it was some sort of handheld console, and I never imagined it could be used for something other than gaming, although the games were the strangest I have ever seen.

It was only when I turned 18 that it entered adulthood with me, and its primary function was enabled: showing the results of my acts to the ultimate consequences.

I know a lot of people have it worse than me, but I never had an easy life. My single mother worked herself to death. My father took me and my sister in, but his house and life were a mess and we were the ones who raised him, not the opposite.

By the time I was 16, I was working double shifts, triple on weekends; my sister left with the first man she met, making me the only breadwinner of our household. Just like mom, I was working myself to death too—but at least I had no children to worry about, and I could save a little for college. What I had wasn't nearly enough when I was 18, but I kept working towards it, and doing my best to keep my father alive and the house clean enough.

My luck started to change when I mastered the use of my special device when I was 20.

"Should I take this gig? I'm so tired," I wondered out loud, and the screen lighted up in green. Curious, I took a look at it.

Run simulation? YES NO

I clicked yes, and was transported to a possible future in fast motion: if I took the job—being a waitress in a fancy garden party—I'd end up meeting the right people and it would end up with me getting a college scholarship. I saw myself in the uniform, making an impression, talking and shaking hands, and then watching some classes.

I went to the party, and things miraculously happened exactly the way I had seen—at first I tried to convince myself that it was a dream but, if I really thought about it, I had no doubt that it all came from the weird video game I had since my childhood.

Two weeks later, I had some sort of gut feeling telling me I shouldn't go home that night. I absolutely had to crash at a friend's. So I locked myself in the toilet at work and I asked out loud, "Should I go home today?"

Once again, I was bathed in the familiar green light.

Run simulation? YES NO

The simulation went only a few hours in the future, and I saw myself in my dark house, finding my dad in a pool of his own blood, his skin already cold. As I tried to scream for help, a man came from the shadows and gagged me, and with a sharp pain in my head everything went dark.

My hands were shaking violently when the simulation faded and I was back in the tiny bathroom stall.

"I don't want it to happen. It has to be another way," I muttered, as if the screen could understand me.

This time, the light was a different shade of green, almost yellow.

Run simulation? YES NO

The second time was even worse: I got home right before my dad was murdered, and I watched him die, being sprayed in his blood and subsequently having my own throat cut.

The pain was unimaginable and unbearable.

"No, no, no, no, no… what if I just call the police?"

The same words appeared in bluish light: **Run simulation? YES NO**

In this scenery, I was arrested for the murder of my dad.

I tried again and again, but the only way to avoid my own demise was to stay away and let him die alone.

He was kind of an asshole, but he was still my father, and he didn't deserve to go this way. Still, the only thing I could do for him was to call him and let him know I couldn't make it home today, and tell him that I loved him for the first time; I don't know if I meant it, but I hoped it made his last moments a little less painful.

The next day, I came home to a swarm of policemen and my old man in a body bag.

2

I felt incredibly guilty, and I couldn't bear to live in the house where he was murdered, so I moved to a small flat in-campus.

It was noticeable that, after my father's death, the device seemed to grow more powerful, and the simulations became longer; I started to see things a couple of years from now, then a decade.

My mental health was declining and the only reason why I kept fighting against the feelings of remorse was knowing that my future was way, way brighter than my life was at the moment.

Still, it was hard to keep up with work and with my classes, especially the ones I deemed less important.

One day, I chose not to finish an important assignment in time and make up an excuse instead; I knew that anyone would be sympathetic to someone who just became an orphan, even if she's not a child.

This time, the apparatus didn't even ask me. Suddenly the world around me sped up insanely, showing me the future that will ensue from this action, while time is paralyzed to everyone else. The scenery changes abruptly so I can barely process each moment, but it's clear that things are becoming darker.

It goes on and on, farther and farther into the future, until 2098, when the civilization collapses earlier than expected.

The world was devastated; the carcasses of dead animals piled up on the streets, along with the human corpses—with way more dead people than living, and with the bodies being incredibly contagious. No one cared anymore about burials and cremations. Humanity became even less humane.

Survivors scavenged around the dead, wearing gas masks and armor made of metal scraps. Most of them were crying, and some mad enough to laugh, and our race was doomed—just because of a mere college research a young woman didn't finish back in 2014, as ridiculous as it sounds.

This is the end of the simulation, the small screen with alien-like technology said in bitmap letters; it didn't use to be this way, and it didn't look like a way more futuristic tamatgochi. **Go back and choose another option? YES NO**

If I did anything other than finish the assignment, horrible things would happen, with repercussions in the far future, until there was no future.

So I made the only choice that was right: I pulled all-nighters to make sure that my paper came to life before the deadline. I even lost one of my jobs, but I was confident that it would be worth it.

Two years later, a pharmaceutical company would start developing the medicine that will keep billions of people alive in a few decades, based on my research.

If I didn't run the simulation, I'd let the human society collapse and I'd be substantially poorer. Although it didn't make me rich, it allowed me to move to a nicer place without having to work two jobs and focus on my classes; I felt chosen, and the device was a blessing beyond compare.

That's why I didn't bat an eyelash when the small green screen showed me a message I had never seen before.
TO MAKE SURE THAT BILLIONS ARE SAVED, A FEW DOZEN HAVE TO DIE

3

Making the choices that lead other people to die, knowing it's for the greater good, is something that I can live with. My hands are bloodied by the deaths of many, and yet they are clean enough to let me sleep peacefully at night. If I was granted a divine power, it's my duty to be level-headed enough to wield it.

I did things for my personal gain, of course—to live comfortably, to meet the man of my dreams, to take amazing trips to exotic islands—but I did so much more for humanity than for myself. I could go way further, but I know how to stop. I'm a reasonable person and I just want to help.

Or at least, that's what I thought before I met this strange woman.

One day, she simply materialized inside my house when I was alone—she was casually sitting by the kitchen island. I tried to scream, but I suddenly didn't know how to use my voice, like in a bad dream.

"You're playing with a cosmic power like a child," her voice was stern and clear, and she didn't sound mad, or disappointed, or even frustrated; she just stated it.

I then noticed that her hands held my device, completely destroyed.

"Who are you? What do you want from me?" I tried to ask telepathically.

If she heard my thoughts, she ignored them.

"I thought you were smarter than that, Patricia. Someone like you should have realized that every time you chose to let someone die, your *Sors* became more powerful, and more bloodthirsty. How long have you seen in the future now? 500, 700 years? This is not meant for the human eye, not even a mildly important one like you."

"What the fuck is a Sors? How I'm only mildly important if my patent will save everyone? Were all the simulations lies?" I mentally asked again, emphatically.

"How many people it said you had to kill, and how many did you actually kill? I can answer that. What was supposed to be a few dozen now amounts to 1,307."

She waved her hand, and suddenly I had my voice again, but my tone was very, very low.

I repeated all my questions out loud.

"Who I am doesn't matter, nor do I want anything from you. It could be anyone, really," she made a short pause. "*Sors* is what we call this thing, it means prophecy or divination in Latin. Once again, it could have been anyone. And it's not exactly lying."

"Then what?"

"This machine is evil and deceiving, and it's actually manipulating you into creating alternate chaotic timelines. Everything you saw as a mere possibility actually happened in real life, Patricia. But they took place in another place in time and space."

"What do you mean? Like a parallel universe?"

"If you don't understand my words or don't believe me, you can see your alternate selves who weren't so lucky," she once again waved her hand, materializing a device that looked a lot like mine.

I was surrounded by all my non-choices.

In the timelines I created but didn't choose, I'm plagued by all sorts of diseases. I'm in a coma for years, but I'm aware the whole time, unable to talk. I'm kidnapped and tortured because of my research. I die in every possible way along with my father, sometimes my sister, too. I go through horrible, horrible things.

After what felt like millions of years, the woman pulled me back.

"Those weren't simulations, right?" I asked, trembling. I could barely talk because my body was completely focused on sobbing and on trying not to go insane.

"I simply transported you to the places and situations you brought to life," she replied. "Usually, someone who meddled this much with the fabric of reality would be sent to a fate worse than hell, but you're regretful. Despite what you did, you weren't completely drunk with power. You remained modest, to some extent. So I have an offer for you."

I didn't have the strength to say anything.

"Become my assistant. Be a guardian to the balance of the multiverse, and help me search and destroy those things. In exchange, you'll get only a small fraction of your punishment. Your eternal damnation will be micro-dosed."

I nodded, and immediately my head became a nightmare of noises—the screams of my other selves.

All of them are suffering in every single hell I created and removed myself from. I hear their voices the whole time, but I wish it was only theirs. No. I can also hear the wails of every single person I ever did wrong in other timelines.

If a domino falls in another reality, does it make a sound? I can assure it does, and it's maddening.

BABYSITTERS

"I only gave the babysitter one rule: if the Christmas lights start twinkling strangely, leave the room immediately."

The man in front of me was your typical upper-middle-class suburban dad, except for the disheveled hair and streaks of dirt and dried blood on his forehead. He was being bandaged by three nurses, including Jo, the one who called me.

Being the only female in the force, I was given the "sensitive" tasks—aka everything that involved collecting the testimony of hospitalized people in the middle of the night.

Ivan Daniels. Everyone knew his wife had died of a degenerative disease at only 32, around five years ago, and was the first person in our town to be cryogenically frozen.

Mr. Daniels then started a foundation under her name to raise funds to help other victims; the illness is incurable, but the palliative care makes a difference, and is incredibly expensive. Recently, there's a promising new experimental treatment too, equally costly.

Their only daughter, Lindsay, is no older than 9 now.

His rule struck me as quite odd.

"Why was that, Mr. Daniels?"

"For her own safety. And my daughter's, of course," he replied, enigmatically.

I know from experience that giving people a set of rules never works. One rule will always be broken—even if there's only one.

"And what's the problem with the lights, Mr. Daniels?" I insisted. He was distressed, so I had to be very clear to get useful information from him.

"Oh, right. Silly me. I'm sorry, Officer, I'm still shaken. That's because I'm convinced that our house is haunted."

"Haunted? By who or what?"

"I… I don't know, honestly. But I'm sure that's why Alice attacked me. She's such a good girl, please don't be so harsh on her when you find her…"

"Alice? Who's Alice and what happened to her?"

"That's Alice Weber, my neighbor, Miss. She's 17 or 19 I think. The babysitter," Mr. Daniels elucidated. "She's the one who attacked me."

The nurses started cleaning him up softly, and I noticed his face was all scratched. His left arm was slightly off—probably dislocated—and there was a larger wound close to his collarbone. Apparently a stabbing wound, but it was clear that this hit didn't connect properly.

"A teenager did this to you?" I asked, as Nurse Jo put his shoulder back in place with a crackle. Hitting like that required a lot of strength.

"Yes, but please, Officer. She was possessed by something evil, I'm sure. She's always so nice to my little girl. Please treat her as you would treat a daughter or a young sister."

Those words didn't appeal to me, as my younger sister stole all my money to escape with her crackhead boyfriend when she was 15.

"And where is Miss Weber now?" I asked.

Mr. Daniels sighed deeply. "Who knows? I think I hit my head or something because after she attacked me I was out of it for a while. I don't know how long. Twenty minutes, maybe? All the while, my daughter was sleeping like an angel upstairs. The first thing I did was checking up on her, but thankfully whatever evil entity possessed her to attack me didn't want to harm Lindsay. Anyway, she escaped while I was unconscious."

Jo made a note to have his head checked.

"Okay, I know you're distressed, but can you please tell me the facts in chronological order? At least superficially, we can go back for the details later."

"Sure, I'm so sorry I'm troubling you," he sighed again. "So I had an important dinner today. I was hoping to get a generous donation to my wife's foundation, are you familiar…?"

"Absolutely, Mr. Daniels. Everyone in this town knows you're a philanthropist. Do go on, please."

"Oh, you're too kind to me, Officer. Getting donations is the least I can do for my soulmate. I'd do anything to have her back, but at least I know she would love to help people like that," he said, filled with a burning passion. He then went back to his mild-mannered self. "I planned ahead and asked Alice to come babysit. She agreed, of course. Alice and my daughter Lindsay really like each other, and I pay fairly for a job well done."

"Alright. How long has Alice been babysitting for you? And was she normal when she arrived?"

"I think around four months. Yes, I think so. She's a quiet and pleasant girl in general."

"One would imagine her relationship with your family was longer, considering how you get along," I remarked.

"Oooh, wasn't Vicky your babysitter?" Jo asked. Mr. Daniels frowned in pain.

"She was, the poor thing. And she had been at my house the night she disappeared too. I think that's yet another villainy caused by my house. I swear I'd leave that hell of a place if it didn't hold so many dear memories of my wife."

"Vicky? Victoria Allister was your babysitter?" I asked. Of course such an important case wasn't given to me, but I knew about it. The girl had vanished a few months ago.

"It does seem like you're cursed!" Jo cooed. She was often insensitive, but I knew that the only way to cope with seeing human misery daily is being cheerful about everything else.

Thankfully, the nurses finished their job and left the room.

"So you left for dinner."

"Yes, it was around seven. Alice arrived ten minutes early as usual, I paid her beforehand and gave her the instructions. I told her it was better to lock themselves in the kitchen and wait for at least half an hour if the lights in the living room went crazy."

"Okay, and then?"

"I was back by 11 or so. Nothing weird happened the whole night and Alice didn't call, so I assume things were fine. The lights of the house were all turned off, but it wasn't unusual. The babysitter usually naps with Lindsay, because my girl hates falling asleep alone. But Alice was awake, waiting for me in the dark dining room. She had a big kitchen knife."

"Are you sure it was Alice? Wasn't the house dark?"

"I am sure because it was dim due to the Christmas decorations. Alice attacked me with such hatred! She wanted to kill me. That's not the girl I know, of course. She was possessed or something, I'm sure of that."

"And what did you do?"

"I did my best to avoid her hits without hurting her badly. I'm stronger than her, obviously, but I was surprised and careful. She was not, so she had the upper hand. I threw her on a coffee table, but I think she was completely uninjured by the time she left."

"Did she say something?"

"I... don't remember. She screamed in struggle, but I can't really remember if she said anything. I don't think my brain processed any words."

"Well, that's to be expected. About the Christmas lights, when did it start to act up?"

"As soon as we put it on, right after Thanksgiving. I bought a whole new set of lights when they first started flickering in a creepy way, but the second was glitching too. I called my electrician and he found nothing wrong. So I left them on. Lindsay loves Christmas because it particularly reminds her of her mom, and it's not twinkling weirdly all the time anyway. It rarely happens."

"Did anything weird happen before that? Regarding the house being haunted, I mean." I decided to entertain his supernatural beliefs. Maybe it would lead to a more rational clue.

His hands were shaking a little now. "There's some sort of presence, I don't know. Something bad. I only feel it when Lindsay is not around, so maybe it only hates me," Mr. Daniels nervously laughed.

"It could be some vengeful spirit, then. Did you wrong anyone, Mr. Daniels?" I asked, dead serious, even though I didn't think so. This man helped people, and ghosts are nothing but an interesting movie trope.

"I sure hope I didn't," he replied very quietly.

"Maybe someone thought you could help them but you didn't," I suggested. "How are the finances going on the foundation? Do you help everyone that looks for you?"

"On the foundation? They're fine I guess. I'd have to ask my accountant, of course. I'm just the guy who shakes hands to make sure the checks will come."

I stopped to consider it all for a moment—we had an injured father, a missing freaked out babysitter, and the former babysitter missing for months. All the while the little girl slept—maybe Alice gave her something to keep her from waking up even with screams and crashing sounds.

But this premeditation is not compatible with being possessed, if there's such a thing.

"Is Lindsay always a heavy sleeper?"

"She can either sleep like a rock or wake up easily, no in-between."

"Is she afraid of the lights twinkling weirdly?"

"It makes her uncomfortable, but I think I'm more afraid than she is."

"By the way, where is she now?"

"With my sister-in-law. I don't want her to set foot in that house again. What if I go crazy next and hurt my daughter?"

"Fair enough. Mr. Daniels, I'm gonna ask for your keys. I want to see the Christmas lights for myself."

"I thought all the cops were skeptic."

I *was* personally skeptical. But as the only female cop in town, I couldn't afford to be like all the cops. I had to be better to be enough.

So I sent Mr. Daniels to be with his daughter and stayed at his beautiful house for almost two days before the Christmas lights started twinkling differently.

Unmistakable *dits* and *dahs*.

Ditdit space dit dah dah dah space ditditdit dah ditdit dahdit dahdit dahdit dah dahdit dah dah

Pause.

Ditdit space dah dah dah dah dit dahditdit dahditdit space dit dah dit dahditdit ditdit dahdit dahdit dit *space* dah ditditditdit dit dah dah space dah dah ditdit ditditdit dah dit dit dahdit space dahditdit dit dah dahdit ditdit dit dit dahditdit ditditdit space dah dah ditdit dah dit dahdit dahditdit dit dit dahdit dit dahditdit space dah dah dit

I took a few notes, then asked for reinforcements and a warrant. The rest was easy.

Mr. Daniels had been skimming a lot of money from his charity. He was using most of the donations in order to try to resuscitate his cryogenically frozen wife; he had hoped that she would live now that her disease could be treated.

Vicky Allister, the former babysitter, was in the wrong place at the wrong time, and was murdered after catching him red-handed.

But Ivan Daniels wasn't an unscrupulous killer. He was actually a good father and husband, whose soul became twisted by the loss of his wife, and he'd do anything to protect the possibility of bringing her back—even killing an innocent girl.

Daniels felt bad for the collateral damage, although not bad enough to stop stealing, so he was always anxious and afraid someone would find out about his worst crime. He felt haunted by Vicky.

The lights flickering made him panic every time because he thought it was a sign that Vicky was watching him.

He wasn't wrong.

According to Mr. Daniels, Vicky was 99% pulverized by one of the Russian substances he was testing in order to resuscitate his wife. But I found Alice in the trunk of his car, a bloodied kitchen knife still in her hand. He had squeezed her neck until she passed out, thus the dislocated shoulder. He then tied her arms and legs, put a bag on her head, and left her to die in a confined space.

There were scratch marks on the inside of the car. She had suffered and fought for her life until the end.

Poor girl, she got some terrifying information and made the wrong move. I wish I found her sooner, she could have survived if I did.

I testified at his trial, making up some plausible story about how I found out about his murders—as I said, all policemen are skeptics. It was clear that the remorse was destroying Ivan inside, and he seemed relieved to pledge guilty for them.

"You don't know Morse code, do you, Mr. Daniels?" I asked. He shook his head no.

But Alice knew, and Vicky's ghost… that was a heck of a genius way to communicate.

After a lot of thinking, I decided not to disclose just one of the secrets that Vicky told me through the lights—that Mr. Daniels believed that he could bring back his wife on his own because he didn't follow the usual protocol.

Because he froze her while she was still alive.

INVISIBLE HAIRS

Working at a psychiatric hospital, I thought I had seen everything. We had a delusional old lady that thought she was Cleopatra for the last 30 years, and absolutely freaked out if you didn't tell her what Marc Anthony was doing. A man that tried to kill his younger brother, drowning him in holy water, because he claimed the child was the antichrist. A teenage boy that firmly believed to be a lawnmower; he never talked, only made whirring noises.

But all of this looked like children's play when I was assigned to Amanda Jameson.

Amanda was only 28. Her crooked figure made me uneasy, but if you looked at her normal parts, you could see she used to be a girl-next-door type of beauty. She was smart too; when all of this started, Amanda was enrolled in a good university.

Others had been assigned to her before, and I had their notes, but I still had to interview Amanda and make her repeat her story to me.

Every single nurse and psychiatrist that took care of her had abruptly quit the job.

I knew one of the nurses, Jocelyn, and called to ask what was going on after she stopped showing up at work. After I insisted a lot, her sister simply told me Jocelyn had decided to move to another state and wouldn't talk to anyone she knew before.

I sighed deeply and entered Amanda's room. She was fidgeting with a small plastic bear holding a red heart.

"Hello, Amanda! I'm Doctor Hudson, but you can call me Lena. How are you today?"

"Hello, Doctor Lena Hudson," she answered, emotionlessly. She was still scratching her left eye, or what was left of it. "Same as always, thank you."

The file said Amanda suffered from an unknown psychosis, but at first glance, she seemed in full possession of her mental faculties. I would do my best to not let it fool me, but she showed no signs of insanity whatsoever. It was an impression hard to shake off.

"I know you have been through this before, but bear with me. I need you to tell me how it all started, if you please."

"I was 20 and living with my college boyfriend," she said, still in a neutral, lucid tone. "I always had allergies, so I was no stranger to feeling my eyes itchy, but it wasn't even spring, and it seemed abnormal to me. You know when you come out of the shower and find loose strands of hair everywhere in your body? It was something like that."

"Yes, I know the feeling. It's really annoying," I agreed.

"I felt a really thin and long hair inside my left eye. I spent some good minutes in front of the mirror, trying to find it and grab it, but I couldn't. I couldn't," she repeated, sounding a little distressed. "Now, my eyes not only were itchy, they were also very red and sore."

"Fortunately, Henry's older brother is an ophthalmologist. Henry was my boyfriend back then," she explained. "I told him I really needed to have my eye examined because something was wrong with it. He started to say I just need to stop scratching it and use some eye drops, but I was physically unable to stop. The itching was so bad.

"When Henry saw how swollen my eye was, he called his brother, Dr. E, and took me there.

"As expected by Henry, Dr. E said nothing was wrong with me. He said there was nothing inside my eye, and that I just had a bad case of allergies. I don't blame Dr. E. He examined me thoroughly and gave me a corticosteroid eye ointment, as well as allergy medicine. I know that usually it would be enough, but it wasn't the case for me. He's really nice, you know? He still visits me sometimes and says he's sorry he couldn't help me."

"I'm glad to know it, Amanda," I sympathetically remarked.

"Anyway, that night is hell. I can't sleep. I put the ointment, but I REALLY have to scratch. And I really need to grab the hair. It bothers me so much. SO MUCH. It's hard to describe how desperate the feeling was. So I do it, and take all the eye medicine off, so I have to put it again. But I also need to scratch again.

"I know how it sounds like. I'm childish. I have no self-control. It's just a normal allergic crisis. I just have to stop scratching it and get some sleep, and things will be fine. But they won't. They won't. I used to have a strong mind. But this is so bad, it's so bad I want to die. I couldn't sleep at all that night, and the itching was unbearable. My eye was so sore and swollen I couldn't even open it. The other eye was completely normal. Why, doctor? Why only one of my eyes was this bad?"

"I don't think you're childish, Amanda," I replied, with sincerity. I had no other answer to offer.

"I make it through the night somehow, but every second is torture. I can't stress this enough. It's pure hell," she flinches, remembering the sensation. "Henry leaves for his classes. I'm desperate for the itch to stop. I do something dumb. Something I know is dumb, but I don't mind, because the only important thing is getting rid of the invisible hair. I grab tweezers and try to pick the hair inside my eye with them."

I do my best to suppress an "ouch."

"It hurt so much. It hurt so much, doctor. I'm starting to go out of my mind. My sclera is completely fucked up, the whole area of my left eye is bleeding, and I'm probably going permanently blind by now. But I just want it to stop. I just want it to stop. I just want it to stop," she makes a long pause.

"I understand you, Amanda. What happened after you tried to use the tweezers?"

"After two hours of agony using the tweezers, for a glorious moment, I feel like I was able to pull the hair off. I never felt this relieved in my life. But then I become paranoid. I can't let it happen again. It will kill me. It will drive me insane," she gestured around the room, with bitter irony. "You know it did."

"You're not *necessarily* insane, Amanda. You just have an unknown problem and you're safer here."

She gave me a half-smile, but unfortunately it was creepier than anything I ever saw. I did my best not to show how her smiling face terrified me.

"Thank you, doctor. Anyway, once again I was being irrational and I knew it, but being rational didn't matter at the time. I only cared about not feeling that terrible agony again. So I got rid of all the hairs in my body.

"Protecting my eyes, I waxed myself. I went bald. I removed my eyebrows and even my eyelashes. I looked like a freaky monster, but it wasn't important to me. I then cleaned the house like a crazy person. I vacuumed everything, I threw a lot of clothes and stuff away, and I refused to let Henry get in unless he had zero hair on his body too."

"Did he comply?"

"No. I don't think anyone in their right mind would do it. Poor Henry went to stay at his friend's house and called my parents. They were surprised, because I had no story of mental issues, nor did anyone in my family," she bit her horrendously deformed lip. "Shortly after Henry gave up on getting in, I realized just getting rid of all that hair wasn't enough. I had to make sure it couldn't enter," she paused.

"I see."

"So I got my sewing kit and stitched my eye."

I shivered.

"When my family found me, I looked awful. My whole body was naked in every sense. I refused to wear clothes because they have tiny hairs. Even now, I only wear seamless plastic stuff. My bed sheet is plastic, I have nothing related to fabric around me. My eye was awfully swollen and stitched. I screamed the whole time that they had to get rid of all their hairs to be in contact with me. I'll admit to you I was a mess, doctor. It was the first time I was put here."

"You're being very brave to share your story, and your point-of-view is very reasonable, Amanda," I encouraged her.

"Thank you, doctor. After that, they treated my eye so what I did wouldn't infect it, and I was put to sleep most of the time. It was a relief, because I know I wasn't in my right mind, and, despite my relief, I was still feeling paranoid. After a few days, my fear proved to be true, and it simply came back. It came back, doctor. The invisible hair, the unbearable itching that literally drove me insane; it was back inside my stitched eye. How did it get in, doctor? Deep down, I knew it would. I knew I wouldn't really get rid of it. I knew things would never be normal anymore," she sighed. "But I wasn't ready to feel that desperation again."

I silently read the notes from her first psychiatrist's notes regarding this moment.

Amanda Jameson had let her nails grow. I felt so bad for her and was naïve to allow it, thinking she simply wanted to feel feminine after getting rid of her hair and eyelashes in a psychotic fit. She was so normal after that—so sane—that I got carried away. But she wanted to hurt herself. She mercilessly dug her long nails between the stitches, clawing at her own cornea, making blood and parts of her sclera come out. Her alien hairless figure made it creepier. I'll definitely recommend completely restraining her if the nurses hadn't done it by now.

"I had to be restrained because I was hurting myself. Now, that was the 9th circle of hell. If I thought before that things couldn't get worse, I was wrong. The itching was awful when I could scratch it, but I can't even put to words how painful to my body and mind it was to not be able to scratch. I thought of suicide the whole time I had to be awake. So I requested to have someone to talk to all the time. Being tied to the bed, it was the only thing that could bring me some relief and distraction.

"It was a very reasonable request, so the clinic allowed it. I was assigned a very sweet nurse, Samira. She would tell me entertaining stories, it was like the book *One Thousand and One Nights*. One day she asked what happened to me, and I told her. She was horrified and ended up quitting after that, but I had piqued the interest of other nurses. One after another, I told them my story so far. This went on for weeks, since I would only be awake for like 4 hours a day. These hours were a nightmare, but having people to chat with really made it less unbearable."

I read the notes of her second doctor.

As abruptly as it started, Amanda Jameson's unknown psychosis seemed to go away. Being restrained is very difficult and we try to avoid it, but it was crucial for her physical well-being. Instead of falling into a depression, the patient fought it, asking to be surrounded by people, and showing positive behaviors. This young woman has a strong and fascinating mind, but I digress. There is strong evidence that her mysterious condition subsided or is cured, so I'll recommend the hospital release her, and the family to keep her under constant but discreet surveillance.

"Somehow, after a few weeks, the itch completely disappeared. They still kept me here for a while, but I didn't need to be restrained. It was the first time in a whole year that I felt normal. My hair was growing back, and even the paranoia that it would happen again was under control. I wanted to enjoy while the peace lasted, you know?

"The first thing I did was to break up with Henry. To set him free. He didn't have the courage to do it while I was here; the poor guy was a mess but still trying to be a gentleman. I liked him, but I wanted to make sure that this thing was really gone before I could think about dating, it just wasn't a priority. I didn't feel ill, but I was still a mess physically, and wasn't ready to go back to college, so I moved back with my parents.

"Things were fine at first. They were so good to me, they got rid of every piece of furniture or decoration with hairs in the whole house. They even re-homed their poor old dog to my sister's house for my sake. They didn't get rid of their own body hairs, of course, but bought hazmat suits to use whenever they were around me. I insisted I was fine and that it wasn't necessary as long and they wore aprons and caps like you're wearing now, but they didn't want to trigger anything bad in me. It was the first time I realized how they must have been suffering because of my condition," she wiped a tear from her good eye.

"This is important, Amanda. You can't avoid a mental illness, but thinking about how hard it is on your loved ones will give you strength to fight it the best you can."

"I didn't feel the hair inside my eye for months. I felt good enough to let my hair grow, as long as my mother washed it for me using a plastic barrier to keep it from falling in my face, and most of the time I kept it inside a cap. But it felt good. It felt like preparing to have a completely normal life again.

For the first time since I was back, my parents felt confident enough to leave me unsupervised. It was their wedding anniversary, and they deserved to have a good time. They went to a fancy restaurant. It would be just a few hours. I could be fine. I knew I could.

But, of course, that's exactly when it came back. I don't know if it was because I was free for months, but the agony felt worse than before. It was like I had now many hairs instead of a single strand. I scratched and screamed and cried, but nothing was ever enough. Finally, I came to the conclusion that the only way to get rid of it is getting rid of my eye itself."

I sighed and read the third doctor's notes.

Amanda Jameson was somewhat a legend to me, but she's real. And she's back. She was left alone at home for a few hours and burned half her face with acid. The older nurses said she was monstrous when she didn't have a single hair in her body, but I bet nothing can compare to what she looks like now.

The left side of her body was better off gone than how it is now: a fleshy, infectious wound, showing more the muscle that should be inside than anything else. There's no skin anymore; part of the flesh of her nose is missing, and her mouth looks like the worst cleft lip I have ever seen. It's like the left portion of her mouth was liquefied, and it was incorrectly reassembled all over the lower portion of her face. In time, Amanda will be left with nasty scars and a very deformed chin, but miraculously, she can still speak, breathe and eat.

I don't know if this fact makes her less or more bizarre.

The eye... I don't how to describe what's left of the eye. The surgeon had to open the stitched mass of gore and remove it, but the first thing she said when she woke up was that she can still feel the invisible hairs moving inside her empty socket.

And she'll still scratch it.

This doctor was right about the nasty scars. It's very difficult to look at her, but as her doctor, I have to. Nowadays, Amanda at least has hair—she concluded that the invisible hairs are not actual hair, so it doesn't matter if she gets rid of real hair or not. Still, worried about making her condition even worse, the clinic forbids the employees to have contact with her without a plastic apron and cap, and she can't wear clothes with hairs, have regular sheets or get plush dolls either.

According to the other doctors' notes, Amanda's condition has been on and off for the past years; sometimes, she will scratch her eye for months straight—she isn't being restrained anymore because, well, there's nothing else to damage. Her eye is completely gone.

Sometimes, she has a few weeks of break from the devastating itch.

"But I don't wanna leave this place. I know it's a matter of time until the itch is back, and I'm scared of what I'll do. I don't want to make my parents even more miserable. I want to keep living and hope that someday someone will discover what is that, and maybe a cure," she said. I noticed that she hasn't been scratching her eye (and I use this term very loosely) for the last 40 minutes.

"Is the itching gone for now, Amanda?"

"Yes, doctor. It seems so," she smiled. I wish I could beg her to never smile again. This sight made me immediately finish the session to throw up. "For some reason, the itching always gets better when I'm interacting with other people."

It's been two weeks since I've been assigned to Amanda, and she is in one of her good, itch-free periods. Besides her deformed looks, she's a very easy-going patient.

It was so hard typing this because I had to stop to scratch my eye the whole time. But I feel like talking to other people will help, at least for a while.

My left eye is uncontrollably, unbearably itchy right now. What about yours?

ONE GIRL AT NIGHT

I learned black magic after Gabrielle was gone.
    She was the most beautiful and kind person you could ever meet. She was also funny, compassionate, and smart. Gab loved animals but hated hikes and camping, so when my friends and I spent a few days in the woods every year, she would wish me luck kissing my face all over, and always make sure to tell me she'd miss me, so I should have double the fun.
    Every time, she playfully rolled her eyes at my childish hobbies and assured me she loved me anyway and that I should never stop being as silly as I wanted because it was part of who I am, and she loved every little bit of it.
    I know most people think their wife is perfect, but mine *was* scientifically perfect.
    The biggest and best part of me died in that accident. I wish more than anything that I died with her, or at least that I was there to hold her hand in her final moments. She must have been so scared, so helpless, so lonely.
    All while I was camping with my friends like a stupid 12-year-old boy. I just cannot forgive myself.
    I had no one else to blame. The other driver, the one who caused the accident, died too. He was lucky enough to be gone instantly, while my Gabrielle suffered all the way to the hospital with a broken spine.
    And without me.
    Her parents and brother lived so far away. Both her best friends live in a neighboring town and didn't make it in time. She had no one. The most perfect being in the world died surrounded by strangers in a cold ambulance.

Suicide crossed my mind many times, and the only reason I didn't take this way out were my parents. I am an only child with no close relatives, and they would be completely abandoned without me, both financially and emotionally. Nothing could even get close to the love I feel for Gab, but they easily get the second place, and I love them very, very much. I could never do that to them, I can't just pass away the pain I feel.

I'll go when they go, I told myself. But I still couldn't bear my everyday life. My empty bed. My empty life. The emptiness and coldness of the world without my sunshine.

Brad, my best friend, was the one who told me about the witch. It was almost silly at the time.

"Hey Jay, I know it sounds stupid, but years ago, an old lady gave me a spell. I had bad stuttering... you can ask my parents if you don't believe me. And it cured me. I swear to God."

I had to laugh a little—a joyless laugh—because Brad had been his class valedictorian, was a teacher *and* a motivational speaker. And he was great at those.

"What did you give her in exchange?" I asked.

"She made me promise three years of my life to her and I was like, "sure, you can have it." I was 17 at the time, so missing three years when I'm old seemed like literally nothing. Still does, to be honest. If the witch likes you, she shouldn't ask for more than five. And I don't even think it's real because I didn't sign a contract with blood or something. But the magic part *is* real."

Brad took me to her. She still lived on the same farm and, according to him, hadn't aged a day; being a teenager at the time, Brad had the impression she was super old, but she was probably in her 50s.

I half-expected the witch to live in a house made of candy, and whole-expected this story to be bullshit—maybe she was a speech therapist, or just gave him confidence to overcome his impediment.

But it wasn't the case.

"Long time no see, Brad. I knew long ago the stars would bring you here on this day and time," she said, simply. She then turned to me. "James."

Quickly scanning me with her deep dark green eyes, the witch seemed to read my very soul, but I wasn't afraid. If something, I felt like I could trust her; she was powerful, the real deal. She introduced herself simply as Circe, and asked Brandon to leave and come back for me in three days.

I didn't sleep for those three days, but they were so much easier than all the sleepless nights I've been having since Gab was gone. I am mentally and physically unable to fall asleep without her by my side, and what little I drowse gives me awful dreams of her screaming in pain and dying all alone. 100% of the time.

In my nightmares, my wife blames me for abandoning her, for not being there to keep her from driving alone on a rainy night.

"You can only use the spell once per person and it lasts 20 hours," Circe said, her voice raucous, but not as much as you would expect a witch's voice to be. It was more of a heavy smoker teacher. "It won't harm your target in any way, but it won't work on the same girl a second time."

"How many years will you ask of me? I'm fine as long as I can take care of my parents until the end."

She snickered. "Good boy. But I won't ask anything for myself. The magic is already too demanding on the caster. Consider this an act of charity."

"What do you mean too demanding on the caster?" I asked.

"You'll find out soon enough, but you'll make it as long as you never use it twice on the same target. Never."

At the time, I didn't care about this ominous warning.

The witch instructed me to never come back to her, unless it was absolutely necessary. Questions about the spell wouldn't be considered necessary, because she already told me everything I had to know. Her attitude was mostly friendly, but as she emphasized this, she looked dead serious. I promised not to bother her.

During my short stay at her shed, I considered many times asking Circe what ulterior motive she had to simply go around teaching people spells to solve their problems. I also considered asking if she would accept money for her helpfulness—I'm not a rich man, but I make decent money. Just when I was about to board Brad's car and depart, she lightly touched my shoulder.

"I need nothing but time, boy. And I'm satisfied as long as I'm not letting ancient magic die."

In three days, just as predicted by Circe, I had completely mastered the spell. After that, my life was a blur of bars, nightclubs, and dates with girls from Tinder. Every night I go out to find my Gabrielle. I desperately need to have someone by my side—someone I can turn into my wife, so I can finally sleep peacefully.

That's why, ever since the love of my life died, I religiously bring home one girl at a night.

Thankfully, I don't look bad and I can afford to go to nice places. It's tiring to flirt and keep some inane conversation for a while, before I can ask a girl to go back to my place.

I don't think I'm a bad person. I just want and desperately need to have my wife. I would never bring a girl home without their consent and I respect them as people, even if most times I don't even care about the sex—I just want to fall asleep holding her in my arms and smelling her hair. Sometimes the girl is not that into me, so I have to quickly find someone else. Once or twice I had to hire a prostitute, but I'd rather not; not coming back for 20 hours is troublesome for them, and very expensive for me.

As soon as we arrive at my apartment, I bewitch the girl, and in a matter of minutes, both her looks and personality are exactly my wife's. Circe didn't explain to me the mechanics behind it—am I channeling Gabrielle's soul or just emulating it?

I don't care if it's an illusion, as long as I can feel at peace, and I do.

The girl won't remember anything, nor feel anything bad or weird. When the spell is almost worn out, I drop them somewhere safe and public like a mall. They will be a little disoriented as to why they are there, but fine.

I don't want to hear about their boring feuds with their co-worker Karen, but I care about these girls' safety. After all, they are the reason why I can spend 20 blissful hours with my Gabrielle.

For a while, I felt fine. Sure, I felt empty and even shameful for chasing after random girls, but I knew this was a small price to pay to have the woman of my dreams by my side again.

Then the symptoms started.

At first, I would wake up with bad bruises and small burns on my body. Although they were hurtful and bothered me, I didn't think much of it. I was probably sleepwalking.

Then my vision started to go bad. I figured it was only the combo being in my late-30s and working on the computer the whole day, but decided to go to an ophthalmologist anyway.

He found nothing wrong with my eyes.

As my vision worsened fast—in a matter of weeks—I thought it was best to try a neurologist and get a CAT scan, but it also didn't show anything wrong.

Now I am pretty much blind. It's awfully hard to drive and work, but the worst thing is that I can barely see Gabrielle's face. Still, I can smell and hold her, and fall asleep peacefully—even if in the morning my body is covered in hematomas.

And it brings us to last night. Last night, the spell went terribly wrong.

I'm more than used to the spell, and the lines I have to recite aren't long. I know I didn't do anything different. Still, as the girl's body started to change, instead of turning into Gabrielle, she grew black wings on her back, and mantis appendages replaced her legs.

As her wings spread, she let out an inhuman shriek, and I noticed her mouth was covered in scars and purple liquid, with fangs coming from her lower jaw, like a payara fish.

Her eyes were completely white, and I never felt more scared in my life; the only thing I could think of was to grab my gun.

As she dashed towards me, I shot her. I had to shoot this monstrous thing six times to simply make it (her?) fall unconscious, then I put her head inside a bag and didn't let go.

It took her four hours to suffocate and completely stop breathing. I was panting in panic the whole time.

I obviously couldn't get any sleep that night, and my desperation was beyond words. Would the spell never work again? Would I be charged with murder? *Are there more creatures like this?*

I felt awful because I had killed an innocent woman after turning her into a monster, but this wasn't even my main concern. All I could think was how I couldn't stand not seeing my Gabrielle ever again. And, like the last time, I didn't even have the chance to say goodbye.

But maybe it was a good thing that I didn't sleep, because by 4 AM Brad was pounding on my door so heavily I thought the whole building was going to collapse.

His tongue had turned into… a giant slug, or a tentacle, all wet and sticky, full of infected blisters. It was something so disgusting, so unholy, that I threw up twice in a minute. Brad could barely stutter some incomprehensible words.

He also threw up, and somehow the revolting mutant tongue detached from his mouth, just to have another one immediately grow to replace it. They both were around 50 cm long and very thick. He was crying now.

I decided this was an emergency big enough to seek Circe and grabbed my keys. I had always been a practical guy, but in that moment I hated so much that Brad was in an even worse shape than me. I just wanted to cry, then plant a bullet in my brain.

But before doing anything selfish, I had to do something about us and deal with the monstrous corpse in my house.

I drove there in the dark, almost blindly, while Brad threw up the sickening thing repeatedly, always growing a new, gooier one immediately.

We found Circe collapsed on her front door, holding her throat with both her hands and choking.

"This was too powerful, James," the witch spoke, between painful coughs and desperate gasps for air. She was drooling something purple and so acid that the skin from her chin was all burnt and fucked up. "I should've never released *it* into the world."

I called an ambulance for Circe and Brad. She stopped breathing before they even arrived, and Brad is under intensive care, but no one can understand his condition. Somehow, I know that he's never going to make it, but at least it's better to die than to live such a miserable, disgusting existence.

I couldn't wait until the night. I tried casting the spell over five or six girls and it just won't work anymore. They don't turn into monsters, but they also don't turn into anything else. They don't turn into my wife anymore *and I need her so badly.*

I'm quickly losing my mind.

Sorry mom and dad, but I guess it's time I join you in death, my adored Gabrielle. I pray there's no heaven and hell, or else we'll never meet again due to my sins.

I hope a machine gun will be enough to kill me, because I shot my head ten times with a handgun and nothing happened.

And I hope that the fact that my apartment was completely empty when I came back doesn't mean that the monster I created is on the loose.

PUMPKIN SPICE

Do you have a friend so reliable you could go to them if you killed a person knowing that they would have your back? I did.

Her name was Kate, and we instantly clicked after meeting in high school. It was one of those friendships for life, no matter how different we became—and we tested that, believe me.

By the time we were 27, Kate had moved to the countryside to a simple but large and adorable house. She worked as an astrologer and spiritual guru in general.

I stayed in the city, living in a kitchenette with my boyfriend, Sean, and working my ass off to finish college and keep a part-time job; needless to say, he was the main provider of our home.

That meant that I depended financially on him. That's the reason why I didn't leave when he started taking his anger out on me—I'd rather be physically abused by someone who'd help me pay the bills than by my parents who did nothing but leech my will to live ever since I was a kid. I saw no other option and I had no one.

"You had me!" Kate would reply softly as she hugged me in her large living room in the middle of the night, the reclaimed wood smelling nicely of incense. "Don't worry, sweetie, I'll take care of everything."

I will not sugarcoat it: after six years of abuse, I snapped and shot Sean in his sleep.

I don't know how I had the mental and physical strength to call my best friend after that.

"What's up, Claire?" she replied on the phone, carefree and unknowingly. I broke down crying, and told her what I had just done.

"I'm on my way. Don't do absolutely anything."

Even without the traffic, the drive from her place would take at least 65 minutes, but she made it in 40.

The way she put him inside a large trunk to carry his body to the car was almost professional; she told me to put the sheets, the gun, and some of his clothes there too, and to make the bed again.

"You're lucky to live in a noisy neighborhood where people go out of their way to mind their own business," she remarked. I nodded—those were the same neighbors who ignored my pleas to call the police every time he punched me senseless, after all.

After she was done putting him in the car, we left. Kate made sure to remind me from time to time that I shouldn't blame myself, and that most people in my situation would do the same. However, the law was flawed enough that I'd be better off hiding it. I nodded, still violently shaking from crying.

At her place, she was an absolute angel, making sure I felt safe. She tucked me in on a comfortable armchair, and I ended up dozing off, vaguely listening to her move around. She then carried me to the guest room and slept in a chair, holding my hand the whole time.

I woke up in the morning feeling like a brand-new woman.

"Rest for today. I'll make us some breakfast."

No more than 15 minutes later, she was upstairs again, holding a tray with a variety of simple dishes and a hot beverage.

"Drink this. It will make you feel better."

The beverage was a pumpkin spice latte, but very different from that one you can get at Starbucks. It both smelled and tasted heavenly, overwhelming my senses with the most intense deliciousness I had ever experienced.

I eagerly gulped down the drink, amazed at how delectable a pumpkin could taste; the spices brought a sweetness and a complexity that I never knew to be possible. The latte was creamy and velvety, with a slightly powdery texture.

"This is so good! I do feel better!" I told her and, like an older sister, she gently wiped my milk mustache with a napkin.

"I'm glad you like it, sweetheart! It's my favorite seasonal treat," she smiled.

***

After that, I ended up staying at Kate's for a few weeks. She'd give me the delicious pumpkin beverage from time to time, and I always felt refreshed after that. Obviously, I begged her to give me the recipe, but she'd just smile mysteriously and say *sorry, but it's a family secret.*

The investigations about Sean's disappearance miraculously didn't turn to me; we lived in an area where urban violence was pretty much the norm and, much to my surprise, most of my neighbors testified about Sean being violent and troublesome, even going as far as stating that he had enemies among the local gangs—something that even I didn't know.

In my testimony, I said that I went to a friend's house after we fought, and that he was nowhere to be found a few days later, when I returned. I also explained that I'm staying at said friend's because I'm afraid to live alone downtown and I can't afford the rent without him.

It feels awful to say it, but my life was the best that it's ever been—Kate even asked me to quit my job, since it was too far from her place and she earned enough to have me stay for a while and heal.

"I'll help you apply for other jobs when you're ready!" she offered, always with a kind smile.

The only thing that I needed for my life to be perfect was to find out that latte's recipe.

I know how stupid it sounds, but when you find the best thing in the world, it's impossible not to become addicted to it. And, when everything else is comfortable enough, it's easy to become obsessed.

So I did the worst thing a guest can do; I waited until Kate had some chores out of the house and spied on her stuff.

It didn't take me long to find a small metal box with a golden padlock inside her kitchen's cupboard, behind a bunch of groceries.

I sighed because the secret was so close but out of reach; after thinking for a while, I remembered how well I knew Katie. She hid all her important things in her plants.

It took me a few tries, since her cabin easily contained over two dozen of them, but I found the small golden key that fitted the lock, all buried in dark-brown earth.

The box was filled with some small jars, made of glass and beautifully adorned. Each of them had a tag.

Cinnamon—Ginger—Clove—Nutmeg—Vanilla—Dearest Lucille—Sean

I screamed while I puked all over myself.

Lucille was the name she had chosen for her daughter two years ago, but she, unfortunately, lost the baby in the 5th month of pregnancy. The gray powder inside it was almost gone.

The jar labeled as *Sean* was the fullest one, and next to it there were a few other human names I didn't recognize. All of them were filled with gray powder, too.

So that's why I was feeling physically stronger after drinking the latte; her secret ingredient was dead people's ashes.

I carefully closed the box and hid the key again.

And, after a few days of feeling absolutely disgusted, I decided that I didn't care.

More than that—it was actually desirable.

***

Months went by.

I ended up getting a job and an apartment closer to Kate, so I'd always be around. I'd always drink the heavenly, witchy beverage.

She didn't offer it often when it wasn't around Halloween, which was frustrating but understandable; she was low on ingredients. Except for Sean's jar, all the others were nearly empty.

So, as a good friend, it was up to me to get her more.

I think she believed me the first time; I called her crying, explaining that I had a Tinder date who tried to assault me and I ended up shooting him.

"Dear Lord, Claire, you're a bad men magnet!" she'd remark, simply. Hugging me. Not blaming me.

Once again, she handled everything for me. She gave me some latte again, and that guy tasted delicious—he tasted like strength, and I never felt better; I was truly absorbing a dead person's energy, enhancing mine.

I craved the drink more than everything now; more than being the best thing I've ever tasted, it was food for my soul. I'd do anything to drink that every day.

That's why I did one of the worst things a person can do. I killed more to get my fix.

The Tinder guy, I thought he'd last for at least a year, but he didn't. I needed to get more.

All the while, Kate made me feel safe and loved. But I got too carried away.

She confronted me.

"I'm sorry, but shooting four people to defend yourself in a year seems like a lot. Is there something you want to tell me?"

No yelling, nothing like my parents or Sean. She sounded concerned, guilty even.

Since the cat was out of the bag, I wouldn't try to deny my intentions.

"I'm just having your back and getting you the ingredients!" I replied, offended that she didn't thank me for that.

"That's horrifying, Claire. Protecting yourself was one thing, but intentionally killing people… I can't condone that. Please stop, that's not how it works," she replied. She was crying and trembling like a fool.

"You think that just because you're some witch you can kill and pulverize people for your recipe but I can't? And you won't even thank me for trying to help you?" I screamed at her, furious.

"Are you listening to yourself?! Claire, I beg you to stop. I didn't kill those people. I just happened to have their ashes."

"This is bullshit! You turned Sean into ashes, and you carried his body like a professional."

I stormed out of her house, never to return.

And then I killed. I killed and burned and powdered but nothing I tried would ever taste like hers. I killed in different cities, different states even. I killed in dates and I killed in dark alleys. I killed businessmen and beggars. I killed men and women, black and white and yellow and red, but no one tasted right.

Frustrated, I started becoming careless.

That was when I got anonymous letters saying things like "stop while you're not too far gone." And I laughed because I knew I was too far gone since the first time I lured a poor guy to murder him and drink his ashes.

It's night and all is quiet. All but some small, small steps moving in the darkness. Carefully, deliberately, just a couple of them every few minutes. They're light, like the soft noise of the wings of a bird watching their prey.

I know it's Kate. I can even sense her smell of wildflowers and incense. I know she thinks it's her job to stop me, and she's here to imprison me so I won't harm people again.

I'll put on a good fight, but she's always been physically stronger. I don't hope to win.

I just hope she turns me into something delicious.

SOMEONE I KNOW MIGHT NOT BE ALIVE

Working at a university library, I'm used to seeing the students looking half dead. But this was completely different.

Heather always struck me as a weird kid, although a very sweet one. She seemed way younger than her peers, like the runt of a litter, but I more than once overheard other students talking about her being some sort of teenage genius.

As it happens to most brilliant people, she didn't seem to pay a lot of attention to the world around her, but she tried her best.

"I heard you had a nasty car accident, Miss Thompson. Are you too hurt?" she asked me just the other week, her eyes full of genuine concern.

"I think you're mistaking me for another librarian, darling," I replied, then went back to reading my own book; our uni was a big complex, with four major libraries with three or more librarians each, and a few smaller ones.

Funnily, all of us lived up to the librarian stereotype very well: thirty or forty-something, tortoise eyeglasses, hair in a perfect bun, a pencil dress topped with a cardigan, so I could understand her confusion.

There wasn't much to do these days, as our collection was completely cataloged in the uni's app; so we were there mostly to handle paperwork and help with the restricted section, one of the only places that remained completely free from the modern world's scrutiny.

Most students had no interest in the library, let alone in the "forbidden books," so I had all the time in the world to just go around hissing "shhh!" if I wanted to. It was the perfect job for any introvert, a quiet place with little to no interaction.

Lately, my days consisted of silently watching over people.

Heather, I heard, was pursuing a scientific career, but she always had a dreamy look on her face when she read our books—we were located in the History Department.

But I became concerned with her hobbies when she started asking for witchcraft books from the restricted section.

"Oh, I'm just… doing some research for fun. Interesting how women turn to magic because it seems to be the easier way for us to gain power, huh?" she gave me a half-smile. She was so pale and clearly concerned about something big.

I couldn't help but peek over her shoulder a little.

How to create a new human body:

- Wax; it must amount to 2/3 of the person's original weight
- An object they held dear in life; this will bind the soul
- The ashes from any book; see above how to ensure that you obtain this material minimizing loss
- As much hair from the subject as possible; this ingredient will give the new body verisimilitude.

Please remember that the above is meant to give a new body to a person that's barely clinging to life. If your subject has already passed, it's crucial to add their own ashes and blood from a living fox. In this case, the fox will act as a recipient for the soul, and must stay beside the person at all times.

Obviously, this was all bullshit—I'm a rational, 33-year-old woman after all. I know better; still, Heather was so pale, her lips were so bluish, that I feared that she was either terminally ill or already dead.

Which is a ridiculous thought, but, come to think of it, I didn't see her interacting with anyone else but me in the last couple of weeks. Besides, she was a smart kid; if she was dedicating this much time to such things, *maybe* they held more than historical interest.

I was intrigued and had too much time in my hands; my fiancé had been staying at the hospital with his sick mother lately and I didn't have any pets or roommates, so I had to admit things were a little too lonely.

So, over the next few days, I helped Heather get some ancient witchcraft books, then casually walked behind her—looming like a ghost, stealthy as a cat.

There was no doubt she was particularly interested in reviving people through old sorcery. The dark circles under her eyes grew bigger by the day. Her hair was matted and tangled, and I started convincing myself that she looked like she was rotting alive.

It was a Friday when I couldn't hold back anymore and decided to ask her if she was dying; I gave the poor girl a jump scare.

"Oh, it's you, Miss Thompson," she muttered. "No, I'm not dying. This is for someone I know."

"They must be really important to you, then," I replied.

"Well, we're not really close, but I think her dying now would be horribly unfair," she replied, biting her incredibly pale lips. Looking closer, I realized she looked so bad because she hadn't been sleeping or eating properly, focused on her research.

"You're a good girl, Heather," I praised her, then started leaving.

"Miss Thompson?"

"Yes?"

"The dying person is you."

I laughed. "I'm not ill, sweetie. Thanks for worrying."

"Yes, you're not ill. You're in a coma with no hope of returning. And your body… is not *actually* here."

***

Heather took me to the hospital, where I saw my own body fading, a feeling so eerie it's hard to explain. There was no doubt it was me, badly injured and hanging to life by a thread.

When you've been in a coma for weeks like I had, it's hard to come back from it. And even if you do, your muscles will malfunction and your body will be so weak that you're prone to catching a myriad of infections and dying anyway.

"My sister is a nurse here. That's how I found out about you," Heather explained, in a whisper, as she cut a huge piece of my hair; I couldn't stop staring at my physical body. It was so pale, nearly lifeless. "Unfortunately, the ritual can only extend your life for a few years, a decade at best. And it can't be done a second time because it won't work with your wax body."

I nodded, paying close attention to her.

"All done here," she carefully placed the hair inside a ziplock bag. "Let's go to your place to gather the other ingredients. I bought the wax in advance."

"Are you sure you want to do this for me?" I asked. "Isn't it something evil? Unnatural?"

"Oh, evil and unnatural is what they tried to do to you. You'll understand when you meet my sister. But first, you know. Let's create your new vessel!"

***

My new body was successfully created; I can't recall a lot of details because my soul was being pinned to the wax and the process can be overwhelming to one's senses, but I remember hearing Heather chanting and a lot of bright lights.

Moving around with it felt natural, almost like it was my original body. However, it came with a number of limitations. Heather recited them to me after I spent a few hours learning how to fully use my new, inorganic limbs.

- Any exam that tries to look inside your body will be unsuccessful and show nothing. You need to avoid getting sick at all costs if you don't want to be studied as a medical aberration;
- Your body cannot take more than five minutes of sunlight a day, and sunscreen doesn't work. The only way is to stay indoors as much as possible, and always protecting your face with a hat;
- You can make your body turn to dust at will and reappear in another spot within your view. However, you'll be even more vulnerable to sunlight for a week after each time;
- Your body will immediately melt if it touches salt water, hot water or acid substances. Keep that in mind even for trivial tasks and always wear gloves just in case;
- At least once a month, you need to ingest wax to strengthen your body. A single candle will suffice.

"Is that all?" I asked. "It isn't that bad."

"My sister Susan will explain the last rule to you," Heather announced, and a woman who looked just like her but several years older and in white scrubs entered the room.

"Miss Laura Thompson, I'm happy to see you well," she greeted me, and we exchanged formalities. "You must recall that your fiancé's mother was very ill before your accident, right?"

I nodded.

"The details are irrelevant, but that family has been doing it for decades: literally stealing people's lives. They approach someone, establish a bond, then suck their life force, leaving their body as an empty shell. That's what your fiancé and his 'parents' (she did the air quotes) have done to you."

"Like vampires? Are they vampires??" it was all my brain could gather. Heather bit her lip and nodded. "And what it has to do with the last rule?"

"The last rule says that you owe a favor to whoever gives your life back. Anything they want to," Susan replied. Heather was sweating and looked so guilty I felt bad for her. "And we want you to dispose of them."

Strangely, it didn't seem an unreasonable request. After all, they pretty much killed me. Why shouldn't I defend myself?

"And what you have to profit from it?" I asked, my brain finally functioning again.

"You see," Susan smirked, and, in an instant, her sclera turned yellow, her irises turned crimson and her skin became purplish, with a leathery texture. Her canines were huge and her whole presence emanated menace and malice. "We are rivals."

ORPHANAGE RULES

Congratulations on your new job! We hope that your time as a resident teacher at the Saint Alphonsus Orphanage is a rewarding and easy experience. To help with the latter, here's a set of rules you absolutely must comply with, as well as make sure all the kids under your care follow.

If you see a child endangering themselves and don't follow protocol, you'll be fired with no previous notice. If you fail to follow the rules for teachers and residents in general, let's just say that unemployment won't be a concern anymore.

General Rules for Residents

Curfew is 9 PM. No exceptions. Adults who need to be out after this time need to let Abbess Johansen know beforehand, and only return after 6 AM.

By 11:11 PM, all the lights should be turned off, except the large chandelier at the dining hall, which should be turned on at ALL times. Every resident is under obligation to report the malfunction of any lamp around the building.

The janitor, Mr. Dracule, is to be called at any moment for emergencies, day or night, except during 3:33 AM and 4:44 AM. If something requires his attention between these hours, Abbess Johansen should exceptionally be called.

It's encouraged to let Mr. Dracule know that the front gate is open if you happen to see it from a window, but don't actively try to see it, and don't ever look outside from any window located on the second floor's south wing.

If the big painting of Saint Alphonsus on the main stairs seems to be moving, ignore it. Walk faster, and don't engage in conversation. He's harmless but can be a handful if you let him escape.

The Mass on Mondays is mandatory for all residents (except the ones from the 4th floor) and eventual visitors. No one is allowed to leave the chapel before 10:31 AM.

Rules for the Staff

Kids under the age of 6 are strictly forbidden from leaving the 4th floor, including for meals, and have to be under the care of Miss Asimov at all times. The staff is allowed on the 4th floor if necessary, but it's discouraged to criticize Miss Asimov's educational methods or question her number of limbs.

The teacher's break room in the basement is permanently deactivated. Don't let the delicious smell fool you, there's no one inside.

The basement is to be used for storage only. If you see a small child there, don't look into its eyes. Retreat without turning your back to it, and immediately call Mr. Dracule.

The playroom on floor 2 is off-limits for adults. We believe in letting teenagers have their own space. Don't let the sound of scratches on the door intimidate you, they know what they are doing.

At the start of every class, you must lock the door and count how many kids you have under your care; at the end of the class, before unlocking the door, count again. If one of the kids is missing, immediately let Mr. Dracule know. If there's one extra kid, read the scroll accompanying this letter as fast as you can until the lights stop flickering.

The Unadoptable are allowed to roam freely around the building, unless there are visitors. It's easy to spot them, as they use very distinctive crimson cloaks. There's no harm in talking to them, they are quite friendly if you don't try to peek under their mantle. However, if you see one of them when you're with potential adopters, just break a bottle of Holy Water by throwing it on the floor; don't hesitate to do it, as your room is supplied with 12 of them per week.

Rules for the Children

Skipping classes is obviously against the rules, but skipping classes on Wednesdays means a fate worse than death itself. If you see yourself outside of a classroom on a Wednesday during school hours, immediately seek shelter in the chapel, and only leave when you stop hearing the chanting.

It's strictly forbidden to shower in the boys' bathroom on floor 3. Other uses are allowed, as long as you're carrying a crucifix on your body. If a boy tries to talk with you from a stall in an unknown language, leave immediately—no matter if you end up urinating your pants or worse.

Bedroom doors are only to be closed at 9 PM, after making sure that all your roommates are inside. Always check their lips, and under no circumstance allow a fellow to enter the bedroom if their mouth is blue, or if you don't recognize them. If that happens, pour Holy Water on them and let Mr. Dracule know immediately.

Food is forbidden outside the dining hall, as well as forks, knives, and utensils made of metal. Food scraps are always to be discarded by the specialized staff; if you're feeling hungry or *snacky* between meals, simply excuse yourself to the dining hall. Mrs. Martel will know how to solve your problem.

It's encouraged to interact with potential adopters, but take a careful look at them. If a man with very thin legs tells you that his daughter is on the 4th floor, do not believe him, and do not give him directions to get there. It's easy to recognize him because his legs are thin like matches and one of his shoes is too small.

When in trouble, you can contact a teacher or inspector to help you find Mr. Dracule, but they are **not** qualified to deal with the happenings described on this list. Observe them thoroughly before approaching them; we don't have a red-haired teacher who's over 2 meters tall on the staff.

Best regards and God bless us all,
Abbess Laurel Johansen

***

This is the letter I've got by mail a few weeks after submitting for my first job. I was straight out of university, with a huge student debt, and decided not to be picky about my options.

Besides, I lived in an orphanage myself until I was 7, and the nuns took great care of me, so it felt like some karmic opportunity to give back.

It's weird to say that, but I really enjoyed my time as a teacher at the Saint Alphonsus Orphanage; it was great to feel like I was making a difference for those kids who had no one else but us. And all of them were incredibly well-behaved, almost like they spent the early years of their childhood under military training.

The staff consisted of 8 teachers, around 20 nuns—commonly referred to as "inspectors," the kitchen/cleaning staff, and the ever-present Mr. Dracule. Despite a name that suggested some creepiness, he was a lovely, hard-working older man.

We teachers had individual rooms, and no strict rules about our free time; as long as we were inside the building before 9 PM and turned the lights off before 11 PM, we were fine.

I got along well enough with the other teachers, but we weren't close, since they were all so much older than me.

Jody, the old History teacher, was the only one who was slightly unpleasant. She took a habit of asking me if I planned on wasting my life on a *nunnery*—her words—and why I had no boyfriend.

As a damn boomer, she was flabbergasted to find out about the extension of my debts, and how expensive it was to rent a small apartment; the salary at the orphanage was below average, but the fact that I had free housing and free food more than made up for it.

Despite the fact that there wasn't a specific rule regarding the nuns, I soon learned the ones I should avoid. Sister Allister was the creepier of them—one of her eyes never moved, perpetually staring at the bridge of her nose. It didn't even blink, so she carried a huge bottle of saline solution with her, dropping it on her bad eye every five minutes.

She looked at least 80 years old, but walked as nimbly as a teenager with half her weight. One day, she simply vanished; her room was perfectly tidy, full of unopened bottles of eye-drop, and no one saw or heard what happened to her.

People disappearing wasn't, unfortunately, a rare occurrence. However, every time it happened, there was a lot of talking between the kids and us teachers for days, until it abruptly stopped. Then Jane Allister was simply forgotten, like she was never there.

To this day, I still don't know if she was some sort of supernatural being or just a misunderstood woman with a simple physical defect.

***

Being a Physics/Science teacher, it took me a while to admit that the paranormal was between us—but not that long. It was only in my first month as a teacher when I first witnessed something that I can't explain.

I was going up the stairs around 10:30 PM—I stayed a little too long at the library, reading the 7th-grade papers. Everything was too empty and quiet.

"What a lovely young lady!" a cheerful masculine voice shouted behind me. Suddenly, there was an otherworldly, compelling atmosphere. I almost couldn't resist turning back to look at him.

I opened my mouth to reply, as a little red light twinkled in the background of my brain. What was it again?

I felt my body in slow motion, then someone shoved me so hard I almost fell face-first on the steps.

"Silly girl! Haven't you read your admission letter? Alphonsus, leave at once!"

It was Abbess Johansen. Her authoritative figure made me feel both scared and relieved, and I remember pathetically begging her not to fire me.

"I'm not firing you. You didn't talk to him. If being about to disobey the rules got people fired, I would need to close down this orphanage."

"Madam, I'm so sorry…"

"Suzanne, you're a good teacher and the children like you. Be more careful and you'll have a bright future ahead."

I was more careful.

Over the next year, the only incident I had happening with me was realizing one of my students went missing during class—with the door locked. I didn't understand how it happened, and I still don't, but I immediately let Mr. Dracule know, and Anthony was found safe and sound.

After the incident with the Saint Alphonsus from the painting, I didn't see Abbess Johansen often, but I somehow always felt her severe stare on me.

***

I had just started my third year as a teacher when I screwed up.

I took the 8th grade on a field trip to the Aquarium. They were to write a simple report about the species they enjoyed the most; sometimes, science was just an excuse to do something nice for the kids—something orphans wouldn't usually be able to do.

All of them used the opportunity to buy themselves some candy, sodas, and other treats we only had on special events at the orphanage.

I forgot to check their pockets and backpacks as we returned. That was mistake number one. Then I saw one of my favorite students eating a chocolate bar on the playground and my first impulse was deciding to turn a blind eye to it. After all, candy hardly qualifies as food, right?

As soon as I realized why I shouldn't do that, I started running towards him, but it was too late. *Something* had awakened.

It's been six years and I still can't forget the crunching sounds as the earth itself seemed to come to life and swallowed Anthony whole, chewing pleasantly on his little bones. I'm tormented by it whether I'm awake or sleeping.

I was terrified to report the incident and decided to hide what I witnessed until I calmed myself down, but Abbess Johansen knew. She knew every single thing that went on in her orphanage.

As to how, I have to mention that, as she summoned me to her office to fire me, I noticed something on the corner of her mouth—the slightest chocolate stain.

REMEMBER ME

Did you know that some indigenous languages and cultures have no sense of past and future? Take the Pirahã tribe on the Amazon rainforest, for example. Their language, also called Pirahã, is considered the hardest known language to learn because of that—and the fact that it involves whistles.

Because they only feel the need to express themselves in the present tense, they disregard anything that they didn't personally see. That's one of the main reasons why they remained isolated and no one was able to catechize them; Jesus is too far in the past for the Pirahã to even acknowledge him.

As a civilization with a strong sense of material and spiritual heirloom, however, one of our most basic social instincts is the desire to be remembered. We want to outlive ourselves, make sure we are important enough to leave a mark on history, or at least in someone else's path.

What would happen if the person you love the most in the world was forgotten the moment they leave your sight? If they always slipped out of your reach, no matter how much you wrote about them, took their picture or used any and every possible tool to register and immortalize their existence?

My story begins outside a coffee shop under the unforgiving rain of mid-April, 2014.

"A change for granny, please?" an old, decrepit lady clucked, the raspy voice of an almost-dying person touching my heart. It wasn't much, but I took a ten-dollar bill from my purse and extended it to her.

She raised her cataract eyes to me.

"Oh, my beautiful child! God bless you! Let me repay by reading your future," she immediately grabbed my hand with her two own, surprisingly strong for a little hunchback lady, no younger than 70.

She ran her dirty, chastised fingers through my right palm, while I held a blue umbrella for the two of us with my left hand, lowering my eyes as people looked at me with annoyance; I had created a small pedestrian traffic jam by stopping there.

What uneasiness I might have felt from the interaction was drowned by the thought that, being an orphan, it could very well be myself in her place, begging for pennies under bad weather, had I not lucked out.

"Your mother is unknown. Father drank himself to death after putting you in the system," she stated.

I was flabbergasted. I had only learned about my father as an adult, and I was still searching for information about my biological family.

"Don't look for your origins. You won't like what you find, might you find something," she added, eerily. I instinctively pulled back my hand, the air suddenly too cold for me to bear.

"Umm, okay, thank you," I managed, getting ready to leave.

"One more thing, child," she nonchalantly grabbed my hand again. "You'll be gone by your 30th birthday. Erased."

"I'll die?" I asked skeptically but as politely as I could. Being 23, the big 30 still felt like a distant possibility, miles and miles away.

"You'll wish," she replied simply, her voice drowned by the lights and sounds from the wet streets, and by the vague but very solid fear that crawled inside my guts.

***

My life has been good since then. Somehow, I locked up this memory and waltzed through the past six years happily, carefree.

Back then, I had just met Dylan, and I was head over heels for him—every bit as I still am. They say the pink flames of love-sickness don't last more than two years before the chemicals in your brain grow used to it and things aren't as shiny and mellow as they used to.

But my feeling for him was way more than a mere dopamine-induced infatuation. It gave meaning to everything I went through in life so I could meet him. Nothing ever felt so real, so sugary, so tender, so deep.

The moment he told me he felt the same and kissed under the moonlight was, along with the day of our wedding, the happiest memory I could possibly have.

Then, a few months ago, when I was still a little way from my 30th birthday, my life started to fall apart.

At first, people would look at me and ask why I was different—my friends, my co-workers, my mother even. I hadn't done anything with my hair, or clothes, or nails—I was the same old Hannah, consistently using the same haircut and general style for over five years.

"I think I misremembered how you look, then," people would usually say, and I'd leave at that, the horrible uneasiness and panic I felt that day all those years ago crawling its way up, bitter and burning like bile, but so much worse.

"Who are you again?" my boss asked, and my face burned in shame. I know that I am very average-looking, and that he only came to the office around once a month, but I had been there for the past three years. He called me by the name many times.

I managed to laugh it off like he was making a weird joke out of the blue. "It's Hannah Davis, sir," I replied meekly.

"I think I recognize you, but I can't remember why," a woman my age with auburn hair approached me in the subway.

I broke down crying, because she had been my best friend in high school.

***

When things progressed to the point where I lost my job because no one knew who I was—not even the face recognition system of the building I worked at—I was miserable.

But I still had Dylan. Dylan still remembered me, although he sometimes looked at me with a spark of unfamiliarity in his eyes, like I had undergone so many plastic surgeries that he simply wasn't sure if I was actually me anymore.

Despite that, he still remembered me. It was all that mattered—we struggled financially, but at least his job was enough to pay the basic bills.

I tried getting a job where no one gives a fuck, but by the end of the month I realized that, even though my co-workers at Walmart had accepted my unfamiliar presence without questions, I wasn't on the payroll.

I was forgotten in every possible way. Nothing brought me more despair than saying something like "I was here yesterday, remember?" and being answered no.

I started frantically looking for the old lady. If she could see it coming, then maybe she knew how to get rid of it.

No luck. I spent days near the coffee shop where I had met her, but I never saw her—as far as I knew, she could be dead already; the only progress I made around that time was finally connecting the dots and realizing that my mother was "unknown" because she had suffered from the same fate I was suffering.

Maybe she still existed but, with no records of it—either legal or sentimental—how would I find her? Was she actively looking for me while I could still be found? What would happen if two forgotten people were reunited?

But soon I realized that my mother was surely long gone. No one could live like this for over 30 years; when you don't exist, nothing is manageable. You have no one and, even if you have money without needing a job, you don't have a bank account to keep it, and you'll likely go homeless because you're unable to be a homeowner or a tenant. Roommates and family will always think you broke into their house. You're not only on your own—you're a crazy person telling lies.

And that was about to happen to me, too.

Whenever Dylan wasn't at work, he was with me, memorizing every inch of my face, or at least doing his best to.

But it wasn't enough, and my husband started to forget me too.

At first, only in lapses. He'd remember me again, although his eyes didn't gleam with love like before, because you can't just love a half-stranger.

I took so many pictures of myself, but my social media accounts couldn't be seen by others, like I was shadowbanned. *I was shadowbanned from life.*

Soon I couldn't even go to the supermarket because people complained that I wasn't there before so I was cutting in line. Small inconveniences became heart-wrenching situations for what they meant, and I finally understood what the old lady meant—the fate worse than death.

I was being erased alive.

***

The worst moment of my life was when Dylan finally forgot completely about me. I was showering when he came home from work.

"Whoa! What are you doing here, lady?"

He calmly said I should get dressed and leave, or he would call the police. I cried, my ugly sobs making my whole body shake, and my husband—always an angel—felt sorry for me and tried to calm me down, even though I was a complete stranger.

When I finally managed to talk, I explained everything to him with such abandon that he believed me.

Dylan—God bless his beautiful heart—got himself a lot of tattoos to remind him of me. My face, my name, what I meant to him, all carved in his skin in an attempt to transcend or at least trick my curse.

But as soon as he forgot me again, the tattoos were rendered useless, turned into mere random images, none of which referred to me.

My only solace was that every day Dylan fell in love with me again; but such a superficial, fleeting feeling wasn't enough. I craved the deepness of his former love, and even though I never complained, he felt guilty. And he slowly started sinking into madness, too.

I considered leaving so I'd be the only one to suffer.

"I can't bear the idea of you not being there, you know?" he replied, when I told him this plan. "Every time I forget about you I feel so despaired. Like someone took off all my organs and filled the empty shell with clay."

I couldn't. I wouldn't.

Back then, leaving his sight for five minutes was enough to be forgotten. He came up with a plan, although he only let me know the second half of it when it was too late.

"Hannah, I want you to use this to our favor for once," he cupped my face in his hands; these days he held me with such desperation, like I was going to physically fade at any moment. "We need to rob some money."

I did it. Under the veil of forgetfulness, I put on a mask, held the poor bank teller at gunpoint, and escaped.

It was the only time I was happy that no one remembered me; still, I felt awful and vomited on the curb as soon as I made my escape.

It wasn't a lot of money; a modest amount, probably enough to live for a year without having to worry.

"What now?" I asked Dylan when I came home, and of course he had already forgotten me. My heart broke from seeing the empty look in his eyes, trying to draw a distant, corroded memory.

I could now recite our story by heart, having told him it so many times. When he finally managed to remember me, he held me in his arms. "I'll quit my job. Let's stay together for how long we have."

Such beautiful words. Such a beautiful angel. But it was getting easier and easier to forget me—now he couldn't even go pee without me. One minute out of his sight was enough to erase the fact that I existed and who I was.

Dylan spent his days watching me and writing notes of his future plans, being very careful not to mention me so they wouldn't be erased.

Then came April 25. My birthday.

And the day that Dylan started to forget about me as soon as he blinked. It was a hell of a day, and by the end of it, through tears and confusion, he put me to sleep in the bedroom and took the living room couch for himself, afraid he would disturb me every time he forgot why I was in the bed with him.

He took it as a personal matter, like the problem was his inability to remember me enough, not the fact that I wasn't allowed to exist anymore.

That's the only explanation for what he did.

When I woke up the next day, I was handcuffed to him. He was sitting by the bedside, staring at me intently.

I screamed.

"If a blink was enough to make me forget you, then I'll never blink again," he announced, the raw meat above his eyeballs glistening, sickly and pink.

Dylan had removed his eyelids to never forget me again.

I cried. While it was heartwarming that he would go to such lengths for me, the vision of his unblinking mutilated eyes was creepy at best—and it was all my fault.

He didn't last long, of course. The infection from the homemade surgery and the fact that he couldn't properly sleep made him fade fast, feverish, delirious, and in despair. By the end, he couldn't stop repeating my name, like it was one last prayer to save his soul.

He died two days ago. I know that eventually his family and friends will notice he disappeared, but there's nothing they can do, because they won't even know who I am. And even if they did, I don't think it will be an issue.

Even in death, his wide eyeballs are still directed at me—the only thing keeping me from nothingness. He's starting to rot so, before his eyes decay completely, I wanted to try one last time to show the world that I am here, that I ever existed.

I know you'll forget this story as soon as you read it. I know it will be swallowed by the other things in your mind and then disappear.

But if you could just make an effort and really put your mind into it—for my suffering, for my mother, for Dylan.

Remember me.

AVA DISAPPEARED

When I was 7, my best friend was a girl named Ava, who was my neighbor. Ava was a sweet kid; I didn't realize it at the time, but her home life was pure hell. We would always hear her father screaming and breaking stuff. I was too young to understand that "stuff" included Ava and her mom.

My parents did what they could to relieve Ava from the burden a girl this young should never carry, but they were honestly afraid to meddle too much and end up having something bad happening to our family, so it consisted in inviting her to eat afternoon snacks and meals nearly every day, and give her some clothes, since Ava was always poorly dressed.

Being sheltered from the violence happening right next door, my childhood was pretty normal, even happy. My father worked an office job, my mother worked from home, and my sister Carly would keep an eye on me. She was 12 at the time and would let me and Ava play in the woods behind our houses as long as there was daylight.

It was 1998 in a small town and life was simple. We loved to play with my Barbies (poor Ava didn't have any), but we also loved to explore the forest and dig the ground. We would usually find bird bones and pennies buried shallowly.

It was an unusually warm November afternoon, right after Ava's 7th birthday. My family bought her a small cake the day before. Now I can't help but think it was our fault she had a swollen, purplish face that day.

"Ava, you're ok? What happened?" I worried to see her like that.

"I just fell from the *stwairs*," she said. Her mouth was so severely beaten up she couldn't even pronounce some phonemes.

But , being terribly young and inexperienced, I believed her and accepted the answer, soon turning my attention to something else. I'm so sorry, Ava.

We decided to use the warm day to bird watch, which I was very into in the last few weeks, since my parents gave me some binoculars. For that reason, we entered the forest a little deeper than usual. We found a beautiful nest of Junco, full of chicks, and squeaked in satisfaction.

I was focused on the birds, when Ava had a distant, intrigued look on her face.

"Are you listening? ...what a beautiful song," Ava was marveling at something, but I couldn't hear it. So I kind of ignored it.

After a few minutes, she started walking deeper into the woods, presumably trying to find the source of the beautiful song. I still heard nothing but our footsteps crunching the leaves on the ground, and the distant chirping of other birds.

Still, I followed Ava without thinking. We walked for a few minutes, when she stopped by a huge, majestic old tree, prettier than any I've ever seen. The sunlight glowed in a different way there. I couldn't quite understand, but it was like the air was sprinkled with glitter. And it was peaceful, a deep, heavenly peace I never felt before.

Ava was looking up at the tree leaves, wonder-struck. Then she frantically waved her hand like she met someone she knew.

I looked up too and saw a woman. Well, it certainly was a female. But she had a really small frame and her skin was glowing lilac. Her long hair seemed to be made of waterfall, and the fabric of her dress was like the wind, if the wind was slightly golden and vaguely shaped like a beautiful lady. I remember thinking she must be a fairy.

She descended from the tree and reached the ground with the softest landing. Her voice was pure sweetness and echoed through my head.

"I'm sorry I took this long to answer your prayers, Ava."

"The song I've been hearing at night, was that you?" Ava gingerly asked.

"Yes, my child." She then looked at me. "You, please leave. It's not your time."

I was hypnotized, even a bit afraid, but I complied. The way she talked was nothing but gentle and benevolent, but her figure held an impressive sense of authority.

I left and, as I looked over my shoulder, Ava started to glow like her. Her hair started to seem like a waterfall as well, and her worn-out clothes slowly turned to gold and air.

***

When I got home, I went to my room and rehearsed what I would answer when people noticed Ava was gone. I was only 7 and couldn't understand a lot of basic concepts, but I had in me both the knowledge that Ava would never return and that people wouldn't believe what I saw.

That night, her father aggressively knocked on our door and demanded to know where she was. When inquired, I vaguely answered that I played with her by the woods until mid-afternoon, but haven't seen her since.

My father was the one who called the cops to report her disappearance, and soon the woods behind my house were swarmed with men in blue, carrying lanterns and using walkie-talkies.

During the investigation, they suspected her father had murdered Ava and buried her body in the woods. Her mother was found severely beaten up at home, which corroborated the idea and got him arrested. Police also found out he had killed his previous wife, so I was more than pacific with my decision of keeping quiet about what really happened. After all, I wasn't letting an innocent man suffer—her father wasn't just nervous, he was evil and dangerous.

I eventually made new friends and even forgot about Ava for a while—it's amazing how fast kids can move on, especially because it wasn't a negative experience. I just remembered this story now at age 27 because I'm back at my family home, and the smell of the trees immediately triggered those memories.

In the last year, I broke up with an abusive partner, lost my job, and was diagnosed with a brain tumor. Defeated, I decided to move back and have my parents take care of me. I still don't know if it's possible to undergo surgery; maybe I'll die within a year.

At night, I pray things will get better. And lately I can hear a beautiful, ethereal song no human voice or instrument can ever make. I think it's Ava's answer, inviting me to leave behind my suffering and join her.

SPIDERS

"Come on, Josh, there's gotta be something you fear," my girlfriend Juliet and our two best friends pressed, after I said I don't really fear anything; we were drinking at home, and the three were way past the point of tipsy giggles, now delving into philosophical discussions.

"Um... ok, what do you guys say you fear again?"

"I fear the moment of my death. Not the concept of dying, but what my last moments will be like," Anna repeated, dead serious.

"I fear finding out that there's no free will and our actions aren't our own," Juliet added.

"And I fear never finding a meaning to my life," said Mark.

Geez. Why can't they have *normal* fears, like sharks?

"Well, I guess I fear giant spiders," I replied reluctantly.

"Come on, don't give us some platitude. A *complex* fear," Anna complained.

"Ok, I specifically fear waking up to a giant spider in my house, like, a spider the size of a person," I said, honestly. Although I don't worry about it on a daily basis, I knew that it *would* be something I'd be scared of. Who wouldn't?

"What is the spider doing in your house?" Mark asked.

"It was walking on the roof like those goats that sometimes climb and fall and kill people."

"You're such an oddball, Josh," Juliet cooed, and the three of them went back to randomly laughing.

This was a long time ago, and the only reason why I remembered this particular conversation was that earlier this year my worst—maybe only—fear came true.

***

I woke up to eight eyes near my face, an uncomfortably intense gaze fixated on me; for a while, while my mind was still hazy from the near-asleep state, I thought it was Juliet, but she was at her sister's.

I thought that, if ever faced with such an absurdity, I'd jump, piss myself, and try to fight, all at once; but, as this happened, I literally felt, thought or did nothing: all my bodily functions were frozen.

It was a black spider the size of a human body, looming over mine, making a pressure that was light but enough to suffocate me with the weight of its giant abdomen—such vision was too surreal, almost like I had wished my fear into existence.

"You really have no fears, do you, Joshua? You're uncomfortable, but most people would die from the shock. I know you don't actually fear us," the spider said calmly. I tried to reply, but only squeaks came from my mouth—I realized I was speaking its language.

"That's exactly why I'm here. To let you know why you're wrong."

The spider stomped one of its legs on the ground, and soon my bedroom disappeared. Now the two of us were surrounded by a cold darkness dotted with countless little lights; it took me a while to realize we were in outer space.

"Some people believe that Atlas carries the world, others that it's a bunch of elephants. So I brought you here to take a look."

There's no normal, logical way to say this: I turned to look, and I saw an immense black spider, a billion times bigger than the one beside me, carrying the planet Earth on its back.

"Lesson number one: your whole world is literally carried by us."

Before I could even process this absurd sight, the spider stomped another leg and now we were in some sort of jungle, the air overwhelmingly damp and hot, the bountiful leaves barely letting the sun in.

"How many spiders do you see here, Joshua?"

I took a good look around but, to my relief, only three small spiders walked around, minding their own business. I replied with a squeak.

"Look again."

Now spiders of all sizes, shapes, and colors swarmed my sight, coming from behind the rocks, from under the leaves, from inside the trees, from under the animals—and from *inside* them, although they were all alive.

"Lesson number two: we spiders can do as we please in the world, and the only reason why we remain mostly hidden is because it's more fun for us this way."

I didn't even know what to think—it was like my very thoughts were stuttering, unable to come up with words that could express what I felt.

The spider stomped another leg.

We were on the top of a tall, tall building, a bustling night in the big city below us. People and busses and cars moved around, and nothing felt odd or threatening.

"This is how you see the world," the spider stated. "Now see how *I* see it."

My field of vision was immediately assaulted by an impossible number of thin threads, coming both from the sky to the land and from under the earth to the heavens.

I squeaked trying to ask what that meant; whatever it was, I knew it would be something uncanny and terrifying.

"Maybe your reality is just a dream a spider is having, or maybe the world is full of thin, thin threads and webs and you're just the meat dolls."

Although spiders couldn't possibly smirk, I knew that's what it was doing. After letting that sink in for me, the spider stomped a fourth leg and I was back to my bedroom, alone.

"I heard a noise in his room!"

"Josh couldn't possibly have come from the window, we're on the 9th floor," I overheard my roommates arguing; it was getting dark outside.

"Holy shit, man! Where have you been? We looked for you all day, and now you just show up in your own bedroom."

I tried to answer his question, but only a squeak came out of my mouth.

***

It's been months now, and I can't remember how to speak any human language; I write everything I need, and I tried to put into words what I went through, but no one believes me—although they can't explain how I disappeared from my bedroom without taking any keys with me, and how I reappeared hours later.

I wrote over and over about the giant spider, but everyone just looks at me with pity, like I am demented. All this time, Juliet was the only one to believe me and try to stand by my side, but I have repelled her violently and no one understands why. Another reason why they think I'm severely ill.

Let me tell you why.

"You know what?" Juliet said. "I believe every single word you told me. In fact, I believe spiders can do even more, like mimic people. It could have trapped you in the jungle or the outer space forever and taken your place if it wanted to."

"Wow, you've given a lot of thought about that."

Juliet then smiled mischievously, glitching into a giant spider.

THE EUTHANASIA SERVICE

I had this idea in my sleep.

I knew that it was very ethically gray, but I always believe that people should be free to quit if they don't want to be somewhere; this includes Alive.

And I knew one person that was perfect for the project.

Saying that my partner Elle was a genius is a huge understatement; she started working for NASA when she was 21, and after ten years there she was able to create our whole equipment by heart. I came up with the boring business details, and in less than two years we had developed a groundbreaking euthanasia model: a one-way trip to outer space for $20,000.

This is our basic fee for simply sending you to sleep forever among the stars; we also have support services such as helping the client organize their life before going—and believe me, most of them need it.

We make a huge profit from death, but what company doesn't these days? At least we only kill the people that want to.

Nine years ago, we discreetly advertised on forums for the terminally ill and people who lost all hope and joy to live. Our main focus was capturing people who weren't approved for euthanasia in conventional facilities.

To my surprise, our first client was a 26-year-old Brazilian girl who had been craving death since she was 13. She wasn't terminally ill, but she believed that life on this planet per se was an illness, and she wanted to break free from this poor vessel and return to wherever she came from. We'll call her T. L.

"I just miss home and the stars," she said, in pretty decent English. She was educated, successful, married—everything that a person supposedly needed to be happy.

"Every good thing I have feels just like the bare minimum so I can tolerate living to see another day," she explained to our psychiatrist. "Death is the only possible freedom, you know? This body, it decays so fast and it takes your mind with it. It curses the soul. Having a body is simply disgraceful."

"You know, people say that suicide is a permanent solution for a temporary problem," the psychiatrist replied.

"Bullshit," T. L. smiled. "We belong out there. Existing is a permanent problem, I hope that quitting the absolute sewer of existence is more than a temporary solution."

"So why haven't you killed yourself yet?"

"I'm a practical woman, doctor. The last thing I want is to put a bullet in my head and end up as a fucking vegetable. I'm not taking any chances. I only get to do this once and I want it to be grand and foolproof. And I got through every day telling myself that one day I'd find this way."

"Don't you have anything unfinished?" the psychiatrist stamped "approved" on her file.

"I took care of everything long ago," the girl smiled peacefully.

I caught Elle watching T. L.'s tape over and over.

"I know that most people don't love being alive, but I never saw someone as passionate about death as her," Elle said once. "It's a need. She thought about this. Not for a year or two, but her whole life. She was so happy that she was dying for sure."

"It really makes me sleep better at night," I replied.

"I never doubt that what we were doing was right, Paul. You need to believe more in yourself."

I suppose there were quicker, cleaner ways to go, but dying surrounded by the cosmos seemed beautiful and grandiose. Who wouldn't want that?

The girl was some sort of micro-celebrity of the depressed and the damned, and it didn't take us long to have our business flourish.

I was obviously very curious to see what's out there, but I wasn't planning on meeting my end anytime soon. Since no one could come back to tell us what it was like, I tried not to think a lot about it.

After two years of seemingly successful trips, Elle decided to go and test her equipment. She was first and foremost a scientist, after all. Her natural curiosity made her crave a deeper understanding of her creations.

"What if you don't come back?"

"I'll coordinate everything. And if I don't, I'll still be happy that I got to find out," she replied, with a determination I only saw before in T. L.

"Well, no one came back to complain about our product, right?" I joked.

Elle was to be sent outside for precisely 7 minutes; the first one, she'd experience without breathing, then our technicians would release her oxygen supply until the last one. The interval seemed like a romantic detail at the time—a reference to seven minutes in heaven—but one of the technicians explained to me that it was how long a body could possibly spend outside without starting to deteriorate beyond repair.

I'm not a science man, but her trip was a success. Everyone said so. However, my associate and friend returned different.

She made no sense, like she had some sort of PTSD, but a happy one. She was literally starry-eyed.

"So how it all went?" I asked after she returned and all the protocols to re-acclimatize her were followed.

"I learned the language of the stars. Did you know that they're constantly screaming?" she asked, at once seeming catatonic and like someone in a blissful daydream.

"And… how it was to see the planet from above?"

"I liked it at first. It was like my eyes could penetrate the atmosphere and I had all-seeing eyes. Like Heimdall, I watched everyone and everything. I pried on seven billion darkest secrets. I saw all the ugly and all the best in people, Paul."

"What about the Earth itself?"

She gave me an enigmatic smile and slid me a sheet of paper. She had handwritten something on it.

It lies under the dust, but you don't know because at some point it is dust itself, one and the same. It is terrifying and larger-than-life, but also life per se, in the most pure, primal sense. It is everything.

Sometimes it is in the air, and it's always in the trees—they are part of it, after all, and the smartest people on the planet tried to make offerings to placate It. I wonder if wood has memory of being part of something bigger. I wonder if it is resentful of being forcibly taken from home. I wonder if It feels that It lost a few hairs, and then lots.

It is growing old and restless. I hope It is merciful to Its unwanted child, although I know the answer. We're nothing but parasitic, stealing everything from the sleeping giant to feel that our pitiful little lives are anything other than tiny and brief and pointless.

After I finished reading this, I gave her a month off.

"You've done enough for this company, Elle. You were literally everything. You should rest, I've got this."

She was sort of a workaholic, but this time she just nodded.

Months turned into years as her mind never recovered. I loyally paid her share every month, visited every other week. I knew she didn't have family or a lot of friends, and I didn't want her suffering to get worse because she was lonely.

She insisted on going back to work but, when she finally did, it was her body that started to fail her. In the end, she was just skin and bones, bald and tremulous, and I dreaded the moment that she would come and ask me to make the one-way trip that made us rich.

She didn't, though. She went the old-fashioned way, gun to the mouth. She left everything perfectly organized, made sure to hide all the documents from our business—typical Elle.

It saddened me deeply that her last letter was just a note for me because she had no one else.

Dear Paul,

I didn't want to go that way because it all felt too infinite.

***

I mourned Elle in a way that my girlfriend and parents couldn't understand. I was always vague about my line of work, but before she was gone I had never realized how much the secret that only the two of us shared meant to me, how big it was in my life. My loved ones knew that Elle and I had been friends since college, but my apathy was so unexpected that it was received with coldness, almost hostility.

I decided to take the trip she took and see what she saw—to test my own product.

"We now know that she got sick because of that, Paul. That seven minutes was too much," my most trusted technician, Natalie, told me. "In the last seven years the scientific community learned so much."

"Then make it six."

"No deal. The most I can give you is two, with half a minute without breathing."

"This way I won't see what she saw," I argued. "I believed she hallucinated from the lack of oxygen and I want to do the same."

"It will be really expensive."

"I'm fucking swimming in money."

"It will damage your brain irreversibly."

"Who cares? I'm not planning to live that long of a life anyway."

Natalie looked at me with sad eyes for the first time. "What will we do if you die too, Paul? You have no one to give this company to. We'll all lose our job. Hopeless people will lose one last moment of fulfillment."

"I'll leave a will in case something happens and the whole team is going to own the company, okay?"

She was still reluctant, but we started preparing for my space trip.

***

The first thing I saw was darkness slightly dotted with white. Like someone had created a movie set that consisted of a black fabric full of fireflies.

Then the stars radiated yellow, and the yellow had a pink halo. The pink illuminated the black and the black turned into rich shades of purple and blue. Finally, a creamy, miraculous deep-green all around, the stars so bright that I probably saw them more with my mind than with my eyes.

The colors were an understatement. Describing them as what we know is the closest that I can get to understanding and explaining how the tones of the universe danced around me, slowly allowing my inferior brain to be a part of it.

It felt beautiful beyond words and, among the coldness, I felt a warmth prickling all over my body.

And then I started to disintegrate.

Little by little, but at an alarmingly fast rate, my body was undone then recreated with stardust permeating my every cell, with the atoms of supernovas and black holes mixing seamlessly to my DNA. I dissolved and was put back together over and over, painlessly, and every time knowing more. Knowing with every bit of my being. Knowing in a primordial and undeniable way. My brain expanded past the mortal capacity into the realms of the gods.

The first thing I learned was the language of the stars. I heard them screaming to one another—they were scared of the Earth.

And then a small star took notice of me. It was our Sun.

"Hey, little bug! I wouldn't go back in there if I were you. She will wake up anytime now, you're safer here."

The Sun sounded as condescending as someone baby-talking to a bee after saving it from death.

"Oh, thanks," I replied. "Who is she?"

"Not she; She. She is… as you'd say, the alpha and the omega, the first and the last. Don't try to understand more than that, it will crush you."

The Sun sounded as benevolent as a boot with no foot inside can sound to an ant. I nodded.

"She can reach you here, of course. She can reach you everywhere. But She has no reason to. She'll deal with the fleas she's riddled with first, that's for sure."

"However, the bug has so much superior matter in it now that it probably could see She," a star even closer to me remarked, uninterested. I think it was Proxima Centauri.

"I'll try. It feels like my very soul changed," I replied, despite the star not talking directly to me. Immediately, I knew the names of all the stars I could see—or at least the names that I could understand.

"Soul? I didn't know that insects had a soul," one of the 61 Cygni exclaimed.

"I think they all share a collective soul," like a chimera, the goat forever disagreeing with the lion, its twin replied.

As the two sisters confabulated, I felt an irresistible pull from inside my belly button. I then spent what felt like an eternity living other lives.

The best way to explain what happened to me was that I lived the lives of every humanoid that ever existed and that ever will exist. I was born as a caveman countless times—we are so new, so tiny. Simultaneously, I was born as great kings and great leaders. I was Moses, the greatest rebel, using otherworldly magic to save his people. I was Gilgamesh, destined for greatness from the moment he was conceived between an Acadian woman and the most handsome interstellar explorer.

I understood what Elle meant by "it all felt too infinite." Not half a minute of our time had gone by and I was everyone and felt everything almost at once. I was both scientists and inquisitors, both daughters and mothers. I loved and was loved, hated and was hated, murdered and was murdered. I learned so much about superior beings coming to colonize us puny demi-monkeys, how the only aliens that dared walk this cursed earth were the scum of other civilizations and the pirates, the fearless and the seekers of glory.

They either didn't know what lies under us or tried to slay She; no one remained indifferent once they knew that they found She's residence.

I can vividly remember being born and born and born, I can vividly remember dying and being immediately redistributed inside the soul of other people, living forever but also living never, too tainted by my own kin to actually possess any thought of my own, to actually exist meaningfully.

And when I made the full circle, learning so much that I felt the spin of every molecule of my body, I looked to the Earth for the first time.

And I saw She's impossible form.

Giant eyelids at the bottom of the ocean, scales and beards and talons everywhere. Nested around an orange ball of melted iron, resting in a turbulent dream, was a reptilian, gargantuan goddess. I wept both from the beauty of Creation and from fear.

"Paul? The oxygen will quick in now."

***

There's so much else I want to say. So much else that I *know*. I know deep in my cells. I know in a transcendental, ridiculously incomprehensible way. I think I'll just have to show you when I'm gone.

Being pulled back to the Earth felt like being born all over again; the sadness of leaving somewhere safe that feels like home, being plucked from the uterus of eternity into the claws of the wolves. I can't get used to anything anymore, not my bed, not the people around me, not even my mother tongue.

I've been too scared. I don't want to have a body in here when She wakes up. She is… literally everything, the Creator and the Destroyer, the inner and the outer, the capital letter and the period. It will hurt. It will hurt.

I can't sleep. I keep thinking about the sleeping giant, the inconceivable god, the unstoppable force that even the Sun and the stars fear. I smell destruction, I despair at people living their lives carefree, not knowing they're about to be painfully extirpated from existence forever.

So I'll fade somewhere better into a sea of light.

Unlike Elle, I'm verbose.

Dear Natalie and everybody else, everything is taken care of. I'll have dispatched myself to lie in a bed of stars where I belong and where the coldness of existence can't get me. The company is yours.

But I urge you to consider joining me instead.

DEMON IN THE ATTIC

1

Whenever I close my eyes, I see him laughing again. Telling me I'll never be able to make it on my own, that I'll starve in the streets and come back begging him to take me back. That I can't do anything without him, and that's why I'll never really leave him, that I have to be guided and disciplined like a stray dog.

He wasn't always like that. He was sweet before he started making more money than I do. Then the humiliations started; he told me to know my place, to quit my job because if I was going to make a puny salary it was better that I only took care of the house and of him. He didn't hit me for the first three years of our relationship. And before the verbal abuse, there were no red flags that I could see.

I spent over six months working odd jobs in secret so I'd have enough money to leave. It's not that I had a bad relationship with my parents, but I didn't consider relying on them because they raised me to be independent. But in the end, I went to them.

I finally realized that not everyone has this privilege, and others would do anything to have the opportunity I had been choosing to miss. Admitting you need help and accepting that you're worthy of being helped takes some courage and grandeur too.

So when he threw me out in the rain, holding all the last four years of my life in a small suitcase, I knew who to call.

Mom and Dad were always good to me, but emotionally distant; they expressed their love in more subtle ways, I suppose. Still, they hugged me tightly for a long moment, then Mom prepared my favorite comfort food and, after I ate it, Dad grabbed some blankets and put me to sleep on the couch, as he kept watch the whole night, sitting on the armchair beside me with his gun next to him.

None of it really matters now, but that's the story of how a 25-year-old freelance writer ended up affording to buy a small and old but otherwise really nice farmhouse.

I always fancied living alone in the countryside. Somewhere peaceful but not too remote, where I could have my own chickens and work in silence, but still see my next-door neighbor in the distance, and only need to drive five minutes to my local farmer's market.

My parents helped me finance this marvelous place; the floorboards creaked in some places and all doors needed a good oiling, but the house was solid, with an old-time charm it was hard to find these days. And it even came with a free cow.

The house was three hours away from where I used to live with *him*, so I felt safer. I was ready to start again.

***

Mom and Dad spent the whole day helping me move and make small repairs and sneezing, despite the allergy medicine and the protective masks.

"Didn't the ad say the house came with fifty chickens? There's only forty-two!" my mom informed; I couldn't help but laugh. It was very like her to count chickens when there were more pressing things to do.

"They probably meant *roughly* fifty," Dad replied.

"But forty-two is roughly forty, not roughly fifty!"

"Or you just miscounted them, Mom. All chickens have pretty much the same face."

When the night came, Dad got us some takeout for dinner in the nearby city. We ate between boxes and dusty furniture.

"Will you two stay for the night?" I asked as we had our meal. The house had a master bedroom, a smaller bedroom that I planned on using as my office, and a third one that needed a lot of work before someone could use it.

They looked at each other, and I could almost see the engines working inside their brains; staying meant they would have a horrible night of sleep, as both were severely allergic to dust, but maybe I'd feel more protected and at peace. Not staying meant having some decent rest to drive back the next day, and maybe I'd feel independent and strong, but maybe not.

"I think we'll just go to an inn in the city," Mom finally replied. I nodded.

I was ready to spend my first night alone.

But not to find out that I wasn't alone.

***

I don't even know why I went to the attic that night. I was exhausted and all I needed was to take a good shower and go to bed early.

I guess I just wanted to take a good look all around my new place, and feel satisfied that I had somewhere nice to live.

"Oh my Orcus, finally!" a very high-pitched voice scared me as I let myself in; startled, I tried to grab something to defend myself. "Whoa, stop this shit," she added, and my silly weapon (a loose piece of wood) fell from my hand.

I shone my flashlight in her direction and saw a magnificent—if extremely odd—female.

Her crimson hair was styled like a 20s' diva, matching her brilliant vermillion dress, full of elaborate embroideries. Her light-brown skin was gleaming, but covered in black scales on the shoulders; her face was beautiful but you could see a pair of fangs partially covering her pouty lips.

Her eyes were weird and mesmerizing; she had feline pupils—two narrow slits almost lost in the immense pale-pink of her irises—and long, thick eyelashes that made her the prettiest woman I've ever seen, despite the fangs, the stained shoulders and (oh my God) the scaly, dragon-like ragged wings.

It took me a while to realize that her bare foot was like the hoof of a goat, and that her hairstyle almost covered two curled black horns.

The tips of her fingers were black too, and covered in dried blood.

I just watched her for a while, not knowing what to do. Her presence didn't feel menacing, just imposing.

She then smiled and whined like a queen:

"Come on, feed me! I only had one chicken today."

Automatically, almost like I was under a spell, I went to the hen house to get her some food.

When she finished eating, she introduced herself.

"My name doesn't matter. It's too dangerous to say it aloud anyway. But yours is Melinda, right?" she asked. I nodded. "Well, girlfriend, your house was cheap because it's haunted. But luckily for you, I'm the empress here, so the lower ghosts won't disturb you as long as you follow my rules. Be smart and you can live happily raising your calves or whatever. Are you ready to hear them? Don't only nod like a dumbass."

"Yes. Yes! I'm ready," I hurriedly replied.

"Rule number one. You'll feed me two raw chickens every day. I don't care where they come from, but if you don't give me them I'll wreak havoc in your little farm and eat alive all your hens and any other animals you have. And then I'll be unwilling to be nice with you for a while. Which means Flying-Head Stu will visit your dreams."

"Right!"

I quivered, but I could live with that.

"Rule number two. No people sleeping over. As the master of the house, you have some privileges, but not your guests. You can have visitors, but if they're here in the darkest hours of the night, I'm under no obligation to be nice to them. So I **will** draw little dicks on their foreheads in permanent marker, grab their foot and their tongue to jolt them awake, and maybe sit on their chests for a little sleep paralysis fun if I feel like it. And don't even get me started with what Legless Linda will do to them."

I laughed a little. Hearing about the other ghosts made me feel uneasy, but somehow I knew that I could believe her—that they'd leave me alone unless she said otherwise.

So that was fine too; I didn't plan to have my parents and friends stay the night, and if I ever got another boyfriend or girlfriend, we'd just hang out at their place.

So far, she had sounded playful, relaxed even. But then her face became somber, and her seriousness was eerie enough to make my knees tremble. For a fraction of a second, I considered that maybe *that man* was right and I couldn't do anything properly on my own. That I was putting myself into a situation far more horrid than the abuse I went through.

When she spoke again, she sounded like a whole different demon.

"Rule number three. I never make noise, even when I roam around. The others are quiet too, except for the eventual pot falling from the cupboard in the middle of the night. So if you ever hear footsteps, *it's not us*. In that case, the only safe place is your bed. Cover your head and wait until I tell you it's okay to come out," her pupils contracted even more. "I might be a beautiful, ancient and scary demon, but there are far greater dangers in this world than me."

2

My first night in the house was quiet, except for the sound of water dripping in the sink; I got up to see what was going on, and realized I needed to install a new tap in the morning.

My parents came back around 10 AM to check on me one last time, told me they were really proud and went back to their place. Mom remarked that now I only had 41 hens.

"Darling, you absolutely should ask for some of my money back, and fix the damn fence. Love you."

I then saw them off and headed to the nearby grocery store. It was almost time to feed my demon tenant and I didn't want to kill another of my poor chickens.

As I was checking out, the old cashier/shop owner started a conversation.

"Two whole raw chickens, uh? You must be the kid who bought Lou's ranch."

Speechless, I just agreed and nodded. Lou was the deceased father of the sellers, and they had been eager to get rid of his haunted property. Had Lou told this old man about *her*?

"No need to worry or explain yourself, lass. Everyone knows that place is strange. Do as you see fit to protect yourself," he winked. "Also, if the raw chickens are back, I'll give you the same deal I had with Lou. It will be too expensive not to buy them in bulk, right?"

I hadn't considered that yet, but I immediately felt grateful for his thoughtfulness.

"Don't buy them from anyone else and you get a great price from me. You'll pay weekly for what would be the full price of six, and I'll deliver them for you, frozen. Rest easy, Lou never had a problem with doing whatever he was doing with thaw chicken," he smiled.

Mr. C—as he introduced himself—was a very fatherly type, with a snow-white beard and gentle blue eyes always partially covered by a worn-down beret. He seemed to be truly worried about a young woman living alone; having him check on me every seven days didn't exactly put me at ease, but it was nice to know that someone cared. He even brought me some cookies made by his wife every other week.

My only recurrent visitor made sure to never enter the house; every Sunday morning, Mr. C honked his delivery truck's horn three times and waited until I opened the automatic gate, then parked keeping a safe distance from the house, going only exactly far enough to pet my goat Lilibeth.

Then, when I went upstairs to feed her the dominical lunch, my fellow demon mocked Mr. C for his fear, then praised him a little for his wisdom.

It's weird to say that, but I didn't think too much about Pandora (since her real name was forbidden, that's how I nicknamed her). She was a graceful housemate so, except for her mealtimes, when she was always incredibly snarky, I was completely unbothered by her presence. I was even happy that she was there because it somehow felt safer, but it was kind of in the back of my mind.

Humans are infinitely adaptable. We can get used to virtually anything and never give a second thought about it again. For that reason, I can say that things went smoothly pretty much all the time.

It was only after two months that I had the first incident involving rule three.

I was washing the dishes from breakfast in the kitchen, feeling carefree and even a little proud of myself. Earlier that day, I had managed to milk my cow, Mary Bell, for the very first time, and drinking it fresh was great. Mary Bell had a lovely baby a few days ago, delivered by the vet from downtown.

I was humming a song when I felt my left ear suddenly go cold; before I could even think about it, a voice whispered on it.

"Melinda, sorry to bother you, but the Master tells you to go hide in your bed," this ghost sounded exaggeratedly goofy, like some Jim Carrey character. I started looking for a dishcloth to dry my hands.

"No time for that, Madam!" a second voice announced next to my other ear, and I felt my body lightly pressured towards my room, like two pairs of hands were trying to move something really heavy (me) and just barely succeeding.

I knew I was in trouble when I heard very slow but heavy footsteps coming from the living room, like a fucking giant had entered my tiny house.

"Go!" voice number one, the goofy one, urged me. As soon as I turned to go to my room, I caught a glimpse of something horrific reflected in the cupboard's glass—a huge, bluish, deformed face with evil lupine eyes.

It opened its mouth like it was ready to devour my body, my mind, my soul, and everything else around. Like there was nothing but endless void and suffering inside this creature, the two at once.

"Close your eyes or it will be too late," voice number two, who sounded like an old lady, warned me.

"We'll guide you, hurry!" Goofy Voice instructed me, and I complied.

Running to a specific destination with your eyes closed is harder than you think, especially when you're really scared and naturally clumsy. I stumbled on some furniture and heard a few things falling and crashing, but I didn't care.

I wanted to follow rule number three at any cost; not only because I trusted Pandora and hated breaking other people's rules, but mostly because what little I saw from that beast was enough to know that I'd rather be dead if I didn't follow them.

I lied in my bed, covered my head, and pretended not to exist, breathing as little as possible.

"I hope our aid was satisfactory," the old lady said politely. "The Master can't come help you at these times because she has to prepare for the battle, so she sent us."

I nodded, not daring to talk. You could hear horrible roars and the unmistakable sound of fighting, despite the decent muffling my blanket provided; I twitched every time I heard the heavy, destructive movements.

"What was that thing??" Goofy Voice asked, astonished. "And don't worry, Madam, the enemy can't hear us. We're pretty much talking telepathically."

"Oh, you weren't here yet when he last came," Old Lady replied. "The Master calls him The Captain. He comes twice a year hungry for souls. He almost got the former landlord, Lou, when he got too old to run to bed. The poor man barely left his room this time of the year."

I was too scared to even open my eyes, so I lost track of the time, but I'm sure they spent at least 20 minutes fighting. I've never been so grateful for not having close neighbors; imagine having to explain that ruckus to other people?

After a long time, Pandora appeared on the threshold, holding a scimitar and all covered in a deep-blue and sticky substance.

"It's safe to leave, housemate!" she announced, in high spirits. "You should have seen me there! Never mind, it would get you killed *horribly*. Anyway, look how his stupid blood stinks."

She put one of her armpits next to my face and laughed; it smelled of sulfur, of course, but the blue patches in her skin had an even worse smell, like a spoiled egg had a baby with a sewer. "It will take forever to clean it up with my powers, so I'll have to do it the old-fashioned way. Get me your best towels and I'll help myself to your tub."

I obeyed, leaving the room to attend to her request. I was pleasantly surprised to see that my house was intact; all their fighting took place immaterially, so nothing was damaged.

I remember thinking that I'd get Pandora an extra meaty chicken for lunch, and that she was actually a good person.

But I was being horribly naïve.

3

Things started to go south when my cousin Alyssa decided to make me a surprise visit.

Pandora knew that I enjoyed a quiet lifestyle, that my only visitor was Mr. C—who knew better than to enter the house—and that my stern parents would rather slit their throats than show up unannounced at someone's house.

Alyssa and I weren't particularly close because, despite being my cousin, she was several years older than me, so I saw her more as an aunt. She was that member of your family that always ends up taking care of the elders, or who cooks for you when you have a horrible flu; the type of person that would always go the extra mile for an act of kindness.

Unfortunately, this extra mile almost cost Alyssa an eye.

I mentioned before that my property has a gate, but it's more of a glorified fence. Despite being electronic, it's just a short thing that keeps the hens from escaping to the road, and prevents the cars from getting too close and running over my animals.

In other words, it's pretty easy for an average adult to just jump over it.

I was still in bed when she crossed the small gate, one of the rare occasions that I wasn't up yet by 11 AM because I had a bad migraine that had been lasting a few days.

"Dammit!" the already familiar voice of Old Lady ringed in my ears. "Stay there and cover your head, Madam, something's coming."

I complied. I didn't pay a lot of attention to the footsteps, as they weren't particularly heavy or scary.

The front door opened with a thud as I heard two feminine voices yelling.

"You fucking bitch! No one allowed you in!" *Metallic noises...* "Shit what is th-ARGHHHH"

I recognized my cousin's voice as the second woman. Afraid to break Pandora's rules, I didn't leave the bedroom, but urged my bodyguard ghosts to immediately explain the situation and ask Pandora to stop.

"Melinda, are you there? It's me, Alyssa. Whatever the fuck happened," she cried a little, two rooms away. "I just brought you some food because your mother said you have a migraine."

I can't recall a time that I felt worse for someone else's kindness.

I ran towards the entrance and saw my really nice cousin all disheveled, sitting on the floor with a line of blood running from her hairline to the side of her face, protectively holding a casserole all draped in a pretty dishcloth like it was her newborn son.

One of her eyes was black and swollen, and my heaviest frying pan — a cast iron skillet made entirely of iron — sat sadly beside her, slightly deformed; on the farthest side of the room, Pandora stood menacingly, still holding her usual weird sword and growling like a rabid dog.

"Bitch can't see me or hear me if I don't want her to," Pandora informed me, in a very scary tone. "Tell her to call beforehand like a normal person, or at the very least stand by the gate. Unless she'd love to lose her stupid head the next time."

She then disappeared. A part of me wanted to scream in frustration at Pandora, but well... horrible supernatural things roamed around the house. Given the situation, I won't say that she was wrong to attack anyone who entered our property uninvited, but she could at least show regret for hurting someone innocent and unsuspecting.

Besides, it would be really hard to explain to Alyssa why I was yelling at the walls on top of everything I had to deal with. I helped my cousin get up and convinced her that she absolutely needed urgent medical attention. I apologized profusely and started putting my shoes on to drive her to the nearest hospital, but she just shook her head sadly.

"My mom is in the car. I jumped your fence so you could open the gate for us to let her in because the doorbell didn't work, but now I guess she'll drive me." She placed the casserole in my hands, defeated.

"I'm so, so sorry, Alyssa. Thank you for being so kind, I hope we can catch up some other day," I awkwardly circled around her, trying to come up with some excuse as to why a 6-pound skillet went flying straight to her cranium the moment she entered my house.

"It's… okay, honey," she managed, but we both knew none of this was okay. "I think some houses are just like that. They reject people. I'm glad you seem to be unhurt here."

"Thank you, Alyssa, I… what can I do for you?"

"You take care of yourself. I saw a suspicious truck taking some leaps near your farm," she replied. As soon as her words entered my brain and I realized all the horrible things that they could mean, I started to hyperventilate.

Great, now I (at the very best) gave Alyssa a concussion *and* made her worry about me over something she said.

"Oh, it's not *him*," she quickly explained. "I saw the driver, it's a way younger guy. Like, younger than you. It's probably nothing but please just… lock your doors and leave alone whatever force that's controlling your house."

I nodded, a feeling a little calmer. Poor Alyssa knew how to make people feel better.

She squeezed my hand and started to leave. "And maybe get a priest to sprinkle some holy water around here."

The world seemed to spin ten times faster as Pandora screamed at the top of her lungs, *"Come back here again and I'll kill you, stupid bitch!"*

And, judging by how Alyssa twitched in fear and ran across my yard without looking back, I knew that this time my housemate meant to be heard.

***

We were both sour when I went upstairs to feed Pandora her lunch an hour later; her because someone violated her rules, me because she was being unnecessarily mean and putting me in a hard situation.

"Good afternoon, asshole!" she gave me a callous greeting. "Just leave my next chickens on the kitchen table and I'll grab them myself. We won't be on talking terms for a while."

My eyes filled up with tears, but I kept my dignity and didn't say anything. If someone enters your yard and you have a violent dog, it's your fault that the person got hurt, right? They had no business trespassing, but you can't blame the animal because it's just how its nature is.

The stupid one was me for thinking of a demon as a friend, when she was more of an intelligent beast.

***

It's funny how the human mind works; during daytime I kept busy and even felt more joyful than not, but as soon I lied in bed, I started having a bad panic attack. It happened for a few nights after my cousin's incident—I was at the same time worried about my family's reaction, frustrated at myself for treating a demon like I'd treat any girl around my age that lived with me, and scared about possibly being stalked.

"It's okay, Madam, soon she'll act like nothing happened and be nice to you again," Old Lady tried to comfort me; it was the first time one of the ghosts talked to me without being ordered to by Pandora.

"Shh, you know you can't talk out of turn. The Master can hear all our thoughts!" Goofy Voice whispered, concerned.

"It's fine, stupidhead. She's not home."

Although the friendly ghosts did their best to help me, my nights were restless, filled with cold sweat and waking up screaming.

Five nights after our fight, I was in the middle of a nightmare, sweating and whimpering. Like in most of my horrible dreams, I was being stalked and tortured by my ex, then his face turned to a younger man I didn't know, but they never stopped hurting me.

Suddenly I felt half-awake, like a light state of sleep paralysis.

"There, there, Housemate. Have better dreams now, will you?" Pandora spoke softly, as she patted my head like an older sister — lubberly but with nice intentions — and I felt her weight getting up from my mattress.

Her gesture was incredibly sweet; still, I couldn't help but notice that her hand smelled faintly of blood and rotting flesh.

4

I almost couldn't believe I'd have the guts to confront her. But I did it the next day. I needed to know if she was attacking more innocent people—people that didn't even break her rule.

"Where were you last night?" I asked as I entered the attic.

"Being a little nice to my roomie," she replied, with a bright smile, exaggeratedly feigning innocence. "I didn't do anything weird to you, though. I wouldn't unless you asked me to."

Was she mocking me / offering to be my friend with benefits to dodge my question? That sly devil…

"I mean earlier. I heard you weren't home," I insisted.

"That's silly. If I could leave this crappy shed what the hell would I be doing here? And even if I could, it's none of your fucking business, nerd."

"Your hand smelled of blood," I remarked. I had learned to discern all her moods: 1. Being really mean; 2. Just playing around and 3. Acting evasively out of uneasiness. It felt like the last option.

"It always does," she winked.

"And of corpse," I added.

She then poked her forehead with her index finger so violently that I swear she created a bullet hole in it for a second. A silvery and ethereal substance in the shape of a tiny circle floated near her fingertip, and with a soft waving movement she threw it inside my temple.

It felt cold and fluffy.

"Take this and you'll see some memories of mine in your sleep. I hope you're happy for being a fucking brat."

***

I looked forward to dreaming of her past, so I even went to bed earlier in my best pajamas. I didn't know what to expect, but I wanted to know more about her.

The dream was pretty clear and in first person. It started with me seeing myself in a mirror, large and with an elegant frame that was clearly very expensive. I saw Pandora's face, even prettier than now. She looked somewhat younger, and *human*—no horns or black patches or wings.

And her eyes sparked with joy, something I never saw before.

I admired my reflection, approving my outfit that consisted of tasteful fishnets, gorgeous hand-embroidered lingerie and a silky corset. I then took a little time examining my exaggerated but beautiful makeup, my perfectly done hair and fantastic high heels. I felt confident, with legs for days and a gracious catwalk.

An effeminate man in a top hat hurried me to the stage.

So Pandora was once human, and a showbiz diva.

She was an incredibly talented performer, not only singing and dancing impeccably but also brimming with alluring charisma. No one in the audience could take their eyes off of her; it was like the other dancers were just part of the furniture. They did everything right, but they could never shine as brightly as her.

It's hard trying to explain how her body moved, everything felt so natural like it was born for nothing else but this moment. Try to picture a mix of Nicole Kidman in *Moulin Rouge!*, Christina Aguilera in *Burlesque* and Liza Minnelli in *Cabaret*, all at once.

I saw flashes of myself as Pandora on the stage many times. But when the curtains went down, she was always a nervous wreck, chain smoking and isolating herself from the other girls.

After I witnessed so many of her glorious moments, feeling thrilled and proud, we suffered together when her worst fears became true.

Her grandfather and brother invaded the stage and took her from it by force, the only place where she belonged and ever felt happy. And her beautiful eyes were never the same again.

***

Being a cabaret dancer was considered utterly scandalous back then, especially by her conservative family; the old red-neck had raised his two orphan grandkids, the boy to his likeness, and the girl to be everything they hated. She wasn't born for that prospectless life, so she boldly dreamed of conquering the city lights.

The two men kicked and punched Pandora all the way back to the farm, calling her a disgraceful whore, and every name under the sun except for the thing that she was—a star. When the three arrived, they threw her in the hen house, where she had to survive on raw eggs, corn, and other scraps they fed the chickens.

She had to spend weeks in some sort of compartment under the hennery installations, a compartment where their waste and loose feathers went to; it was barely 20 inches tall.

All the while, they had long discussions about what to do with her, like she was just an inconvenient piece of trash dirtying their path. I was so mad. They went out of their way to ruin her dreams and it was literally over nothing but their stupid and ridiculous pride.

First, they considered marrying Pandora by force to have her be someone else's problem; then, establishing that she was probably impure by now, they decided she needed penance. So they kept her tied to a pole for ten days and ten nights, naked and filthy, being fed just some soybeans once a day.

She talked to the chickens to avoid going crazy. And she still dreamed of going back to her stage, even if it was only possible through violence. Her skin bled from harshly rubbing against the rope as she struggled to keep her muscles working. To make sure that someday she could still walk, to make sure that someday she could still dance.

Nothing drove her but anger. That's how, malnourished and nearly dead as she was, as soon as she was released, Pandora went on a rampage and strangled her grandfather; his soft age-worn skin easily gave in to her hatred like wet paper.

He barely had time to scream hoarsely and horribly before his eyes bulged out and his body became still. Afraid to be incriminated, her brother buried the old man's corpse in the woods near the property.

Maybe if he wasn't an addict, he'd let her go. He'd pretend that she didn't exist. She'd then go back to the cabaret, take some pills with whiskey every night to put herself to sleep and momentarily forget all that she had gone through so far. She'd tremble all over when she wasn't dancing, but still do her best to keep her demons under control.

But the worthless redneck couldn't keep a job so he'd at least have money to drink himself to death.

"Since you went and became a slut, you might as well make some money for me," he said, as he physically, literally put her on a leash, afraid that she would murder him, too.

And oh, she would.

***

I cried in my bed as I witnessed all the terrible violations her body and mind went through. She spent two long years like that, having to take clients for her brother. The bastard just wouldn't die, and by then all the dreams had fallen from her head, letting her feeling empty and dry.

The only thing that kept Pandora alive was the idea of vengeance, and seeing that she outlived her parasite of a brother; she didn't have any plans for what to do with her life after that, as she was now too ugly both on the inside and on the outside to come back to the cabaret. She just wanted to punish her persecutor.

Then one day, after one particularly unspeakable abuse, she broke. She grabbed a shard of glass and was ready to bleed herself to death. That's when *the creature* showed up in front of her, seeming to paralyze time; no one else moved or spoke but the newcomer and her.

The thing looked both like an elephant and like a fat pig, and its body was bulbous and scaly at the same time. It had long horns, twirled many times, and a giant tail made of fire.

"I come on the behalf of Orcus, the Prince of Undeath, and we have an offer for you," he announced.

"I'd do anything. I just want my freedom back," she replied, and the thing gave her a joyless smile with its mammoth-like mouth and fangs.

"You get your revenge. Kill whoever you want, bathe in their blood, and no one will ever know what happened. You'll be allowed to carry eternal vengeance, reanimating your brother's and grandfather's bodies as many times as you see fit to torture and kill them again," the thing mechanically read it from a long scroll. "Then you'll disappear without a trace. No one will remember that you even existed, for all purposes. You'll spend eternity neither dead nor alive, as a property of Orcus. You'll become a demon chained to this place, having to survive on raw chicken and whatever humans or other things—dead or alive—you might desire to consume."

Pandora signed the scroll without a second thought.

By then, she knew that it was the only option she had. She didn't hope to return to the stage, because two years is a long time in showbiz. Because she was tainted. Because there was nothing for her except for washing the sorrow from her heart with the blood of everyone who did her wrong.

She'd only learn decades later that Orcus rejoices on offering horrible deals to desperate people like her, so they can give him their soul and improve their still miserable existence through violence.

She then carried out a carnage that not even Stephen King could put into words. She hunted, tortured and killed every last abuser, every last person who could have helped her but didn't, and people she's never seen before.

Still, I don't blame her, and I'll never blame her; fictional women who are abuse survivors are pictured as badasses that grew and became strong because of their suffering, but Pandora is real; she's not Sansa Stark. She has every right to feel nothing but hatred after her spirit was broken for pointless reasons. She has every right to become the only thing that she could—a pulsating mass of fury and heartache. A monster. A demon.

A being almost as evil as the men who did this to her.

***

The day was almost breaking outside when I woke up, startled and with my sheets and pillowcase dripping wet with tears. I heard her laughter coming from outside my window. And then I heard a horrifying scream that I now knew very well.

The exact same scream that her grandfather let out as she murdered him in my dream.

5

As time went by, we had a tacit understanding about not mentioning the memories she showed me and their implications. I did my best to be nicer to her without making it obvious that I felt sorry for her; one of these days, I asked Pandora if she wanted to watch a movie with me.

She seemed pleasantly surprised. "Don't go thinking of me as a human woman, okay? But I guess that would be cool."

We watched it together in the living room, Pandora saying "ahhhs" and "ooohs" for everything. Just then I realized that no one ever treated her like someone that might have interests or want to see the world; now that I knew that she did, I both wanted and had the duty to give her some exciting things to do.

After I dreamed of her tragic story, I saw some flashes of her with previous owners of the farm. Lou was the only one who lived peacefully with her, but he never approached her the way I did.

Maybe I am the fool, but I don't like the idea of just tolerating each other.

After that day, Pandora started to spend her days binging every single movie, sitcom, and anime that I could find for her; and she thought that everything was great, no matter how cliché or low-effort the story was.

Since she didn't need to sleep, eat anything but the two daily raw chicken meals, or do chores other than to protect the house from invaders, Pandora went through the streaming services' catalogs in a heartbeat, and I soon saw myself going back to old-fashioned, illegal Torrent.

Her daily routine consisted mostly of watching a bunch of things then, after dinnertime, having me watch her favorite thing with her so she could make comments about it with me; I thought this was really sweet.

Being a binge-watcher myself, we often spent hours in that activity. And I think that's when she started to really warm up to me, in her own demonic way.

"Pandora?"

"Yeah?"

"I love you and you're my best friend."

She laughed. Her face said you don't have to be extra-nice to me just because you know I have a tragic past.

"Okay, nerd. But that's because I'm your *only* friend. You're lonely and lame."

I laughed too; if she was mocking me with such gusto, it meant that she was feeling at ease.

"Can I ask you something?"

She nodded.

"What would happen if I hypothetically one day got married and had kids?"

"You'd be lamer."

"I mean about the house."

"First of all, you only go outside in those ugly jeans, so you getting a man is not a real threat," she smiled. "But I think you'd better sell the house. I'm unruly, you know? I can't promise to not harm more than one person at a time, it's not a demon's nature."

"Would you be fine without me?" I asked, truly concerned. She laughed again.

"Bitch, I've been here since your great-grandmother was a cutie and I'll be here forever. But thanks to you I'll give the next owner a fourth rule: get me a Netflix subscription or I'll kill you."

***

We didn't talk about specific details of Pandora's past, as I didn't want to be hurtful or rude. It must have been really hard for her to even share all those memories with me. I didn't ask a second time about what she did when she left the house (but not the property per se, as she couldn't).

According to what that strange demon told her, I assumed that the putrid smell meant that she had been reanimating her grandfather and brother to beat the shit out of them again, but I don't really know how or where she kept the bodies. I can only assume they are buried somewhere around the farm, because her nails are always full of dirt when she comes back.

Every once in a while, I considered telling her about my ex but telling a woman that went through all the seven hells that I lived my life in fear because the man I trusted humiliated and slapped me over the course of a few months simply didn't feel right.

All abuse is hurtful and terrible and wrong, but I thought it would be like telling someone who lost their two legs that my bruised knee was hurting. Besides, my ex hadn't tried to contact me all this time, and Pandora would attack any intruder anyway, so I thought it was best to leave it at that.

In other news, I bought her a pair of expensive, flamboyant shoes, and was waiting for an opportunity to gift them to her. I also started renovating the third bedroom using any spare money and time I had available. I wanted to decorate it in a way that looked like a stage and a fancy dressing room, so she'd feel at home there.

And, to try to avoid getting more people attacked by Pandora, I had a personalized warning sign made in the nearby city.

FOR YOUR OWN SAFETY, DO NOT TRESPASS
The house itself might hu*rt you. Ring the doorbell.*
If it doesn't work, call me: XXXXXXXXXX

Regarding my poor cousin, I called my mother to ask about her state daily. Luckily, Alyssa's concussion didn't leave any permanent damage; her eye was swollen to the point of not opening for a few days, then her vision was blurry for a few more, but other than that she was fine. Even the awful bump in her head was completely gone after two weeks or so.

I imagine that Pandora didn't hit Alyssa with all her might because she didn't seem particularly menacing, or because the trespasser was a woman.

I felt horribly guilty nonetheless — especially because the casserole was delicious —, so I spent roughly 1/3 of my monthly income sending her nice stuff like a fruit gift basket, then a chocolate gift basket, some sunflowers (they were her favorite), wines and cheeses from my local farmer's market, and even a balloon and a plush bear holding a heart that read *get well soon!*.

Since she was always the one doing kind stuff for others, I hoped that being a little pampered once could make it up for the awful incident at least a little. However, I'll admit that confrontation always made me panic, so I avoided directly talking to her (and to my judgmental aunt) like the plague.

Unfortunately for me, one day Alyssa's mother was at my mom's house and they called me. I was taken by surprise and couldn't avoid talking to her; I hate sisterly bonds and schemes.

She lectured me for half an hour about how dangerous it was for a girl to live alone in the woods (*"It's not in the woods, Shelly, it's a farm and you know it's pretty close to the town,"* my mother corrected her in the background), especially in a damn haunted house, and that if I was in such a financial pinch she'd help me sell this awful thing and find a decent apartment to live.

Aunt Shelly made nonsensical suggestions, like having me stay at her place ("It's less than two hours away! I could really use a bridge partner when Alyssa leaves, and my guinea pig *will love the extra company"),* making all the family pitch in to help me buy a property that's not haunted, pawning her grandmother's heirloom, and even that I immediately find a husband so I can move in with him.

("Come on, Shelly, you know she's been *through a lot!"* "... or *a wife!"*)

Wow, Aunt Shelly. Thanks for being a progressive crazy person.

I said I appreciated the concern (honestly, I didn't), but I was really happy there. She then said that maybe the house put a spell on me to make me *think* that I'm happy and insisted that I leave it immediately; she'd even help me pay the rent.

My aunt isn't a bad person, and I know that this came from a place of worry, but she can be a handful. Talking to her — or rather, listening to her long monologue with my mother's director's cut — gave me an awful headache; both my writing job and the chores of the farm were relatively taken care of, so I indulged myself in a marvelous aspirin-induced late-afternoon nap.

I woke up to a sound that could only be described as a tank invading my yard.

"Holy shit, it's the Colonel's Army!" Goofy Voice announced, sounding really concerned. "Sorry for the language, Madam. Please stay very still and quiet."

"We'll have to go this time, Miss Melinda. It's all hands on deck today," Old Lady announced, gently, then yelled like a general. "Flying-Head Stu, Legless Linda, Burnface, you're allowed to act today."

6

It's hard to describe the noises that followed.

What you could hear the most were the chains and the moans of agony; it was like all the souls of the damned from the whole universe decided to hold a conference in my yard.

Then Pandora kept yelling things like, *"How many times do I have to tell you that son of a whore Colonel isn't here? Just go to the fucking light you morons!"* as she dashed with her strange-looking long sword, clank-clanking it against the chains.

And there was Legless Linda's laugh, among some other strange noises that I couldn't identify. She sounded like (and I think she was) a particularly vicious old witch.

It took Pandora over an hour to come fetch me, something that had never happened before.

"Ugh, I'm beat. Let's watch that super silly musical again," she announced by my doorframe.

"What happened?" I asked, concerned. It wasn't like me to ask about her business, but it was mostly because she could deal alright with the other invaders.

We sat on the couch and I put *Grease* for us.

"Menaces that are pitiful are the worst. Did you know that this used to be a farm with over 1,000 slaves?"

"I figured this land probably had slaves, but I couldn't imagine how many."

"Of course this used to be a way bigger farm, extending to the neighboring properties too; but the slave-owner's mansion used to sit right here where we are, including most of your yard and the hennery too."

I nodded.

"When slavery became illegal, that horrible Colonel invited all the slaves he had at the time—I was able to count at least 80—for a banquet at the mansion. *Supposedly*. What actually happened was the racist scum locking them inside and burning the mansion to the ground, because he thought that, if not to serve him, they didn't deserve to live."

It took me at least 20 minutes to let that sink in, and I'm not ashamed to say that I broke down crying. My brain couldn't even process such cruelty, especially because — since the government didn't offer any aid for recently released slaves who had literally nothing — most pro-slavery farmers, when forced to release their slaves, ended up just hiring them for pennies, and they lived pretty much the same life, but now legally as free people.

But this Colonel didn't even think that they deserved that infinitesimal change for the best. He was evil and rotten.

"For a long time, even before me, they have been returning; no one knows when they'll show up. It could take months, years, even decades before the next raid. But they always come back so full of sorrow and angst. They are so blind that they firmly believe that the Colonel is still here, and they want to destroy him."

"That's understandable," I replied.

"Yeah... I know all that because, every time their chains touch me or my underlings, we see and feel it all. All they went through. That's why the battle is always so slow. This and because I avoid destroying them completely, so they have one teeny chance of just moving on and going to the frigging light."

"That's awful!" I whimpered. "So the Colonel's ghost is not here anymore?"

"Nope. Went to hell or whatever else a long time ago. Isn't it unfair how he gets to move on with his afterlife while all these people have to suffer as shadows? They look so awful... all burned down, pieces of their bodies falling as they move. And it's not only the 80 or so that were burned that come here. All the slaves he ever owned want to destroy him, and we have to fight more as the first ones fall and more enter the property."

"It sounded like a tank entering the yard," I remarked, still fighting back the urge to cry over all this senseless cruelty.

"Oh, that's because some of their forms are so mangled and wry that they fused with their chains and with each other, working as a vehicle for the ones that are (more or less) in one piece above them," she explained.

We watched the movie in silence for a while; Pandora seemed more relaxed because she started letting out small laughs and muttering "her hair is ridiculous" every time the camera closed in on Sandy. On my end, I was still trying to process these incredibly dark pieces of information.

"Uh... Pandora? Is it okay if I give you a little something I bought?"

"Is it an extra chicken? I'm good. I just eat them because of the contract, I actually hate it."

I shook my head and grabbed the brilliant pink box that I had been keeping hidden for a few weeks. I then got on my knees to help Pandora put her brand new shoes on.

"Shit, what are you doing? I can't get married!" she seemed truly concerned that I was going to propose.

I laughed and showed her a pair of very artistic, flamboyant high heels. Something that Lady Gaga would wear, but in a more affordable price range — I'm still only a writer with a mortgage to pay, after all.

It was weird to choose the ideal size because she didn't have toes, but then I figured that with hoofs it was way easier to wear extravagant heels, since those always hurt your toes the most.

She was so happy. She even started criticizing every hairstyle in the movie with more scorn and gusto than ever, and she never took them off.

"Melinda?"

"Yeah?"

"Uh, I... suck," she seemed like she wanted to say I'm sorry, but couldn't bring herself to do it.

She seemed to be gathering some courage to go ahead.

"I shouldn't have attacked your relative. It's just that her mentioning the p-man and the h-thing..." I inferred that she meant *priest* and *holy water* "Those really hurt me, you know? And the others too. It's physical torture, and it won't banish us no matter how much they try, because the house — no, these very grounds... well, it's time Lakota tells you about all the complicated shit that's way above my pay grade."

"Lakota...?"

I screamed as a very tall Native-American older female in typical clothes and braids suddenly materialized in the living room; unlike the other ghosts, who had names like Legless Linda or Burnface that suggested a lethal injury, neither her name nor her body carried anything suggestive of her *causa mortis*.

Lakota was beautiful in a sense, like an old and intelligent aunt you look up to; everything in her suggested a strength that wasn't unlike a force of nature, and she looked calm as the eye of a hurricane. She carried herself in the manner of a wise and compassionate leader.

"Hello, kid. I am what you'd call a shaman, and I've been tied to this place as an eternal observer since before your people first walked these lands." Her mouth didn't move, but I heard her pleasant and energetic voice inside my mind. "You see, the leader of my tribe, contradicting the belief of nearly all the other Sioux, didn't think there was an afterlife. To him, the only way to put our souls to rest was to tie them to a piece of land that was specifically made for the dead. A cemetery for your spirit, one could say."

I nodded. It sounded... like something that would go terribly wrong.

"Over the millennia, that ended up creating some sort of magnetic field that attracts lost souls, especially the ones who died wishing for vengeance; a drain for those that are neither alive nor have crossed whatever there is to cross; and, most of all, a raft that beings on journeys in the outer planes end up using as a patch, or as a door to wreak havoc in the world of the living."

"To sum it up," Pandora intervened. "Your place is cursed as fuck."

7

I asked Lakota a bunch of questions. She was the most knowledgeable being I've ever met when it came to history and old witchcraft, but she didn't know much about anything else—after all, the poor lady lived many centuries ago.

She explained to me that there were two types of resident ghost in the house, and then the third, Pandora, a unique type.

The first group were the ones like her; they were neutral observers tied to the land itself, so they could move around a little (pretty much only to the nearby properties). They couldn't fight, but their very presence provided as much balance and protection as possible to the area.

And that's why it didn't have an evil atmosphere, and why supernatural intruders appeared once a week or so, instead of swarming my place every single minute.

This group was a vast minority; except for Lakota, there were only three others, and they were shamans, too. I asked if I could meet them too, but she explained that they very rarely interacted with anyone but themselves, not even the other ghosts; I could try, but she was the spokesperson of the group.

The second group was there because of the "drain"—they died in resentment and hatred and became wandering lost souls; the house, which is the epicenter of the distortion caused by Lakota's tribe leader, provided the only vibrational frequency that was comfortable to them.

Those ghosts—like Goofy Voice and Old Lady—were technically able to leave the house, but it's in their best interest not to; if they cross the limits of the property, they either have to be ready to go to the actual afterlife, or their spirits will be dissipated into energy and assimilated by the land.

Unlike the shamans, most of these ghosts don't have a lot of mental clarity, and they don't recall much of when they were alive; they mostly remember the circumstances of their deaths—most of them tragic and violent, as you might have inferred—and the reason why they seek revenge.

I asked if they were able to move on eventually.

"Over time, some ghosts have graduated from Sioux Manor, so to speak," Lakota said. Pandora interrupted her to explain that this is how most of them call the house. "But most refuse to leave until they can have their vengeance, and most times it's not even physically possible anymore. They're all simply too lost and confused to realize they have a choice."

"Have you done something to help them?" I asked. Lakota sighed.

"The other shamans and I are guardians to the land, not to its people; so we can only go so far as talk to them, hoping to pass down some wisdom that leads them to enlightenment little by little."

I nodded.

"Now, regarding our Pandora here, it's a special case, even among all the peculiar stuff I've seen in my long life here. She made a deal with one of the highest servants of Orcus while still alive, and the unique magnetic field of the house makes this contract pretty much indestructible. She willingly accepted the terms—driven by despair, of course, but a demon doesn't care about that."

"Trying to leave the limits of the farm, or sometimes even thinking about it, makes my skin burn," Pandora explained, like it was no big deal. "It's unbearable. I wish I could just be dissipated, you guys. Non-existence would be bliss to me."

I felt sad about the idea of her not existing, but of course it would be so much more merciful to her than living this miserable half-life feeding on raw chicken and attacking monsters.

"I see that you've been secretly researching it, and of course I don't know everything there is to know, even regarding witchcraft, but I know this much: there are only two ways to free Pandora, and she already knows them. But one is worse than her current situation, and the other is nearly infeasible," Lakota explained.

I blushed. I didn't want Pandora to know that I've been buying obscure e-books on the internet to try finding a ritual to free her from Orcus (and failing).

"Can I hear them anyway?"

Lakota then nodded and disclosed them; here's what I learned from her long explanation: Pandora either had to ask Orcus to break this deal and have a different one, but he'd give her something even worse, or have someone take her place under very specific conditions.

***

A few nights after the Colonel Army's raid, something very unpleasant started to happen: stupid teenagers learned of my haunted property, and daring their friends to trespass became a common trend.

Of course, one thing was harming invaders that came to hurt me or take my soul. But it would be both too cruel and too troublesome if my personal demon slashed some dumb 16-year-old that meant no harm.

It was really fortunate that, while in town that day, I heard some kids talking about going to my property at night; that way, I could prepare Pandora to not kill them.

"There's a fucking warning, Melinda. If they can't comply with such a simple thing that is none of their business, they're better off dead."

"They're not bad, just dickheads," I replied; all these months living together really got me used to expressing myself like a thug.

"Can't you just scare them? I don't know, just do the non-lethal things you'd do if I had overnight visitors? I agree we should teach them a lesson, but not too harsh."

"These little shits are thrilled to experience a haunted house, right? Oh, I'll haunt them alright," she smiled, then yelled. "Burnface! Tonight is the night you shine."

Burnface materialized before me, and I retched.

I half-knew what to expect, because when we watched a Batman movie Pandora said *"he looks like Burnface, but cuter"* about Two-Face. Still, nothing could have prepared me for how horribly deformed his face was—and not only his face, every visible inch of his body was full of terrible burns and open scars; like he was made of pinkish lava after it hectically condensed... and he smelled horribly of charred skin and rotten flesh.

"Pardon me," I managed, covering my mouth and nose.

"Go, but don't run too wild," Pandora ordered, and, from the smell, I knew that he had left. She turned to me. "I know you're feeling super bad because you're a pathetic cutie-pie, but he's used to these reactions. He even grew to like them. Makes him feel powerful or whatever."

Pathetic cutie-pie was one of the loveliest things she ever called me.

"I wish he went to the fucking light already," I retorted, finally able to breathe properly again.

"Oh, don't you worry about *him*. Burnface is having the time of his life. But now that you know how the ghosts work you might want to have a word or two with some others."

Burnface was a total rock star, making the trespassing teens pee themselves—or worst—in fear, what I considered a fair manner to be taught a lesson and to think before they willingly put themselves into a potentially dangerous situation again.

But youth is a curse, and it's contagious; finding the exact thrill that they had been looking for, the news spread like fire, and my house became a hotspot for all the biggest assholes between ages 14 and 17.

So, for the next month, there was a ruckus on my property almost every single night. I had to increase slightly the use of non-lethal force (like making them trip and fall face-first in cow shit), or else I'd be just running an amusement park attraction for free.

Never a dull moment in this accursed farm.

This seemed to be finally curbing their obsession with Sioux Manor, but one of these nights things almost ended tragically.

8

The Captain showed up for the second of his yearly visits right as the young dumb-fucks were being scared off by Burnface, Legless Linda, Flying-Head Stu, and even Mentally Challenged Rob (a fat ghost that licked everything he saw and almost drowned you in saliva; he sucked for real battles but was great to chase people away).

Those that were trespassing on my property that night had no idea of the true horror they were experiencing, and how close to being reduced to nothingness they were.

Luckily, Pandora single-handed defeated the soul-eater once again—he wasn't as strong as he was scary. Still, I was always terrified when I heard the sound of him approaching; just listening to his heavy steps, or remembering the glimpse I caught from his face the other time was enough to send me into a panic attack and nearly crush my mind.

Up until this point, I've been relatively laid back about my otherworldly visitors because most things are just bizarre and I know that Pandora can always handle them, but this unnatural creature was one of the most horrific things that my mind could conceive, and its danger was overwhelmingly real.

I'd feel so guilty and angry if The Captain caught one of the foolish teenagers, and not being able to do anything but lay in my bed and wait made me horribly anxious. I'm ashamed to say, but I broke down that night.

"Hey, hey, it's okay, sweetie," Old Lady immediately made me know that she was nearby, as I trembled under the blanket. The already familiar presence helped a little bit.

"Can I ask you a favor?"

"Anything I can help you with, as long as it's within my reach," she replied, solicitous.

"Can you tell me what brought you here? Or anything you remember about yourself when you were alive?"

I felt a gentle pressure over my hand, like she was grabbing it with her two; she reminded me a lot of my late grandmother in this sense.

"Of course, dear. There isn't much to tell, but I'll be glad to share it with you if that's what you want," she slightly raised her voice to superimpose the uproar outside. "I hear most people are here for bad reasons, but I'm just passing the time until my son returns from the Vietnam War."

"But didn't you know--"

"It's fine, darling. People insist that the war has been over for a long time, and everyone has already returned if they could, but he's always been a forgetful boy, and so clumsy, the poor thing. That's why I need to be patient," she sighed and paused. "Maybe he has passed too, but that's all the more reason to wait so we can cross together. He'll come, I'm sure. A mother's heart knows."

I used my other hand to squeeze the air where I imagined hers to be.

***

That night, when Pandora came to tell me it was safe to leave the bed, she asked if I had a moment to talk—something that never happened before.

"You see me with too kind eyes, but I have to burst this bubble for you, roomie. You should know that I killed the previous owner of the house."

It took me a while to process it. As far as I know, Mr. Lou was an old widow, beloved by the community if a little eccentric, and he was very fond of the Sioux Manor—that's why he refused to leave such a dangerous place and go stay with his relatives.

"Did you have a good reason for it? Was he bad to you?"

She laughed. "You really think that whatever I do is justified, don't you? If I tell you that I just ate a puppy, you'll say *'Okay, I guess the puppy was actually Cerberus.'*"

"I just know that you're smart enough to not act senselessly," I retorted, without hesitation; Pandora seemed shocked.

"Well, you're surprisingly right this time. You do realize that the farm was extremely cheap even for a creepy property, right? Old Lou's family wanted to get rid of it as soon as possible because their dad was murdered."

Pandora sucked at explanations, so she just picked an icy and fluffy memory from her head and implanted it in mine.

This dream was completely different from the other; it was somewhat blurry and poorly lit, like something recorded on a cheap disposable camera.

I watched Mr. Lou, a likable old man, limping slowly around the property; these days he had an employee to run the farm, because he himself couldn't do much. The man, around 40 years old and always wearing a cowboy hat, took care of the animals and helped him with some tasks around the house too, like basic cleaning and cooking, but he wasn't allowed to stay the night.

Mr. Lou treated Pandora with an awkward gentleness, like she was an estranged daughter he had been recently reconnecting with; since she didn't have a name, he called her Girl—not very imaginative.

I watched in horror as Mr. Lou uncovered his head when he heard the heavy footsteps entering his bedroom; Goofy Voice had told me that the old man didn't leave the bed when it was likely that something bad would show up, because he couldn't escape quickly anymore.

But it seems that, assuming that he was almost dying anyway, Mr. Lou's curiosity took the best of him and he decided to steal a glimpse from the aberration that had chased and intrigued him over the last decade.

He let out a hideous scream; The Captain was a giant animalistic black smudge, that somewhat merged with the natural shadow of its surroundings, consuming everything.

The horrid ghoul let out a satisfied roar when it realized that Mr. Lou was taking a peek at him; with atrocious, unavoidable speed, it caught him and started eating—no, suctioning—his leg; it started disappearing completely, leaving no blood or chewed bones behind.

Pandora smashed his protégé's head to kill him before he was completely devoured, so at least his soul could be saved.

After that, chaos ensued; the employee found Mr. Lou's body the next morning, and thank God he had a solid alibi for the time of death—besides, there was nothing to inherit but the property, so the cowboy didn't profit from his boss' demise.

Mr. Lou's family hated the house with all their might, even more now that they suspected it had killed him, so they decided to sell it for pennies. And that's how I ended up here.

The next morning, I let Pandora know that I watched everything and that she did the best that she could. She brushed it off.

"Thinking about it, that's pretty much how Legless Linda died; she was a previous owner, and she hates her nephew's guts because she thinks he murdered her, but it was just us trying to save her partially."

"That's awful! Have you told her that?"

"Of course, dumdum. But she won't believe me, even after seeing Old Lou suffering from a similar fate. You should have realized by now that the ghosts here are all biased and stubborn."

I had a somber look on my face. She then added: "Cheer up, sunshine! You might die from that too, but I'm getting more powerful, so I'll probably only fail to save your feet."

***

After Lakota patiently clarified all my doubts about the Sioux Manor, I finally understood why The Captain returned from time to time: unlike our ghosts, who still belonged to the material realm, The Captain and other entities like him belonged to an outer plane. So, even if Pandora slashed him to bits, he'd just reform on his natal plane (Hell, Abyss, Hades or something like that) after a while.

But, having Pandora and the other resident ghosts around to protect me, I was able to deal with even that.

There was only one thing in the world that I couldn't handle, and it hit me like lightning the day after The Captain came.

An unknown number called me; I figured that maybe some door-to-door salesman saw my warning sign by the gate and wanted to be allowed in, or even one of the kid's parents called to apologize—it wouldn't be the first time for both things.

But it was my ex's sister.

I can't bring myself to say the name of my ex-fiancée because it makes me tremble, so forgive me for not reproducing her every word here.

"Melinda? Are you with <*him*>?"

"Why would I be?" I replied, somewhat harshly. I used to be friends with this woman, but when I told her about the aggressions, she was dismissive and said that all couples are like that. She's the reason why it took me so long to ask my parents for help.

"Because my brother said that he would make things right with you. And now no one has seen or spoken to him for over a week."

9

Asking Pandora if *he* had been on the property was one of the hardest things I've ever done.

At first, I started describing him physically. But then the next thing I knew, I was crying in her arms as I told her how he slapped until I said his name and begged for forgiveness every little time I made a small mistake—or anything that he considered to be wrong.

"I saw you quivering in fear every time you dropped a glass or something. You apologizing frantically for that, even if there was no one there. So yeah, no need to tell me anything else if you don't want to," she awkwardly ran her fingers through my hair.

"So, has he been here? Have you killed him?" I asked, panicking for a million different reasons.

"Oh, hell no. *He's still here.* I'm keeping him under the hen house, a cozy spot for some torture as you could see from my review. I'm breaking him nice and slowly."

"Shit. Shit, shit, shit, Pandora, I can be arrested for that. You know the police won't just believe that a dead person did it."

"It's fine, roomie. He's the one who tried breaking into your house to kill you. And do worse things too."

I was completely freaking out, and nothing she could say would ever make it better.

***

His sister had told me that she called the cops on me, so they could search my farm.

"You don't mind, right?" her voice dripped the same venom that *his* did every time he hurt me. "If he's not there, you're just being a good, cooperative citizen."

I hate this bitch with all my might, but that isn't the point.

***

"Will you kill him?"

"Of course I'll kill him! And then probably revive him to suffer more and kill him again," she replied coldly. "I might be cool, but you keep forgetting that I love to make humans feel pain, especially when they are such horrible assholes."

I urged Pandora to think this through. "What if he dies and becomes tied to the house forever? It will be so much worse than having him live. Why the fuck didn't you tell me that he showed up?"

"I really didn't think I'd have to worry you about him being here. I didn't want you to relive all the abuse. You have a beautiful and strong demon to take care of such things to you after all."

She was too laid back about it.

"But now you made it all even worse!" I yelled, exasperated. "You might be a demon and have your damn rules, but you can't make the rest of the world bow to it. I'm so fucked up, there's no way I can claim self-defense if he didn't even come near me."

"I don't give a fuck about the little shitty laws you humans created. I give a fuck about protecting you," she replied.

And I wanted to say "okay, let's think together. Let's figure a way to deal with this. There must be a way out." But I was too far gone in my panic and despair.

Just like when I grew apart from all of my friends. They begged me to leave and I got angry at them, I downplayed the abuse because those things don't happen to women like me, right? Educated, middle-class, strong-willed women like me? It only happens to vulnerable girls who didn't know better, right?

Just like when I cut contact with my parents to a minimum because it hurt to lie that everything was fine. It hurt to be asked how my day was and be unable to think of a single nice thing to say.

Just like when I cut my hair and threw away all my make-up so he wouldn't have reasons to feel jealous of me.

Just like when I yelled at my neighbor because she called the police on him; I said that it was none of her business and *all couples are like that*.

Just like when I started hurting myself to punish me for not leaving and not taking my first opportunity to be helped.

I was too far gone into my trauma, into my pain, into the ugliest part of me that he so thoroughly fed.

"Is that so?" I didn't sound like me. I was so bitter, so angry, so utterly unable to act like myself. "Because ever since I moved in you have been a total bitch and treated me poorly, so fuck you. I never asked to get a cursed poltergeist trying to boss me in my every move. This is serious and I don't want to rot in prison, so this time I'm not sitting around and letting you do as you please."

"Fuck *you* and all of you humans. You piece of shits are all the same anyway. You think you're some shit but you'll live for 50 more years, 60 years tops, and when you turn to fucking dust and manure, I'll still be here, and I'll have things my way."

"Then I hope you disappear," I retorted. I wanted to stop myself. I was being so childish, on top of everything. But I couldn't. Not in that moment; right then I was the frail, the loser, the pitiful person that *he* had convinced me that I was.

"Great, because that would be a fucking ray of sunshine in my miserable eternal life." She made two heavy thuds as she took off her shoes, one of the many pairs I gave her, and dematerialized. "So have it your way, stupid bitch. I'm turning off my telepathy and going dormant because I'm too fucking mad and I don't want to recklessly hurt you."

***

I know what you're going to say. This is too out of character for you, Melinda. Considering all that's happened so far, there's no way that you are this dumb. You're better than that.

You're lucky to not know first-hand that, when it comes to our abusers, sometimes we'll display incoherent and self-destructive behaviors, and coming back from it is not linear. You're broke in a way that, no matter how good of a job you do to mend yourself, you're forever at risk of snapping again. The risk can be small, but it's there, and given enough pressure, it's unavoidable.

You're lucky not to know that a piece of your abuser grows on you like a parasite and it becomes pretty much a ghost limb, acting up and hurting yourself every now and then.

My irrational behavior came from a place of fear, from manipulation and from hating myself for having been manipulated. When you feel like that, it's hard to do anything but act on the belief—so carefully seeded into your heart—that your abuser will always be in control and you're just a sad Pavlov dog.

I am not. I am strong. I am a survivor.

But it didn't keep me from freaking out and deciding to go to the hen house before the police arrived.

It didn't keep me from having mixed feelings when I saw him. His throat ripped out and his vocal cords all destroyed so he could never again scream at me, his face filthy with chicken crap and dried blood.

Does he really deserve it? Isn't it my fault that I accepted to be hurt? I*sn't it my fault that I'm too clumsy and incompetent?*

I am strong. I am a survivor.

But I'm also the woman who made the worst possible choice at that moment:

I set him free.

10

I didn't release him because I am weak, or forgiving.

I have admitted that my lingering trauma played a big part in my decision, but here's what the rational part of my brain said:

He might be getting a deal with Orcus right now.

And boy, I was right.

***

As soon as I pulled *him* from the space under the hen house and went outside again, there was a giant figure towering over me. Even the vision of its back was enough to terrify even someone like me, who considered herself to be used to the creepy and the supernatural.

Still with its back—nearly naked and completely scarred—turned to the hennery, the fat pig of a demon that bound Pandora to this godforsaken place rotated its neck to watch me, with a smile that was both cruel and delighted.

Seeing it in person instead of only in a memory was a sensorial overload: I'll never get over its stink, how it moved like a legged ooze, how its whole skin was made of infected blisters, its voice, its *wrongness*.

Have you ever seen a being and thought "this shouldn't exist. This is not only an aberration, but a proof that there's no God looking after *us?*"

This is how I felt about The Captain. This thing right in front of me was on a whole other level.

He was outraged. Apparently, the demonic envoy had given his voice back partially so they could make a deal.

"Come on, you rabid bitch! Tell this fatso who he's messing with," he spitted his words in raucous rage.

Lovely words to say about the being who granted you the ability to speak, and to the person who just freed you from a life of having chickens shitting all over you.

And he didn't stop: "Fucking tramp, you always ruin everything! Can never do anything right, can you?"

The demon patiently read from a scroll: "Let's make a bet. If she leaves you here to perish, I'll release you myself and guide you to the h*ouse where you can kill her as you please. But... if she shows up within the next three hours, I win. She wins. I'll rip you apart piece by piece and eat your soul."*

The scroll did have a bloodstain that was clearly a fingerprint.

But *he* wasn't worried about the 9-feet-tall otherworldly creature and the deal he did with it. He was worried about destroying me.

"You'd better start saying my name and begging that I forgive you."

And through everything, I smiled.

"You know... I spent all this time thinking that I couldn't say your name because I'm scared of you, but it's just that. No. I won't say your name. Ever again. Because I refuse to acknowledge you as a person."

The demon spit on his forehead, and it wounded him like a bullet. He whimpered.

He was then punched repeatedly until the two of them were inside the hennery again; the demon held his head against the chicken crap and used his face to smudge it, laughing maniacally.

The demon didn't care who it was, as long as there was someone suffering.

And luckily, through all my bad choices and regrets, this someone wasn't me or a person I cared to protect.

***

I watched it torture him for long minutes, and even decided to record it with my phone for good measure. Pandora had explained to me that powerful outsiders like this demon can't choose to make themselves invisible for some people while visible to others, that's why the time kind of stopped when she made her pact with it.

I knew that the demon wanted me to see it all to maximize *his* humiliation; so I let it put up a show for me.

Things started to get troublesome when it started whipping its fiery tail against the old, dry, and very flammable hennery floor.

Without thinking it through, I jumped inside to save my chickens, but the demon mistakenly assumed I was interfering with its job.

"Just watch it quietly, fool!" its thunderous, disgusting voice roared.

It was just a small slap. It was just throwing me out of the way.

But the thing was an emissary working under Orcus himself, and I was just an average woman; it almost killed me.

As my lacerated abdomen bled enough to leave me unconscious in a matter of seconds, I smiled weakly, and I counted the chickens; forty-one, just like my mother had counted. At least I was able to evacuate all of them.

***

I don't know for how long I blacked out. I just know that, when I came to again, I was dying in her arms, as she spoke to *him*—still being devoured bit by bit by the demon.

"Oh, you're scared? Scared enough to beg a winged woman you don't know to save you?" she chuckled, talking to *him* as she held me. "You deserve to be way more terrified for all the hell you have put Melinda through. Consider yourself lucky you're only getting a painful death once, if it was up to me I'd murder you hundreds of times."

"She's strong now because of me!" he mumbled pathetically.

Pandora laughed again. "You didn't make her stronger. You tried to destroy her and it's all on her that she's still standing, that she's still kind, that she held on to every good thing you tried to take from her, that she became an even better version of herself. That she's the woman I love and am proud of."

I wanted to pretend I wasn't hearing, but tears started streaming from my eyes.

"Hey, roomie, you're up," she said softly. Just then, I realized she had ripped off a piece of her left wing to stanch my bleeding. "I've been thinking about something you asked me once."

"Yeah?"

"If you ever got married and have kids. I'd protect your babies. I'd protect your guy too, but if he pissed me off, I'd still draw little dicks on his forehead."

I tried to squeeze her hand, but I realized my body was too weak to do it. Every surface of Pandora that I could see was covered in my blood.

"Sorry it took me a while to come get you. If I go dormant the other ghosts go too because I'm their boss, so I tried to stop being mad quickly. I hope you don't mind that I punched a few holes in the walls."

Although the pain was unbearable, I smiled.

"Sorry I stormed out like that. I was scared," I feebly apologized; I didn't want to die without doing so.

"Yeah, girlfriend, I was scared too, in a sense. But I guess even scared you were able to figure out something that I couldn't. And hey, now we're in kind of a pinch that I can't solve myself. Aren't those stupid officers coming? I need someone with a body and able to leave the property to get you to the hospital."

The fat demon continued eating the last bits of *his* body carelessly, paying no mind to Pandora or me. Soon, *he* was going to be just a miserable head, and then completely erased from existence.

"The hennery is on fire, so I guess the neighbors will notice it all soon," I replied; it was also hot as hell where we stood. "But I don't know if I can make it until they come."

"Let me tell you a little something about being physically hurt by a demon. The problem is not your body, but your soul. You're surviving because you have a strong soul," she put her hand on my sweaty forehead. "But I don't know if it's strong enough to make it through completely."

"I'm sorry for dying on you, Pandora."

"Although... there must be a way," she hesitantly added.

***

Circumstance number one: the person has to be entirely familiar with the terms of the contract, word by word.

I saw her memory in my sleep over and over, and I can recite every word from it.

Circumstance number two: the person has to be alive and unbounded by other contracts.

I'm a freelance writer. My mortgage was put under my parents' name—they insisted their credit score was better so I'd get to save some money.

Circumstance number three: the person has to be willing to not only take Pandora's place, but to become Pandora herself.

This one is easy. I feel that we're so connected that we're already part of each other.

Circumstance n*umber four: the person has to agree that Pandora takes the person's name and life for herself.*

And there's nothing I'd like more than to have her live a normal life, at least for a few decades.

Circumstance number five: the person must have been touched by *the bearer of the contract.*

So there we have it. The final requisite.

***

"All this time I didn't want you mortals to get close to me because I know you're reckless. I feared someone would offer to take my place, having no idea what it means, but…"

"But what?"

"But letting you take my place to save your soul is different."

"So let us do it," I said softly. Despite her magical tourniquet, I was fading again.

"You stupid fuck. You know what that means for you, right? Forever. For the rest of eternity. You're damned and a slave to Orcus."

"Pandora… I lived a fulfilling life. I had loving parents, I liked my job, I got this great farm and was able to meet you and all the others, even Mentally Challenged Rob," we both chuckled. "I don't have big dreams or plans, but I still don't want this life to go to waste. So please, let me offer you a little kindness to make it up for all the horrible things you went through."

"You'll be chained to this house forever."

"Yeah, but you get to be free. Plus I quite like this place."

She hesitated for a while, then smiled. "Well, I do think that you'd make a great leader for the ghosts."

"I have so many ideas! Anyway, how do we do it?"

"That's pretty cheesy, but you know how they say that every time you kiss someone you two exchange a piece of your souls? It's like that."

So she leaned towards my face like a Prince Charming, giving me the kiss of immortality, and we held hands as we swapped.

***

It's been two years now. The soul could take the wound, but the body still ended up with a nasty scar; luckily, it didn't take long for a few neighbors to come get us help.

I used to be someone a long time ago, then I lost the right to have a name, and then she came and named me Pandora. Now I inhabit a body named Melinda. The body of the prettiest, strongest, weirdest woman I have ever met.

I left the farm for the first time in forever to go to the hospital, and I've been leaving it daily. Even the most mundane task like grocery shopping amazes me. I just make sure to never spend too much time away from my savior—not because she will get lonely, but because I will.

I'm working on my rage because it is such a waste to treat poorly the life that she so kindly gave me. Thanks to her, I look forward both to living and to one day, in a few decades, finally dying and finding rest on the other side.

Although we couldn't break the curse, I think we at least weakened it, because two things changed:

The first is that she doesn't have to survive on raw chicken; we think that it's because she kind of died protecting a few dozen chickens, but she can eat pretty much anything now—of course I've been improving my cooking skills so she can dine like a queen; it's the least I can do for her.

The second is: part of the original deal was that I was forgotten, but now she's in my place, and I'll never, never forget her.

Now I, the former raw chicken-eating demon, am a writer with a mortgage, and she—Melinda One, the most amazing woman that ever lived—has hoofs and fights against invaders. You should see how cool she is, fighting with two khukris; she's a better me than me.

So much that she has gained the favor of the other shamans and even convinced many of the ghosts to go to the light, including all the former slaves. Of course, more will always come, but they will be in good hands.

It's funny how you can be broken into a million pieces and still find someone who's broken too but whose pieces match yours completely. Melinda One likes to say we saved each other, but she's the one who saved me. She's the one who saves everyone.

And when I die, she'll still be here, taking care of whoever erratically walks around this place like a fallen angel. Maybe you humans were right in your fairy tales, and true love actually can break curses somehow.

Or maybe she has always been more than human.

My beautiful demon wife.

MORE CREEPY READS FROM VELOX

Printed in Dunstable, United Kingdom